THE NORTHERN DEVIL

THE NORTHERN DEVIL

DIANE WHITESIDE

BRAVA

KENSINGTON PUBLISHING CORP.

BRAVA BOOKS are published by

Kensington Publishing Corp.
850 Third Avenue
New York, NY 10022

Copyright © 2007 by Diane Whiteside

Brava and the B logo Reg. U.S. Pat. & TM Off.

ISBN-13: 978-0-7394-8585-9

Printed in the United States of America

For Kate

Fierce-throated beauty!
Roll through my chant with all thy lawless music, thy
swinging lamps at night,
Thy madly-whistled laughter, echoing, rumbling like an
earthquake, rousing all,
Law of thyself complete, thine old track firmly holding,
(No sweetness debonair of tearful harp or glib piano
thine,)
Thy trills and shrieks by rocks and hills return'd,
Launch'd o'er the prairies wide, across the lakes,
To the free skies unpent and glad and strong.

—Walt Whitman,
"To a Locomotive in Winter,"
Leaves of Grass, 1876

Chapter One

Boston, Christmas 1867

The party was magnificent—if one enjoyed weddings or the company of respectable women.

Lucas Grainger took another swallow of excellent champagne and counted the hours until he could catch a train back to Kansas, the cavalry, and dependably uncivilized Indians.

Anglesey Hall's great ballroom was full of Boston Brahmins, swooping and swirling across the dance floor under the glittering chandeliers, chattering from the gilded chairs along its edges, or making a hundred deals in the corridors just beyond, which would shake America's business world in the months to come. Even the rich fragrances of fir, balsam, and roses from the wreaths and garlands couldn't hide the reek of money and ambition—especially the thwarted avarice behind the polite congratulations given to the married couple.

But Lucas had never seen anyone happier than Elias Davis in his life, nor one who deserved it more. Congressional Medal of Honor winner and the man who'd taught Lucas everything about being a cavalry officer, Davis should be looking forward to life with a beautiful, young bride—no matter how few years that would be.

Of course, that was the real reason for this enormous party. Child of his father's old age, Davis had always been given what he wanted, including a West Point education and military service. After a Rebel's bullet had torn Davis's lung during Sherman's last great wartime battle, nobody had expected him to live more than a few months. But his wealthy, powerful father had brought him home, where he'd been nursed back to this approximation of health—and fallen in love with a senior servant's daughter. Rather than arguing the choice, Old Man Davis had clearly recognized he had very little time to waste if he wanted to see his grandchildren. So he'd chosen to invite Boston's most snobbish members to the wedding, calculating that if they attended the ceremony they'd be unable to attack the union later.

Now Davis stood proudly next to his Rachel, whose cameo-pure beauty—even at seventeen—was enough to make great portrait painters stop in their tracks. They were clearly physically comfortable together, something Lucas wasn't accustomed to seeing in a married couple. Rachel was forever tweaking Davis's coat or shirt or stroking his cheek, touches that made him beam fondly. She was intelligent, too; she'd conversed quite sensibly about the new railroad bill at dinner last night. Its fundamentals were so coated in bribery as to defeat all but the most perceptive.

Their union was almost enough to make Lucas rethink his objections to falling in love. Certainly not to marriage—never that!—but love might be worthwhile if it brought joy and physical comradeship like that.

The music changed into another dance. Two matrons immediately collected their daughters and bore down upon him from opposite directions, their intentions clear. Lucas snorted silently in derision at the matrons' poor choice of tactics; they wouldn't have lasted an hour against Bedford Forrest or the Indians. He straightened and strolled toward Davis and Rachel, his dress sword clanking softly at his side.

He caught Davis and Rachel during a temporary lull in the flow of guests. The crowd shifted around them, forming a wall of backs and an illusion of privacy.

Davis was chuckling. "My apologies. I can assure you from personal experience that Bostonian matrons are not always so blatant. Pincer movements like that have been old hat for centuries."

Lucas joined in the laugh, although he mistrusted its febrile quality.

Rachel smiled and moved closer to her husband on his left, the side that hadn't been wounded. Unfortunately, he was very dependent on his right hand and had never learned to do much with the other, even to shoot.

"I'm glad you stopped by now, before we all leave," Davis said quietly enough not to be overheard. "There hasn't been time for the three of us to speak together privately."

Lucas inclined his head, the old wartime habits of obedience and respect coming back. He'd only been eighteen the first time he'd followed Davis into combat. Their company had been one of the very few to survive that bloodbath.

"As you may have noticed, my handwriting lacks—a certain elegance."

The younger man kept a straight face and Davis chuckled again. "I thought you'd enjoy that description of it. In any event, my darling Rachel has graciously agreed to serve as my secretary especially for my private correspondence, copying out my letters to ensure their legibility."

He coughed and she came alert, snatching up a glass of water and watching him warily. But the spasm was over in seconds and he went on, after taking a sip of the proffered drink. "She has my full confidence. But if you would prefer that our conversations remain strictly *entre nous*, then say so and you may continue to decipher my scrawl."

Lucas glanced at her, wondering what she thought of all this. Would the reminder of her husband's ailment be a painful burden or something to be forgotten?

Her eyes were shining and hopeful.

He looked back at Davis. "Of course."

"Excellent."

"If I may ask a personal favor of you, Lieutenant Grainger?" She had a very gentle, melodious contralto voice.

"Certainly. If it is in my power to grant it, then it is yours." The gracious words flowed from his mouth without conscious thought, the first time he'd ever offered any such gift to a woman.

"Oh, this is nothing so very big or important, Lieutenant. But could you please slip in a few observations about the West into your letters to my husband?"

He bowed, oddly touched. No one in his family had ever asked him that in their occasional letters, instead focusing solely on their doings and his failures. "It will be my pleasure to do so."

"You may also write directly to each other on the subject, if you'd like," Davis approved. "My darling will be spending far too much time caring for invalids, between my father and myself. Visits to the outdoors, even if only on paper, will do her a world of good."

He lifted a finger and a servant immediately appeared with a tray of fragile champagne flutes, the golden wine shimmering within.

Davis looked around the small circle, his skin the color of old parchment except for splotches of color burning high on his cheekbones. "To friends and comrades!"

"Friends and comrades!" Lucas and Rachel echoed and they drank together.

Now he could have Rachel as his friend, his only female friend.

Fort Union, New Mexico Territory, September 1870

Lucas knocked politely before entering the house he'd rented for his mistress. He'd never fought with Ambrosia before, but he'd heard enough from other men to know that women should be approached very cautiously after a fracas—especially a major quarrel like this one.

He'd thought that after two years together, she'd have realized he would never marry her, although he had said he loved her. That had been God's own truth, too, even though they'd met in a New Orleans brothel.

She'd sworn she loved him, too, enough to follow him to the edge of civilization, first to Kansas and then here—over a hundred miles from Santa Fe's musicians, as she described it. He'd loved her all the more for it.

Dammit, he'd enjoyed having a smile on his face when he looked at a woman. Davis had looked like that and the sound of it still came through in his letters.

Last night, Ambrosia had said that she wanted a wedding just like her friend Sally Anne's. He'd been too exhausted after a three-month patrol to guard his tongue, so he'd told her the truth: She'd have to find another man to give it to her. She hadn't believed him at first but when she did, she'd started throwing things and he'd retreated to the bachelor officer quarters.

This morning, he'd visited Erickson, the bartender—and unofficial banker and pawnbroker for most of the gamblers. Lucas had come away with a remarkably fine diamond necklace that should put a smile back on her face. Ambrosia was very fond of trinkets. Even if she was still furious, the stage back to Santa Fe didn't leave until this afternoon.

Coming out of Erickson's, he'd noticed that Muldrup and Livermore were passing through Fort Union, probably to go hunting in the Sangre de Cristos. He'd have to privately warn the Provost Marshal to keep an eye on them, although Jones had probably heard about the old scandal. Court-martialing and convicting two officers of rape was extraordinarily rare.

It was very quiet now in the tiny adobe house.

The hairs on the nape of Lucas's neck stood up.

"Ambrosia? Ah, angel?"

He took another step forward, his Colt shifting against his hip as if ready to be drawn.

The main room was completely empty. The silence pushed

at him, whispering of ghosts, telling him to hurry. But the threat didn't seem to be aimed at him.

Still, he twisted his wrist, bringing his dirk into availability. He'd spent months learning how to use knives, first when he was a common trooper, and from Little, his very good friend and an Indian scout. Recently, the top wagon master, William Donovan, had shown him some other tricks. God forbid he had to use them now.

He went into the bedroom warily, prepared for anything except the sight that greeted him—a single sheet of paper, staked to the pillow with an enormous hatpin.

> *Lucas,*
>   *You are a fool. Did you really believe I was in love with you, a young man with little experience and no skill before I met you?*

He flushed angrily, resenting the description while acknowledging how much she'd taught him.

> *I have stayed with you because you are rich.*

Ambrosia! He gave a low, ragged sound and sagged back, clawing the wall while his dreams shredded around him. Good God, how she must have laughed at his declarations of love.

When he began reading again, he was standing stiffly erect, his chest filled with a cold rage that admitted neither tears nor hope.

Elias and Rachel Davis were now the only happy couple he knew.

> *If you will not marry me and give me your money, then I will return to New Orleans where I can have men who are both rich and charming.*
>   *Do not follow; I will only spit in your face.*
>   *Ambrosia*

Returning to New Orleans? When he'd visited Erickson, he'd walked past Smith's, where civilians stayed while waiting for the stage. Nobody had mentioned Ambrosia and Jennie Smith was a notorious gossip.

So where was Ambrosia?

This wasn't a safe town for a woman to be alone in—even though it was a very large military post—not with Muldrup and Livermore present. He knew damn well just how much those two bastards were capable of and how cleverly they could skirt the law, with the aid of their friends.

Worse, there was nothing they wouldn't do if they thought it would hurt him in any fashion.

Where the hell was Ambrosia?

And where the devil were Muldrup and Livermore?

He dropped the note on the bed and headed out, his spurs jangling furiously.

Sangre de Cristo Mountains, Colorado, October 1870

A flock of dark-eyed juncos flashed across the forest's edge, making Lucas's big stallion toss his head. Lucas absent-mindedly rubbed his old friend's neck and crooned reassurances too softly to be heard even a few steps away. All the while, he scanned the valley below, looking for his prey and making sure they hadn't spotted him and his companion first.

They stood high on the steep mountainside within a heavy stand of fir trees. Below them, the little river wound its way down icy rocks and through snowy meadows. Its passage slowed at a still pond, glazed by early winter's first crystalline coat of ice and bordered on one side by a long stretch of frosted, golden grasses. That meadow would be a perfect setting for what Lucas had planned.

Downstream, the river gathered itself to race past a handful of huge boulders and hurtle over a knife-edged cliff in a torrent of roiling water. Even from a mile away and almost a half mile higher, Lucas could hear the river plunging into the abyss beyond.

Old memories stirred, of when he'd stared at another water-fall and forgotten the pond behind it, with the girl he'd promised to guard. Cold slashed deeper into him, an ancient pain more profound than anything that had touched him in the past few weeks.

He closed his eyes, his fingers opening and closing on his Colt. Inside his jacket, a velvet jeweler's pouch rested over his heart.

A horse whickered and pawed the trail behind him, its tack jingling delicately. It belonged to William Donovan—the one man he'd wanted with him on this hunt, who'd accepted immediately when he'd heard Lucas's reasons. A friend, to whom he now owed a blood debt beyond measure.

Lucas opened his eyes.

"Campfire over to the west," Donovan remarked calmly in his California drawl, an entirely fitting accent for the owner of one of the West's great freighting houses. He carried a shot-gun in his rifle scabbard, a bit of foresight that had made Lucas blink and then grin mirthlessly. "Just inside that aspen grove. I'd say they only recently lit it."

"They definitely haven't spotted us yet," Lucas commented, gathering up his reins. He shot a glance at Donovan, shaping his mouth into a smile's travesty. "Shall we invite them to the party?"

Donovan's smile was as predatory as his own. "Definitely. After all, they are the guests of honor."

When Lucas and Donovan arrived at Muldrup and Livermore's camp, they didn't bother to make any pretense at amiability. They wore the rough clothes of hard men moving fast through difficult terrain in bad weather: Heavy wool coats, broad-brimmed hats, leather trousers, heavy gloves, and high boots. Their weapons were prominently displayed.

Muldrup and Livermore looked like what they were: two

THE NORTHERN DEVIL 9

Army lieutenants on a hunting trip in the high mountains. Their neat white tents, fir bough beds, wooden camp stools—everything bore silent testimony to years successfully spent under the roughest of conditions. But then Lucas had always known these two were good travelers and good fighters. They also had the forms of the perfect gentlemen they'd always claimed to be. Muldrup had dark hair and dark eyes, with the speed and agility of an expert dancer—or a back-alley knife fighter. Livermore was slightly taller, famous for his enjoyment of any pleasure offered, whether or not he'd paid for it. A neatly dressed elk carcass hung high in a fir tree, well back from the camp. It was probably Muldrup's handiwork, not Livermore's.

Seven years earlier at the siege of Vicksburg, they'd appeared to be everything Union cavalry officers should be—until he'd caught them raping a young Southern gentlewoman. They'd threatened to break him back to sergeant if he reported them, thus destroying his month-old officer's commission. Driven by the need to protect all women, even a rebel, Lucas had called their bluff and seen them convicted by a military court-martial. But *military necessity*, in the form of a long campaign which needed every experienced cavalry officer, saw their sentences officially reduced to pre-war rank, time already served and, unofficially, to the loss of their so-called *honor*.

Still, Army regulations, which forbade deadly combat between officers, had always stood between them—until now.

The two men stood to meet Lucas and Donovan, Muldrup leaning against the tent frame with one hand resting casually on his hip. Livermore stood farther off to the side, making it difficult to take them both down with a single exchange of shots. Not that it mattered; that sort of party wasn't at all what Lucas had in mind.

"Good morning, Grainger." Muldrup's tone was polite, if not welcoming. He gave Donovan an abrupt jerk of his head, nothing more.

"Grainger," Livermore echoed, managing a nod.

"And a good morning to you—murderers." Lucas was finally free to let all the contempt he felt infuse his voice.

Muldrup's eyes narrowed briefly. "Watch who you're talking to," he drawled, as certain of his own superiority now as when he'd first left his family's century-old South Carolina plantation fifteen years ago. He'd bragged for years about his kinship to John Lyde Wilson, governor of South Carolina and author of *The Code of Honor*, which provided the American rules for dueling. "If you weren't a fellow Army officer, I'd challenge you to a duel for calling me that."

"Hadn't you heard? I resigned my commission days ago." Savage satisfaction flooded Lucas's veins at Muldrup's evident shock—and rapid reconsideration of the situation. "After seven years, you've finally gained the duel you wanted. Donovan, will you act for me?"

The only man he could trust at his side in this fight, because of both the subject and the possible weapons, bowed. "It will be an honor."

"Name your weapons, Muldrup, either guns or Bowie knives," Lucas snapped.

"I thought Philadelphia aristocrats raised their sons to act as gentlemen, Grainger. But resigning your commission? Naming an *Irish teamster* as your second? What the hell are you planning to do?"

Good; he'd rattled Muldrup out of his usual arrogant calm.

"Leave your bones for the vultures, just as you left Ambrosia."

Too many women had gone through too much because of these bastards. He could have shot them down, like the curs they were. But no—they were going to see the gates of hell slowly open for them and know exactly why they died.

Muldrup's eyes searched Lucas's and found only murderous intent. Something passed between them, a communication beyond words, two fighters measuring each other before the bout for who'd be left standing at the end. It jarred him into speech. "The courts won't do anything. There's no proof that Livermore and I—"

The damning words hung on the clean mountain air for a long minute.

Lucas watched him stonily, his fingers a hairsbreadth from his Colt. He hadn't needed the admission; he'd recognized their bloody handiwork from seven years ago in Mississippi.

"What the hell are you challenging us to a duel over the likes of her for?" Livermore broke the taut silence. "Duels are affairs of honor among gentlemen. She was only a whore!"

Lucas flung his arm out, his heavy Colt cocked and pointing straight at Livermore. He'd loved her too long and too strongly to have her called that by anyone, even knowing how much truth rang through those words.

He'd probably never be lucky enough to get the drop on Muldrup. Didn't matter; he'd kill Livermore here and now for insulting his late mistress, and worry about destroying Muldrup later. "If you call her that again, I won't even grant you the courtesy of a duel before sending you to meet your Maker."

Livermore growled, unfortunately not quite elitist—or stupid—enough to openly challenge Lucas.

Donovan shifted in his saddle, clearly bringing his own weapons close to hand.

"You destroyed our careers back at Vicksburg," Muldrup snarled.

"I reported you for outraging and nearly killing a young lady of good family," Lucas snapped back. "The Army meted out justice when it court-martialed and convicted you."

"Based on your testimony! You broke the code of silence when you informed on us."

"What code of silence exists when a woman's life and honor is at stake? Even so—after all that, you still managed to have your sentences reduced to pre-war rank and time served, in light of the wartime emergency."

"Our services to the Union were recognized."

"In other words, you skirted the law and your friends rewarded you for it."

"Not much of a reward, when the damn conviction still hangs over our records like a shroud, preventing us from being promoted beyond our pre-War ranks!"

"And this time you won't even have that much grace," Lucas snarled.

"I choose revolvers," Muldrup announced silkily, picking up the gauntlet.

"To send you to hell," Livermore sneered, falling in behind Muldrup as he had since West Point.

"To become vulture bait," Lucas corrected and swung down from his horse.

"While you and I, Livermore, will make sure that this duel is conducted with all propriety," Donovan added, his voice edged with the same crisp menace that had made millionaire mine owners reconsider double-crossing him.

Livermore opened his mouth, shut it after a look at Donovan's shotgun, and reluctantly joined his fellow second.

"Code Duello or Wilson's Code of Honor?" Donovan inquired, as if arranging a duel was an everyday occurrence for him. His accent was now as purely upper-crust English as if he was standing in the halls of Westminster.

Livermore hesitated.

"Oh, make it the Code Duello!" Muldrup exclaimed, pulling on his heavy overcoat. "We can't reach any sandbanks without wading through icy water and there's no question of sheriffs or prosecutors to chase any of us. So we'll use the older code."

"The Code Duello then," Livermore repeated obediently.

"As the challenged, I select the ground. We'd best make it that meadow between the river and the forest."

"And I select the distance—ten paces," Lucas snapped back.

"I presume that the time will be here and now." Donovan remarked, taking up his duty as Lucas's second to fix the time and terms of firing.

Muldrup looked up from unloading his Colt. The seconds would also reload their principals' weapons in each others' presence. "You *presume* correctly."

"Firing will be done on the count of ten, which either I or the lieutenant will give."

The two officers glanced at each other.

"I'll be happy to let you do it. Your voice carries better than mine," Livermore said silkily.

Lucas's mouth thinned. *Was that when they hoped to do mischief?*

"I believe only one weapon for each of the principals. Livermore?"

"Certainly. It specifically says the second weapon provides the second shot. We'll fully load the revolvers instead."

The eighteenth-century Code Duello had originated when pistols had only one shot. It therefore allowed participants to choose between one weapon or two. If one weapon was chosen, then it could be loaded with a single bullet or fully loaded.

"Excellent."

The two seconds bowed to each other in full harmony for the first time.

Lucas hadn't carried six bullets in his six-shot Army Colt since he'd ridden against the Rebels during the War, thinking it far safer to carry five. Any misstep could make his gun go off unexpectedly, causing damage to himself or others. At the prospect of doing so now, the old, familiar coolness of combat settled over him.

"The Code Duello also provides for the seconds to be armed," Livermore suggested.

Lucas stiffened, caught in the middle of unloading his Colt.

"But not to fire. An excellent idea," Donovan agreed.

Lucas took a deep breath and shook out the last few rounds. At least he could be certain that Donovan was a far better shot than Livermore.

The great golden carpet of frozen grasses ran long and narrow beside the frozen river just before the great waterfall, with the aspen forest crimson bright on the other side where it flowed up the mountain. They left the horses back in the trees, well away from where they'd fight. The four men stood slightly apart in pairs on its edge.

Donovan handed Lucas his revolver. "No tricks in how the Colts were loaded," he said softly. "No guarantees about anything else."

Lucas shrugged. He'd removed his gloves, for accuracy and speed. "Just keep Livermore out of my way and I'll deal with Muldrup."

"You have my word." The Irishman's smile turned edged. "If things were different, I'd fight you for the chance to gut the bastard Apache-style."

Lucas chuckled. "If I don't finish him in six shots, your Bowie knife can have the rest."

Donovan slapped him on the back. "May all the saints be with you, boyo."

Lucas walked out into the meadow, time slowing until he could hear his watch ticking off the minutes and seconds. The grass crunched under his feet and stabbed needle-sharp against his knees, golden and tipped with sparkling ice crystals in the rising sun, like a royal carpet.

He took up position with his back against Muldrup, both of them holding their heavy Army Colts pointed into the air.

Donovan and Livermore stood at the meadow's edge near the horses, but more toward Muldrup's direction. Still, Lucas turned his full attention on Muldrup, confident that Donovan would handle any threat from Livermore.

"Gentlemen, is there any chance of a reconciliation between you?" Donovan called. A pro forma request but his duty as a second.

Livermore snickered.

"Hell, no!" Muldrup shouted. "Will you hurry up and start?"

Lucas took a deep breath, centering himself in the moment as Little and his Indian scouts had taught him.

"One," counted Donovan. "Two, three. . ."

Lucas listened for his enemies with more than his ears, using more of the skills Little had given him. Muldrup's footsteps crunched through the ice, their rhythm carrying steadily through the ground and into his own feet.

"Five, six . . ."

What the hell? Lucas's eyes flickered to the side. Livermore was edging away from Donovan, into a spot where Muldrup could easily see him.

"Seven, eight . . ."

Muldrup's footsteps were no longer solid. Ice crackled briefly from where Livermore stood.

And Lucas knew exactly where the first attack would come from. He dropped facedown into the frozen grasses.

Livermore's shot rang out, drowning Donovan's count of "nine." It would have taken Lucas's head, if he'd still been standing.

Booted feet ran for the forest.

A shotgun's distinctive boom echoed around the high valley. Livermore's scream trailed into silence. The seconds had played their hand; it was time for the principals to act.

Lucas sprang to his feet. "Muldrup!"

The murderer halted, a handful of strides from the blood crimson aspens. He turned slowly to face Lucas, defiance written on his face. Muldrup had lost his advantage of faster speed on the draw. Now it would be a contest of pure marksmanship.

Lucas leveled his Colt and lined the sights up on Muldrup's chest, matching his enemy's movements. Time slowed until every beat of his heart, every pulse of blood through his veins, was a distinct event. Even the waterfall behind him seemed to hold its breath. He saw the puff of smoke from Muldrup's Colt, but it was distant and unimportant.

He exhaled softly, his hand and arm finally perfectly still—and fired. His enemy's bullet whizzed past his ear.

Muldrup dropped onto his face and didn't move.

Lucas slowly holstered his Colt and pulled the velvet jeweler's pouch out of his heavy jacket's inside pocket.

Donovan came up beside him, his shotgun slung over his shoulder.

Moving slowly now, his fingers stiff with more than just the mountains' chill, Lucas untied the strings and tipped the magnificent diamond necklace into the palm of his hand.

He held the jewels up to the morning light. They sparkled with all the colors of the rainbow—but were ultimately as lifeless as the river beyond.

"A woman may one day be very glad to wear those," Donovan commented in a completely neutral tone.

Ice settled more firmly into Lucas's bones. He'd always known Ambrosia would never marry a man who made his life so far from civilization, thus keeping intact his vow of never taking a wife. But, sometimes, he'd wondered about his wisdom. Now he'd never know.

"No woman of mine, either wife or mistress, will ever have the chance."

He hurled the jewels far out beyond the cliff, where they glittered for a moment against the spray before disappearing amid the rocks.

Chapter Two

Jersey City, New Jersey, January 1873

The small, grimy carriage lurched through another pothole, sending it swaying in the other direction. Two voices cursed from the box above, one in a distinctly Jersey accent and the other Bostonian flat. Both vocabularies held the casual, vicious certainty of men who knew violence all too well.

A cold wind ruffled the carriage's frayed curtains, bringing the memory of the previous night's deep freeze and the promise of snow. It was far better than the stench of mackerel and sardines, which had infused every inch of the fishing schooner they'd been forced to spend the last few days on.

Inside, Rachel Davis held her mother's hand as tightly as if she were three years old, instead of twenty-three. From the opposite seat, her younger sister Mercy held both their hands, completing the circle. She was bitterly glad her father had died three years ago—from pneumonia after saving a child from drowning—without seeing them like this.

She'd married Elias six years ago for friendship and to protect her friends, the other servants that she'd grown up with. She'd found more joy in her marriage than she'd ever hoped for. But she'd never expected a hell like this.

"Remember," Rachel whispered. Her heart seemed to be

somewhere closer to her throat than her ribs. "When we reach the train station, no matter what happens, simply run and don't look back. Do you understand? Don't look back."

"But—" protested Mercy, as mulish as ever.

"Hush," begged their mother, her voice choked with tears from behind her veil. "They'll hear you."

Mercy reluctantly lowered her voice to just above a snarl. "There must be another way!"

Rachel closed her eyes, able to offer her sister little hope. She was grateful for the concealment of her own, very fashionable veil. She might have hated being forced by Albert Collins to accept a new wardrobe, as a sign of ending her mourning and therefore becoming open to his son's advances. But its more fashionable—and wider—variety of hats did have some benefits.

"We'll be together," insisted their mother.

Rachel noted she didn't say when. God willing it would be on this side of the grave. But, even if it were on the other side, she'd pay the price just to see her family finally safe from the Collins men.

The hollow reassurance made quick-witted Mercy shift restlessly. It was obviously time to reiterate the plan. All of them knew how dangerous this would be. But Mercy had to be strong and fast for Mother or there was no hope at all.

"Just remember, Mercy: All you must do is flee, as soon as you have the chance," Rachel managed, despite her unhappy stomach. "After that, catch a ferry to Manhattan and buy passage on the Cunard packet we saw. Even if she's going to Canada, she will still sail within the hour, on the next tide. I'll follow you as quickly as I can."

Happier with concrete details, Mother listed their resources. "We're lucky they've never searched all of us at once, so we'll have cash for our fares."

Mercy sighed and accepted the bitter choice. "And we have a few days' clothing in our carpetbags, plus the jewels Elias gave Mother."

Thank God Mercy had kept her voice down this time. If Collins's thugs on the box had heard anything... Rachel shuddered, remembering past punishments meted out most severely to Mother and Mercy. Dear heavens, she'd thought Mother would never recover after that forced ice bath.

The wall of noise from outside suddenly started to grow, anchored by the great rumble of iron wheels, clanging bells, and the high notes of steam whistles.

Rachel closed her eyes in grateful prayer. She'd been right: The Collinses were taking them to a train station, not another boat. There'd be a chance for Mother and Mercy to escape this hell.

"Correct, Mercy," agreed their mother. "You know what to do. Now if we all do exactly what we agreed, everything will go very well."

She gave Rachel's hand one last squeeze, just as the carriage came to a jolting stop, then released it.

"God be with us," she whispered.

"Amen," her two daughters breathed.

The door was yanked open, admitting a burst of frigid air and a great, black shadow. "Mrs. Davis?"

Rachel inclined her head and rose, adopting her haughtiest attitude. Her one satisfaction over the past year was that the Collins men had always seen her behave like a lady, as opposed to their frequently crude and outrageous demands. No matter what they might say of her family tree, her manners were as good as or better than theirs.

She exited slowly, lingering on the step to survey the almost deserted station. At this very early hour in the frigid weather, there were almost no people around except Albert and Maitland Collins, accompanied by two of their thugs. Every ruffian was a sailor from their shipping line—and utterly, blindly loyal to the Collins family. She'd have as much luck persuading Plymouth Rock to melt, as she would convincing one of those brutes into helping her or her family, as past events had painfully shown.

At the end of a long platform, a single station attendant was busily seeing off a passenger train, almost invisible in its clouds of steam.

Beyond a long ramp, an overhead sign proclaimed FERRIES with a gilt arrow pointing to MANHATTAN. Beyond that, she could glimpse a clerk taking tickets from the last men to board a ferry, while a sailor prepared to cast off.

"Mrs. Davis." Even with a half-century lifespan behind him, Albert Collins was a very dangerous man. He stood just above average height, built strongly enough to stand his ground against any mob or howling nor'easter. He had piercing gray eyes that missed nothing, above highly cultivated muttonchop whiskers and between a gleaming bald scalp. He was superbly dressed, as befitted the head of one of Boston's oldest shipping dynasties, even if his firm now owned less than a half-dozen ships.

He'd always reminded Rachel of a water moccasin—dark, extremely poisonous, lurking in the swamp's shadows until he could strike and quickly kill.

Behind him and a half-head taller loomed his son, Maitland. Maitland was an undeniably handsome young man, something he knew all too well and expected to provide him with every advantage. In him, his father's patrician features were sharpened to a knife edge, his father's solidity turned into a cobra's leanness. His eyes were a dark, almost charcoal gray, considering the world with a calculating charm—like a butcher considering cattle and their owners in the marketplace.

Yet their family reputation had been polished and refined throughout the centuries that Boston had stood. As the last two Collins males, they were men of considerable standing—and Rachel's feet always started edging for the door every time she saw them.

Rachel gave Collins a cool smile and nodded slightly, completely ignoring his son and praying to God for strength. "Mr. Collins."

She stepped down off the step and strode briskly away, heading for the only private Pullman in sight—and forcing as many men as possible to follow her. Thankfully, the railroad car wasn't very close, especially when she took the longest possible route through the station's stairs and platforms.

"Welcome to Jersey City, Mrs. Davis," Collins observed.

"Really? How long will we be here?"

Behind her, she could hear Mother making a great show of climbing down slowly from the cab, no doubt assisted by Mercy. The distant train was pulling out, loudly announced by its whistle. The sailor had untied all but one of the lines attaching the ferry to the dock.

"Not long, I'm afraid. The locomotive's got a full head of steam up and is ready to pull out."

She raised an eyebrow, carefully not looking at an empty luggage cart only a few steps away. "Why take me?"

"Your charming company?"

Maitland, pacing behind his father, snickered loudly.

Mother and Mercy were definitely out of the cab now.

Rachel smiled, allowing her teeth to show slightly. "You'll forgive me if I don't believe you."

She grabbed the luggage cart and shoved it into Collins, the less nimble target. He staggered back with a curse into his son, who stumbled, thereby knocking down one of their thugs.

Rachel picked up her highly beribboned, flounced skirts and ran for the departing train. She'd never make it very far—an hour's freedom would be unbelievably lucky—but the longer she was gone, the harder Collins would have to work. And the less attention he could spend on finding her family, reducing the odds Maitland would ever be able to terrorize and attempt to outrage Mercy again.

"Come back!"

Rachel crossed the tracks in a most unladylike leap. Ahead and at the top of the stairs where she'd entered, Mother and Mercy's escort came running down the platform to capture her.

Behind him, the two women were racing up the ramp toward the ferry, where the ticket-taker was waving them aboard. Thank God, their plan had worked so far. Now to give them some more time . . .

She dropped onto the tracks and began to run, dodging an incoming freight train.

Collins's feet pounded behind her. "Stop her! She's mad!" he shouted.

Of course, he'd still claim, to anyone and everyone, that she'd gone insane from grief over Elias's death—the same logic that had enabled him to lock her up for the past six months. She was probably giving him additional reasons to do so. Not that it mattered, if it would save her family.

A locomotive thundered past, half-deafening her. She sidestepped, dodging it like a door slammed in her face.

The air cleared, quieting with the engine's passing. She took a deep breath and turned, returning to the route away from the station.

Maitland stood square in her path, smirking at her like a cannibal with a tasty new treat. "And how are we feeling today, Mrs. Davis?"

Her skin turned to ice, despite the hot sweat pouring under her dress. Was that the look he'd given Mercy, the one that had left her unable to move despite his coarse words—until he'd started to lay harsh hands on her?

Rachel swallowed hard and tilted her chin up, determined not to show fear. "Maitland."

Collins thundered up behind her and gripped her elbow hard, the granite warning of someone who wouldn't hesitate to do violence. "I'll take her to the railroad car."

"Father—"

"Maitland, get the men and look for the other women. If they're gone, we lose our best lever against Mrs. Davis; you know that. I'll manage the situation here."

Maitland nodded curtly and ran off.

"I'd let him punish you except he hasn't learned discipline yet," Collins warned, hauling her back toward the Pullman. "I'm not ready yet to explain to the other trustees any serious injuries you might have. But don't push me too far; you can always have a riding accident that would cause any such problems."

A whistle blew—the rich, mellow sound warning of a boat's departure. With a great huff of steam, the ferry pulled away from the dock.

Rachel held her tongue, refusing to add fuel to his temper's fire. So far, there'd been no sign that they'd found her family.

Collins nodded and waved at the station attendant in a very jovial, patriarchal fashion and twirled his finger by his temple in the universal sign for madwoman. The other man hesitated but finally touched his cap.

"I'll have to pay him off," Collins complained bitterly. "You clumsy cow, I wonder how much this escapade of yours will cost me?"

He marched her onboard the private Pullman and shoved her into a seat. Two of his thugs followed them in, regarding her with sincere dislike. "You two," he ordered, "watch her until I return."

Rachel sniffed and closed her eyes, listening to the station's noises. God forbid they'd reveal her family's capture.

Two hours later, Maitland leaped up into the railroad car's drawing room, completely ignoring the damage his muddy boots did to the superb carpets.

"Well?" demanded his father. "Where are they?"

Maitland came to attention. "I'm not completely sure. But a cabbie took two women of their description to the Cunard packet, which sailed for London more than an hour ago."

Thank you, Lord! Mother and Mercy are safe at last.

Rachel started to smile, flexing her fingers for the first time.

Collins slapped her across the face, knocking her sideways.

For a brief moment, she saw stars—and then nothing at all.

Chicago, two nights later

"Good evening, Mr. Maitland," came the words through the night's blackness. The flat down-easter accent was harsh, suggesting a face and throat ruined by years of fighting in back alleys.

Rachel's subconscious recognized it immediately—and who her jailer greeted. She jolted awake, lying tense and still in her hotel bed, listening to her enemy's return.

Ever since Elias's death, she'd been held captive by Collins—first at Anglesey Hall, the Davis family estate, and later on at Collins's Ledge, the Collins family's private island in the Elizabeth Islands, after he'd convinced the other trustees that she'd gone completely mad from grief. Long months of never going outside without at least one guard, of being allowed solitude only in rooms the size of a large pantry, of having every message scrutinized—even under the guise of spurious concern for her welfare—had taught Rachel more than she'd ever wanted to know about cages. Her parents had always given her the freedom, both physical and intellectual, to go where she pleased and to think as she pleased.

After Mother and Mercy had escaped, her captors had tightened the noose around her even further. Now—now even her dreams were frantic.

She'd guessed that Collins planned to head south to Philadelphia or Wilmington, taking her away from the other trustees and closer to his family's allies. But without any explanation, the private Pullman had been hitched to a western-bound train in Pennsylvania. She still didn't know why they were in Chicago, but being a thousand miles away from anyone who knew her or might help her left her extremely worried.

"Evening, Silas. How's the bitch doing tonight?"

Rachel flushed angrily, hating yet another reminder of Maitland's opinion of her.

"Sound asleep, sir, like always. Went to bed early, she did."

Rachel smiled slowly, her fingers curling into the quilt's

fine needlework. *But I was victorious in this much, at least: I smuggled in and read Susan B. Anthony's latest treatise on women's rights. Something that would undoubtedly infuriate both of you. And someday, I'll manage to attend Mount Holyoke Seminary. Somehow.*

Maitland chuckled nastily. "Good enough. She wouldn't offer anything interesting to a real man, in any event. Good night."

"Good night, sir."

She hissed softly, wishing yet again that Elias was still alive. He'd been well pleased with her attractions and he'd been a great hero. Both Grant and Sherman had praised his deeds and he'd even been awarded the Congressional Medal of Honor.

Whistling softly, Maitland entered the room next to hers, the suite's sittingroom.

Rachel started to lie back down.

The doorknob creaked next door.

She stilled, startled by the metallic screech. Due to some quirk of the hotel's construction and nighttime echoes, she could hear every sound from inside the suite's sittingroom.

"Good evening, son. Close the door and sit down," ordered Albert Collins.

Maitland hesitated, obviously not expecting to see his father. He recovered quickly enough. "How was the opera, sir?" he asked, shutting the door and coming forward.

His handsome face bore all the expected signs of dissipation, plus some indications of brawling. He was still the finest son a man could hope for—strong, clever, handsome. Pity he couldn't have gone to sea to smooth out some of that temper, as five generations of Collinses had done before him. But the Panic of '57 had nearly wiped out the great Collins shipping line fifteen years ago. Maitland's grandfather had killed himself for failing the family, leaving it up to Collins to rebuild everything.

He waved off his only child's inquiry. "Well enough, for

such a benighted frontier town, and I made some good business contacts. They've rebuilt quickly after the great fire, but done little for their music's quality. Still, we'll be able to leave on schedule tomorrow. And your evening?"

Maitland shrugged, settling into a chair with a cup of black coffee as he eyed his father over the rim. Good; he was a smart lad and was trying to sober up. "Won a little more than I lost. That makes up for last night."

He'd wasted so much money that he had to admit it? Good God, had the boy been paying no attention to any of his father's lectures all these months?

Collins slammed his fist down on the table next to him, rattling the china. "You should be courting the widow, not spending your time at the cockfights!"

Maitland looked genuinely baffled. "Why? We control her money now."

"We do not. We only have the purse strings. You need to sire her brats so we hold it forever."

His son glared at him and set the china cup down all too carefully. "Rachel Davis is a bookseller's granddaughter and no fit mother for the next generation of Collinses."

"Her ancestry matters little, compared to the money."

Maitland seemed disinclined to drop the argument. "It's hard to imagine why the other trustees protect a servant's brat so thoroughly. Old Man Davis must have been mad to let his only remaining son marry her."

"Her father was Davis's secretary and most trusted confidant. All of his friends—especially all of those trustees—knew her father as well as they knew Davis. I personally praised the match to high heavens, in order to stay on the trust's board."

Maitland muttered something under his breath but not loudly enough that his sire was forced to rebuke him.

"As for Davis's opinion of the marriage, I suspect he'd have accepted any woman his son wanted to marry, given the immense hole in the boy's lung."

"So her blood's poor, but she's somehow accepted by society," Maitland complained. "Even if I could tolerate that, she's a cold bitch, with more interest in books than men. Unlike her sister, who'd always go into a flutter whenever I squeezed her tits. There's nothing in Rachel Davis to heat my blood."

"Who cares as long as you breed her? Just marry her and get some heirs off her," Collins snapped. "For that much money, you can close your eyes with her and find your pleasures elsewhere."

Maitland rolled his eyes. "If it's so important, why don't you marry her?"

"I'm her *principal* trustee, not her *sole* trustee. A three-quarters vote of the other twelve trustees could remove me at any time. I've already been warned that if I married her, they'd remove me, certainly as principal trustee and probably from the board as well."

"They threatened a Collins?" Maitland's face darkened. "Buy them off! Kick them out of the board!"

Collins's heart warmed at his son's instinctive backing. But it was his paternal duty to bring common sense into the discussion and raise his son to full manhood. "Even a Vanderbilt couldn't bribe all the men Old Man Davis selected. Only her blatant grief at the whelp's funeral gave me enough ammunition to keep her sequestered for so long." He tapped his finger on the table to emphasize his next point. "It would take a combination of wealth, great power, and superb family reputation to obtain enough votes on the board to become sole trustee. Someone like a Grainger of Philadelphia could do it, but nobody else."

Maitland frowned, recognizing the impasse. Always swayed by deeds long past, Boston's upper crust still included the Collins men in their inner circles, as they had for the past two centuries. But today's Collins clan lacked the cash and barefaced political clout to throw a serious contender off the Davis Trust's board—unlike, say, one of the Pennsylvania

Graingers with their ancient name, immense banking and railroad fortune, and vast web of political connections. They were so powerful that they might even be able to publicly bribe a Congressman.

No, he'd have to seize the Davis fortune more subtly.

Collins stood up and poured himself a fresh cup of coffee, then carefully stirred cream into it and waited to see where this setback would send his son's thinking.

"What's the rush? Why can't it wait for a month or two?" Maitland asked slowly.

Ah, now his boy was showing some maturity! Putting the pieces of the puzzle together, instead of simply wanting to hurt someone.

Collins propped his hip on the heavy central table, deliberately rewarding Maitland's insight by relaxing and treating him as part of a team. "The other trustees keep a close eye on the trust's funds, at least the ones they understand."

"So?"

"It seems young Davis invested in a very rich Nevada silver mine, an unusual investment for the Davis family. I've been skimming every bit of cash out of that Bluebird Mine for the past year."

"Somebody's asking about it?"

Collins nodded, silently urging his son to probe.

"One of the other trustees?"

"That I could handle, dammit. No, it's the other partner, a Californian named William Donovan. I told him we'd spent the money to explore a new discovery of silver."

"A big tunnel to nowhere, eating up his money without a trace? Good idea."

Collins smiled, savoring another example of a Collins's ready ability to stretch the truth. Then he shrugged and returned to telling the facts, as was due to his own flesh and blood. "Yes, except Donovan didn't believe me. He's in Seattle now but has demanded proof upon his return from there, when he'll visit the Bluebird. If there isn't a big silver find or his money, there'll be hell to pay."

"Who does he think he is? No Californian can do that to you!"

Collins smiled wryly and clapped his boy on the shoulder. "Thank you for your confidence in me, but you'd best know who your enemy is first. He's the owner of Donovan & Sons, one of the largest western freighting companies. He's a partner in the Bank of California and has a seat on the San Francisco Board of Trade. He most certainly has us over a barrel, should he demand that the Davis Trust repay him."

"Hell," Maitland swore softly, his face darkening.

"Exactly," Collins agreed—and twisted his wrist, instinctively testing to make sure his old seaman's dirk was still ready for action. No matter how much attention Donovan's sudden death would draw, he still saw red whenever he heard the fellow's name.

"Do we have the money?"

"Not in cash; we've spent too much on rebuilding the shipping line. But marrying Rachel Davis would rid us of Donovan—and give us the rest of the Davis fortune as well."

Maitland flung up his hand, like a fencer acknowledging a hit. "Touché. I'll do it tomorrow."

He grabbed the brandy decanter and poured a slug into his coffee cup. "We should probably kill Donovan anyway. It would be cheaper than paying him off."

"True," Collins agreed, rather pleased by this blatantly bloodthirsty train of thought. It was the first time Maitland had used his natural viciousness to help the family. "My man in Nevada should be able to arrange his death, probably in an ambush."

Maitland lifted his cup. "To the new Collins fortune, built on the foundation of the Davis Trust!"

"To the new Collins fortune!"

Their cups clinked.

*   *   *

Rachel's fingers clenched and unclenched in the embroidered coverlet, wishing she could throw something at those two demons in the other room.

William Donovan's life was in danger and she was the only one who could warn him.

She needed to escape soon, just as quickly as possible. They were headed west to Omaha, where a western freighting company should have a depot. Maybe there she could get word to William Donovan.

Or she could cable to her friend Lucas Grainger, who worked for William Donovan now.

She and Grainger had remained friends ever since they'd met at her wedding to Elias, their relationship rather like those with the young men she tutored in Latin. Their letters had grown into a personal correspondence that endured beyond Elias's death. Always friendly, never intimate, and certainly infrequent given Grainger's erratic movements about the countryside, his often blunt thoughts, about anything from political scandals to how Indians followed wolf tracks, had been her one refuge from Elias's slow, dreadful spiral into death.

Afterward, she'd wished bitterly she still had the solace of his letters, given the Collins clan's increasingly direct attacks on everything she held dear: First, to force her to give them control of Elias's home, and later, to drive her into marrying Maitland.

But Grainger's letters had stopped when she'd arrived at Collins's Ledge, undoubtedly because Collins had blocked them like every other contact with the outside world.

He'd be Rachel's last choice to help her with her real dilemma, of course. But he might be able to find her a man who would.

Also, he came from a very compassionate family. His mother, for example, was a great patroness of children's charities, although her private life was whispered about.

Surely he'd ensure a warning would reach his employer, once she managed to send it to him.

If she only knew where he was.

Across town, Lucas Grainger followed his father, Thomas Lawrence Grainger IV—or T.L.—through Chicago's best hotel and wondered what trial the old devil was planning for him this time.

At least Mother wasn't here. In that case, he'd have been certain he was about to descend through the nine circles of hell.

Christ Almighty, how clearly he recognized signs of the old trap closing around him, starting with the Old Man's false cordiality all evening. He'd always fought battle after endless battle with his parents, usually about what role he'd play in the family business.

He'd been tutored throughout his childhood, rather than going to prep school like his brother Tom and other boys of his parents' social circle. The greatest fight with his parents had come when he'd learned that they expected him to attend the University of Pennsylvania and live at home, rather than follow Tom to Princeton. Unable to dissuade them, he'd run away and joined the western Union army, the farthest from Philadelphia. He'd taken great pains to become a private in a state militia as close to the front as possible, in order to remain isolated from any of his father's contacts in Washington. It had worked: By the time Pinkerton's men had found him, he'd become a hardened veteran and his parents were no longer willing to display him to their fashionable set, since they abhorred the reek of common soldiers. Later, he'd transferred to the regular Army's cavalry, having found a life that he loved.

It had been two and a half years since their last battle, caused by his father's fury that Lucas hadn't resigned his Army commission in order to return to Philadelphia and join the family empire.

If he didn't need his family's business contacts, he'd leave now. When Donovan had suspected the Davis Trust was swindling him, Lucas had vehemently objected, given his prior service with Elias Davis during the War. He'd suggested that Albert Collins, the principal trustee, was more likely the fraud's author, not Rachel Davis, Elias's widow. She'd corresponded with him, first as a proxy for Elias and later in her own right, primarily discussing politics and books. He found it impossible to believe that anyone with such pungent opinions about political bribery would have embezzled money from one of her beloved late husband's business partners. He knew damn well she hadn't lost her wits from grief either, no matter what the gossips said.

And she was so young, little more than twenty-three years of age. Too damn innocent to know how to protect herself from fortune hunters who'd stop a lady's correspondence . . .

A muscle ticked in his jaw.

Dammit, if he hadn't been traveling so much, he'd have realized her letters had ended abruptly with no explanation and would have helped her. But first, there'd been that expedition into Colorado for the Spanish gold, then he'd brought the horses safely out of Memphis, and settled them in California. Somehow, yet again he hadn't been able to help a woman who needed him!

Donovan had agreed that Lucas could be correct and sent him to investigate it further. So Lucas had cabled his brother, asking for the loan of a private railroad car and the Graingers' commercial connections to test the Collins clan's desperation for money.

Given assurances of those resources, he'd come to Chicago with a wardrobe suitable for Boston's finest circles; a logical precaution, if he was to seek out all of Collins's weaknesses. He hadn't expected to find waiting here both the *Empress*, the Grainger family's legendary private Pullman—and his father.

But by then he'd already learned that Albert Collins and his son had also journeyed to Chicago, a thousand miles closer to the Bluebird Mine. Why? For them to come here, when they'd never gone more than two hundred miles west of Boston, stank to high heaven.

Worse, there was Rachel Davis, who for some impossible reason had traveled to Chicago with Collins. Her idea of an enjoyable winter evening included translating Cicero, singing with her mother and sister, or ice skating. None of those could be performed on a cross-country train trip, especially alone with Collins and his son.

So why was she here? To marry one of the Collins men, as so many rumors said? He doubted it, given her acute intelligence and the son's unsavory reputation.

If gaining an answer to that question meant being polite to his father, he'd manage to do it, by God.

So here he was, to learn what the devil his father really wanted from him in exchange for the *Empress*. He'd guarantee that almost any request would start another fight between them, given their past record. The only question was whether the price would be too high for him to stomach.

He was slightly grateful—although wryly unsurprised— that the demand hadn't come during their dinner in that *public* dining room.

As befitted his father's view of the Graingers' role in society, the luxurious sitting room was the centerpiece of the best suite in Chicago's best hotel. The large room was a rich tableaux of brown and gold masculine comforts, from the lavishly upholstered chairs to the large marble fireplace, the thick Brussels carpets, and the lamps casting hissing, golden gaslight over all. Even the brilliantly polished spittoons were well placed to ensure that a gentleman could always find one, while not having to worry overmuch about knocking one over if under the influence of Demon Rum.

Lucas dropped his top hat onto a side table and carefully

draped his evening cloak beside it. The elegant display should remind him to be patient, rather than use his typical street language over the old autocrat's demands.

T.L. Grainger IV was often held up as a fine example of what the world called "the splendid Grainger men." He stood a few inches shorter than either of his sons, his once black hair now white, but his features retained their eaglelike sharpness. Few had ever successfully tricked or cozened him into doing anything he didn't choose to.

His youngest son usually acknowledged the family likeness.

T.L. handed Lucas a fragile crystal balloon glass, half filled with a rich golden elixir, and settled into his own chair with a similar glass.

Despite himself, Lucas sniffed appreciatively. Courvoisier cognac, the finest brandy in the world. Perhaps there might be a few good reasons for reentering the Grainger fold. He leaned back in his chair and pretended to admire the cognac's color. Even so, damned if he'd start the conversation.

"You've done very well for yourself out in California," the elder Grainger mused. "Those Central Pacific shares you bought five years ago have gone up noticeably."

Lucas somehow managed to show only polite gratification, rather than shock. His first compliment from his father? *What was this leading up to?* He inclined his head. "Thank you, sir."

"I understand you're traveling a great deal throughout the West. Are you searching out more investment opportunities for yourself?"

Lucas frowned slightly. How could he tell him that he was the chief troubleshooter for Donovan & Sons—the most challenging, enjoyable position he'd ever held? That any opportunities to make money by himself, for himself, were merely the icing on the cake? "I, ah—"

His father leaned forward. "Or are you seeing a young lady?"

Lucas stiffened. Dammit, couldn't they be alone for five minutes without restarting that old inquisition? Was it already time for a lecture on returning to the family fold and finding the proper breeding partner? "Certainly not."

"Indeed," T.L. mused, his gaze very sharp on Lucas's face. "I understand there are some beauties in California."

Lucas gritted his teeth, recognizing a conversational pit opening in front of him. He smiled slightly, adopting the gentlemanly countenance used when declining to discuss a lady in any terms whatsoever.

"At least you're not chasing some female with more looks than breeding."

Lucas very nearly threw his expensive brandy in his father's face at this dismissal of every woman in California, including all of his friends' daughters and sisters. The only thing more predictable than his father's demands was the Old Man's snobbishness, his absolute certainty that only a very few families produced daughters suitable for inclusion in the Graingers' bloodline.

At least his father forbore to pursue the topic further, permitting Lucas's pulse to resume a normal pace.

T.L. grunted and swirled his cognac, letting the light dance in its depths. "The family's Wilmington branch just bought a very fine bank. You might have heard of it—Tallmadge's Bank."

Lucas didn't quite blink. It never paid to show the Old Man when one of his topics alerted you, as did any direct mention of money by the old banker. "Really? That must be worth at least half a million."

"Closer to a million." His father lifted his glass in salute and all but purred when he drank the fine brandy.

Lucas sipped at his drink, warily considering the gambit. "Why did old Tallmadge decide to sell out?"

"He wrote off his son-in-law as a bad investment and decided one of my brats would be a better bet."

Every hair on the nape of Lucas's neck stood up. Settled for only two generations in Wilmington, the Tallmadge family was barely accepted at Mother's larger parties. Surely they weren't good enough for the family dining salon, let alone the family Bible. "What does Mother say to that?"

"She gave me a matched pair of bays, in thanks for finding the chit."

Lucas raised an eyebrow and waited, waves of ice rippling over his skin. If his mother was pleased, it wasn't because he'd enjoy it.

"Miss Tallmadge will be the perfect daughter-in-law," Lucas's father pronounced, hoisting his brandy snifter in celebration. "It's taken me years to find someone like her. Young, rich, virginal—and, best of all, her name is Martha."

The name sent the old misshapen guilt roiling through Lucas. He fought it back, as desperate and nauseated as the first day he'd tasted its sourness, until he could stare at his father—and saw triumph written across the older man's countenance.

"No." His voice was little more than a rasp. He would rather die than have the name Martha uttered daily in his own home. He'd lived too long with his mother hurling it at his head.

The Old Man considered him for an instant, like an auctioneer studying an unbroken horse. Then his expression shifted to coaxing.

Lucas immediately shuttered his countenance, as if he stood in a gunfight. His fingers tightened on his glass's fragile crystal stem. His dirk's long, lean blade pressed against his forearm and his pocket Navy Colt hung against his hip. If he wasn't wearing fancy dress, he'd have the joy of his heavier Army Colts to deal with this. The world narrowed to the all too smug man watching him from across the table, encircled by a red haze.

"A million dollars, Lucas," T.L. crooned softly. "Think it over carefully."

He didn't need to; the money wasn't a bribe—it was closer to poisoned bait. Lucas swirled his brandy, until his breathing came back under control. He took another sip, set his glass down on the table and pushed it away, not wanting anything to cloud his senses. He wouldn't speak—couldn't think—of Martha.

"My brother Tom," he pointed out carefully, "is married with four children and another on the way." Sweet Jesus, did he really hope that the Old Man was speaking of Tom?

"Possibly all of them girls. Someone else needs to provide sons to carry on the Grainger name and you're the only one who can," his father snapped out.

"Like hell!" Lucas slammed out of his seat, his fists clenching and unclenching. All the shouting matches he'd had with his parents over the years roared through his head, deafening him. Did his father still truly think of him as only a means to an end, the breeder of the next generation?

A moment later, T.L. also rose and spoke more sweetly, offering what he must see as inducements. "Tallmadge's Bank has excellent western connections—in St. Louis, Denver, especially San Francisco."

Lucas sucked in a deep breath and tried to relax. It would take every ounce of public and private influence to learn why Rachel Davis was in Chicago with the Collinses, not in Boston, where she belonged. He could not afford to throw aside the Grainger family, no matter how little his father had ever accepted him.

"And old Tallmadge's granddaughter is a pretty young girl. You'd be able to mold her into whatever sort of wife you want."

"Dammit, sir, stop!" As if a pliable virgin would ever—could ever—interest him, even under these circumstances!

When he could finally control himself, he enunciated every word very clearly. "I swore to you back in 1862, before I ran off to join the War, that I would never provide the world with another example of the farce known as a Grainger marriage."

"It's your duty to settle down and start a family," his father roared. "You must end your whoring around."

Lucas pounded the table, making the crystal dance. "Why do I need to stop? Did you, at any time in my life? Did Uncle Ned or Aunt Alice? Or Grandfather? Did Mother, even if she calls her paramours 'solace for past sorrows?' When did any of you honor your marriage vows for longer than a few days? We're a family of notorious adulterers and I have it in my blood from both sides."

His father flushed, his head jerking back as if struck. Lucas had never spoken so bluntly about the family vice before. He wouldn't have done so now, if Mother's longing for another Martha hadn't been so harshly brought up.

There was a long, angry silence.

The Old Man gathered himself back together and glared at his son. "At least consider your duty to the family name! Your older brother has provided only females, thereby endangering us. As a girl, your sister Hortense is of no help."

Lucas flung up his hand. "My brother has four daughters, which proves he and his wife are young and fertile. There's time aplenty for them to provide an heir for *your* branch of the family. After that, my cousins are doing more than their share to provide the next generation of Graingers. Do you have anything else to discuss?"

"Uncle Barnabas should never have left his fortune to you. Independence has gone to your head." The older man glowered, looking like an angry bear. "You must come home to Philadelphia and start a family, Lucas. It's where you belong."

"No." Only loyalty to his older brother, the one family member he'd ever been able to speak somewhat freely to, kept him from saying *never*. He'd always dreamed of a warm family that would welcome him home every evening—but not at the price of marriage or a return to Philadelphia.

"I came here for our family's private Pullman and her entire crew." He repeated his demand. "Are you willing to discuss that—or do I need to ask Fisk or Vanderbilt for one?"

"You wouldn't dare! The gossip would be appalling if you asked one of them for aid."

Lucas lifted an eyebrow and waited, keeping his expression impassive. In some ways, it didn't matter what his father answered. Fisk and Vanderbilt, those two great railroad tycoons, would leap to give him a private railroad car, whether freely—to tweak the Grainger patriarch's pride—or hired.

But a small part of him, hidden deep within for decades since a summer afternoon by a still mountain pond, hoped his father would help him on this adventure.

T.L. Grainger IV stared at him, as if clearly seeing him for the first time as an adult. "Very well," he said slowly, "you may have the *Empress*. I'll cable Stewart in Philadelphia, telling him to make sure you have the maximum assistance possible from the railroads."

Lucas bowed slightly, hiding the unaccustomed relief flooding his veins. "Thank you, sir. I am deeply appreciative of your generosity."

Chapter Three

Western Iowa, the next afternoon

Another gust of wind slammed against the train, making the luxurious private Pullman shiver until the fringes on every sofa and chair's arms and skirts danced madly. It was the latest—and frighteningly, a dying example—in a year of wicked storms. The lamps' crystal shades clattered, sending the gaslight skittering across the overhead murals and bouncing across the room through the series of mirrors. Only the lavishly upholstered furniture and opulent Brussels carpet were stable, like boulders too massive to be affected by a storm.

Albert Collins stared blindly at the flat, featureless landscape outside, alternately hidden and revealed by billowing snow. Maitland Collins paced up and down the aisle, shooting impatient glances at Rachel.

Rachel considered him from under her eyelashes, careful to pretend an interest in her Bible. So far that had been enough to prevent a proposal of marriage and her subsequent refusal—and Maitland's almost inevitable angry eruption, which she'd seen happen far too often when he was blocked.

She desperately needed a more permanent alternative.

She hadn't been able to escape from the train. Every time it stopped, there'd been at least three of the Collins's thugs watching the private car's exits. A mouse might have disappeared into the surrounding prairies but not a cat, and certainly not a grown woman.

If only she'd been able to study Latin at Mount Holyoke and be valued for her wits by someone, instead of her bank balance. But she'd known when she married Elias that she might one day find herself a widow beset by fortune hunters. She simply hadn't expected them to be so vicious and persistent.

The train jerked again, rattling china and silverware until cutlery jumped across the table. The teapot teetered and she grabbed for it, barely stopping it before it fell into the aisle. The cream pitcher fell over, splashing everything in its path with rich white droplets, including both Collins men.

Maitland spun, brushing at his sleeve, and roared, "Clumsy cow, how dare you ruin my new suit!"

She jerked her head briefly, not directly answering the unjust accusation, and began to rapidly reassemble the tea tray, gathering up the cutlery and china from where they'd slid perilously close to the table's edge. Albert Collins clucked his tongue at the damage to their extraordinarily expensive suits and handed his son a napkin.

Maitland started to jerkily mop himself up, every gesture telling of leashed rage. "Once we reach Omaha, we'll find a preacher and . . ."

Rachel stiffened, startled and frightened. Was he about to simply announce that they would marry? Without even a courtship—or asking her to accept him?

She played her last delaying card, hoping it would work. "When we arrive in Omaha, I must send a letter to Mrs. Biddle."

"Mrs. *Horace* Biddle?" Albert Collins questioned, coming alert.

Thank God, she'd caught the senior, more powerful man's attention. Her ploy just might save her. *This* time.

She adopted her most docile, studious expression, which would certainly have made her mother extremely suspicious. "Yes, sir, she gave me a most impressive study guide for the Gospels. I have been sending her my answers weekly, even from the island."

She prayed they couldn't see how her pulse was hammering. Her statement wasn't quite a lie; she hadn't told them exactly what day of the week she usually wrote to Mrs. Biddle.

"What the devil do we care about a Mrs. Biddle?" Maitland demanded.

"Her husband is *the* Reverend Horace Biddle, of the Cambridge *Clarion Call* and one of the Davis trustees," Collins snapped, quelling his son with a peremptory flick of his fingers.

Maitland subsided, muttering under his breath. Rachel managed not to sigh in relief; she'd never seen him openly disobey his father.

"Mrs. Davis, we would not dream of interfering with your religious studies," Albert Collins intoned graciously. "We will be happy to send your letter as soon as it's ready."

She smiled and nodded at him, hoping she managed to seem appropriately grateful rather than frantic to escape. Dear heavens, she'd dodged Maitland once again, but for how many more times? "Thank you. I'll write it in my compartment and give it to you."

Maitland growled something unprintable and slapped the brass railing overhead. She nodded to his father, waved her hand in Maitland's direction without directly looking at him, and departed rapidly for her compartment's sanctuary.

She had a small carpetbag and a few other necessities packed and well hidden deep in her trunk. Would she ever have a chance to use them and escape this prison?

Albert Collins automatically braced his feet a little wider and took another sip of his whisky-laced tea, staring after Rachel Davis. He'd be damn glad when he could celebrate her capture with a bottle of champagne, even in this weather.

A knock sounded at the door. "Enter."

The Negro steward entered, precise and self-effacing in his uniform. "Telegram for you, sir."

Collins's skin prickled, the infallible instinct that had always warned him of a change in the weather. He snatched the neatly folded paper and began to read it, his free hand impatiently waving away the servant. "Damn."

Maitland watched, bracing himself on an overhead rack. "Who's it from?"

"Our spy in Donovan's camp. I paid his telegrapher to tell us everything the Irishman does."

"And?"

"Donovan just left Seattle. We're advised to make all haste to the Bluebird Mine, if we want to arrive first." He began to impatiently refold the cable, without bothering to match any of the original creases. "Damn, I'd hoped the bastard would stay in Seattle or Victoria through February before he returned to San Francisco."

"I thought there weren't any railroads into Seattle yet."

"There aren't. Donovan and his wife will be traveling by steamship to San Francisco, then by train to the Bluebird."

Maitland frowned. "But that will take days at this time of year."

Collins fought the temptation to snarl, reminding himself that the boy simply lacked contact with the harsher side of Mother Nature. "So will travel by rail for us, since we're crossing in midwinter. Why, last year, it took one train more than thirty days to cross Wyoming in the winter."

His son clenched his fists. "Hell, he could reach the Bluebird weeks before us."

Collins nodded, his stomach roiling as it never had on a ship's deck. "Exactly. We need the Davis fortune now."

"Damn, I wish we could pay to have him killed as soon as he sets foot in San Francisco."

"A very poor option: it would be extremely expensive to have a leading citizen assassinated in his hometown."

Maitland cursed under his breath but fell silent. He swayed back and forth on the ornate brass plaque, his feet remaining in the same place, his expression thoughtful. The wind howled mockingly outside, while Collins reviewed options ranging from knifings to poison to . . .

"The Union Pacific's yards in Omaha are along the river bottom, aren't they?" he asked at last.

Collins raised an eyebrow at the non sequitur. "I'd think so. That would be the cheapest place to find enough flat land."

"In this weather, it should have the worst conditions—the most exposed to wind and snow."

"Probably. What are you thinking of?"

"Since it's also where the lower orders work, it should be surrounded by their diversions—saloons, brothels, and similar dives where someone could become lost forever."

"And?"

His son's eyes met his, flat and deadly. "When we reach Omaha, have our private car parked there, far away from anyone or anything else, and dismiss all the servants. After you depart for the evening, I'll have a chat with Mrs. Davis, who'll be alone with me. I guarantee you that, by the time you return, she'll have promised to become my wife."

A frisson ran down Collins's spine and he searched his son's expression. "You wouldn't harm her, would you?"

Maitland made an impatient movement. "How can I do that? She has to be able tell the other trustees that she's willing to marry me and to have at least one child, doesn't she? So don't worry about her."

Collins hesitated. The words were comforting but the tone and the glint in his son's eyes weren't. Still, he didn't have a better plan to offer and surely Maitland's courtship would win over Mrs. Davis this time. "Very well."

They arrived in Omaha shortly after nightfall, the snow falling in the delicate swirls that marked a major storm's passing. Rachel's New England-bred eyes reckoned it as having left a foot of new snow. Her gut warned her that the coming night would be bitterly cold.

Albert and Maitland Collins departed almost immediately thereafter, well dressed and calling loudly for cabs.

Rachel peeped out from behind her compartment's drapes to watch them go. They obviously intended to spend the evening here exploring the town: Collins on some sort of business venture, as had been his practice on this journey, and Maitland deeply engaged in the more unsavory pursuits. At least they'd left her behind in the private Pullman, beyond their sentries' constant stares.

After that, the Pullman was uncoupled from the passenger train and taken to a siding deep within the railroad yard, its exact location hidden by darkness plus all the equipment, steam, and coal smoke of the yard itself.

By the time Rachel left her compartment for the dining salon, she could hear all the sounds of a working railroad—steam whistles shrilling, trains rumbling past, heavy freight cars banging into each other as they were coupled and uncoupled to form new trains for new destinations. Farther off, machinery was repaired or tracks were laid to a new destination. Throughout all of it, men shouted and cursed in a startling variety of languages.

And all of the noises were alternately vividly exposed or muffled by the blowing wind, while the sound of a great river ran underneath everything, ice cracking and grinding against itself.

But the Pullman itself was silent, except for the faint creaking of its wooden walls and the faint rattle of glassware. It wasn't the usual pattern, which told of supplies coming aboard, of fresh linens handed in and soiled ones going out, chefs urging caution while heavy blocks of ice thudded into the lockers under the central kitchen, Collins's valet demanding better brands of brandy. Rachel's maid—hired in Philadelphia and rightly terrified of the Collinses—had disappeared as usual, immediately after dressing Rachel.

Rachel glanced out the window, hunting for signs of her guards. Maybe, if they weren't here, she could grab her hidden carpetbag and run for the railroad depot. If she could just get far enough away, fast enough . . .

Fog, built up from steam plus wood and coal smoke, obscured the view outside, its eddies occasionally swirling to offer glimpses of the Union Pacific's workmen. A high steep bluff, dotted with lights, loomed in the distance—Omaha. And, as always, Collins's thugs watched every exit, this time apparently strolling around about the Pullman rather than leaning against a convenient wall to chat with each other.

Why on earth had Collins left the private Pullman here? He'd have to cross the railroad yard and probably some nasty parts of town, as well, to reach it. She shuddered, imagining the sights, somehow quite sure that Dickens had not told everything horrific he knew about gambling dens and filthy slums.

The private Pullman creaked again, a cold draft fluttering the draperies' velvet fringe like a ghostly hand.

Rachel gasped and jumped back, dropping the curtains. For an instant, she wished she had a genuine weapon for protection against the lurking threat.

Then she laughed at herself, ignoring the sound's hollowness. She didn't need anything deadly, such as a gun or a knife, when she'd be the only passenger tonight. The only aid which might come in handy she already had—her brown promenade dress, far more demure than any evening gown, which would turn male eyes from lascivious thoughts. Around the Collins men, the dress' merino wool, soft and fine as any cashmere, also soothed and comforted her, its bustle enabled her skirts to swish in a most authoritarian manner, and its full, bell-like sleeves allowed her to hide how her fingers often curved into claws.

She tilted her chin at the importunate draft and proceeded down the corridor, determined to let nothing else stand between her and a good dinner. Heaven knows she'd had very few quiet meals since the Collins men had begun trying to steal the Davis fortune.

Rachel paused at the dining salon's door and found a properly set table for two—but no uniformed waiter, with a napkin over his arm.

Only the chef glanced out of the kitchen, looking extremely uncomfortable—and untying his apron. He wouldn't meet her eyes.

She frowned slightly.

Maitland came forward, suave in his formal black frock coat and an edged smile gleaming in his eyes.

Ice jolted up Rachel's spine and her knees started to weaken. Dear God in heaven, what was Maitland doing here? Where was his father?

She locked her knees, keeping her face calm. "Mr. Collins."

"Please sit down, Mrs. Davis. Charles here will serve us— and depart, leaving us alone together on the train. I'm sure you don't want to keep him from visiting his family in the city."

Alone—with Maitland? *Oh, dear Lord, what was he planning to do now?*

Lucas leaned over the desk at the Cozzens Hotel, a golden half eagle barely visible between his fingers. He'd received William's cable during the trip from Chicago, saying that he was leaving Seattle for the Bluebird Mine. Given those dates and this year's hard weather, Collins needed to travel straight through to Nevada without any delays.

So why had he unhitched his private car from the passenger train tonight and had it taken across the Missouri River to Nebraska? That decision made no sense whatsoever, since the other cars would be crossing the river in the morning to gain daylight's advantage for crossing the plains.

The most obvious advantage for Collins was that he'd spend the night isolated from anyone who knew him and his son. Of course, he might intend to rest here from the journey's hardships, since he hadn't taken the typical few days' rest in Chicago. Omaha was hardly known as a scenic retreat, though.

At least the Grainger family's connections had garnered Lucas a very rare private train from Chicago to Omaha, after his father had delayed him in Chicago. He was now only an hour behind Collins.

"Are they staying here?" Lucas asked the clerk quietly.

"No, sir. But Mr. Collins is having dinner with three other gentlemen in the main dining salon." The clerk's eyes barely flickered toward the coin. "If you'd like, I can have one of the porters show you the way."

Every nerve in Lucas's body came on full alert. *Rachel Davis wasn't here?* Instinctively, he shifted subtly, checking his guns' locations. "No, thank you, that won't be necessary. I'll speak to him later, after he's finished eating. As a surprise."

He slid the gold across the desk, where it quickly vanished from sight under the clerk's hand.

"Whatever you wish, sir," the fellow agreed smugly. It was probably the largest tip he'd received that day or maybe that month, certainly enough to keep him from speaking to Collins about this inquiry.

Lucas touched his hat and headed back out into the snow, jostling his way past the hotel's patrons. Why the hell had Collins let Rachel Davis, his golden goose, out of sight? And if she was alone with the young brute, Maitland—well, he'd give better odds on a lamb strolling out of a lion's den.

Cursing under his breath, he started jogging toward the railroad depot, where he'd last seen Collins's Pullman.

The exit door slammed shut beyond the kitchen, announcing the chef's departure and completing their isolation.

Rachel looked around, telling herself once again everything was entirely normal and nothing—nothing!—would, or could, go wrong here.

The center table was set for two with a cold dinner composed of meats, cheeses, breads, cold soups, cold salads, and other side dishes. One sideboard displayed a few light desserts, such as custards and pastries, flanked by a great coffeepot and teapot, with their attendant china. Everything was all so reassuringly ordinary, just as it had been on the entire journey, down to the curving sugar tongs and the long, sharp lemon fork used to select the perfect flavorings.

The sideboard on the opposite side held a spectacular array of fine wines and brandies, their bottles, decanters, and glasses glittering in the lamplight.

The other tables hadn't been set for dinner and were stowed away, leaving the room filled with heavily upholstered settees and chairs. Only a few end tables were scattered among them with lamps. In other words, instead of the typically crowded arrangement where one would tread on a stranger's foot every other step, there was enough space for Rachel to twirl and not have her train strike a stranger's knees. All the curtains were tightly drawn against the nighttime chill or a stranger's casual glance.

Rachel straightened her shoulders. Hopefully, Maitland only meant to converse with her. But, given how he'd attacked Mercy, she wasn't extremely optimistic.

If he wanted to discuss marriage, she would explain yet again that she wasn't ready to consider a union with anyone. He didn't have to know she meant a union with anyone *present in the room*; Elias was long dead and she'd promised him to spend the rest of her life in sunshine, not walking in his tomb's shadows. So far that explanation had kept Maitland from laying a hand on her.

"Good evening, Maitland." She held her head high and stepped forward, keeping the table between them and refusing to show any weakness despite the multitude of gnomes gnawing at her stomach. "Would you care for some coffee or tea before dinner?"

Maitland leaned back against the far sideboard and eyed her, glass in one hand and bottle in the other.

"Why waste time on that swill?" He poured himself a tumblerful of brandy.

Her brows knitted. Why was he drinking so much? For the first time, she seriously measured the distance to the exits. There were two doors from the dining salon itself: One close at hand and another far beyond all the tables and conversational nooks. No exit could be easily reached in the face of his displeasure.

"What do you want, Maitland?" she asked more cautiously, trying to maintain a rational atmosphere.

He blew out his breath. "Not you—but I'm going to have to take you," he stated crudely.

"What?" Her breath stopped in her throat and she froze, her hand on the back of a chair. She didn't sit down.

"You're a scrawny brown rabbit—"

She stared at him, unable to believe her ears. Surely he could not be openly discussing her physical attractions. "Maitland, shouldn't we be discussing the relative merits of cold turkey or ham? It's suppertime, after all."

"No, we're going to be married and you're going to birth my sons." He took a very long swallow of brandy. "Somehow I have to mount your cold hide tonight because the other trustees won't start paying over any real money until you're pregnant."

Rachel couldn't have said how she stayed erect, given the spinning in her skull. Her fingers tightened on the carved wood, reassuring herself that there was still something predictable in the world. "Maitland, surely you're joking. You haven't proposed to me, for one thing." Could she scream loudly enough to draw the railroad yard workers' attention? Probably not.

"Not necessary. You'll marry me even if you're unconscious at the ceremony and the preacher's drunk and well bribed. My family needs your money too much." He guzzled more brandy, his Adam's apple bobbing up and down steadily—inexorably. "Damn, I wish you looked like more fun, though."

Rachel tried to think of other saviors. Collins's ruffians? Maybe if she screamed very loudly?

She'd have to play for time until someone came close enough to hear. Perhaps some carefully applied reasoning would be able to dissuade him.

She shot a quick glance at the nearest door. He stood between her and it, closing off her best chance for escape. *Oh God . . .*

"Don't think of running. Or screaming," he added, setting down the empty decanter. "The guards are all Father's men. They've been well paid to ignore anything that goes on in here."

She swallowed hard. Not that she'd truly believed those thugs might become her allies but, still, to know that they'd ignore a woman's screams was a most horrifying thought. She fought back the voice that whispered *run!* and tried again for logic.

"If you force me into marriage," she tried again to reach him using a firmer tone, "that's cause for a divorce."

He snickered at her. "Only if you tell somebody—which you won't, because you'll be locked up, waiting for me."

She froze. *Waiting for him? Dear God, that tiny island and Mercy screaming as she ran from him, blood pouring down her throat from where he'd ripped her earring out . . .*

He chuckled, a happy sound of purely wicked intent. "I thought that would catch your attention. You'll live on Collins's Ledge year round, alone except for the servants and whatever brat is in your belly at the moment."

No, never. Please, God, not him and that prison . . . "Maitland, the other trustees—"

He smiled all too sweetly—and poisonously—at her. "Will believe you have firmed your preference for the pure ocean air. As you must remember, it's a difficult place to reach, given the Atlantic's currents, and the ferry only runs four months a year." He filled his glass with more brandy.

Dear heavens, the last time she'd stood in that closet which passed for a cellar, she'd sworn the walls were falling in on her every time a wave crashed onto the beach. If she had to go back? Her pulse was racing and her skin cold and wet under her once-warm dress.

Bear his child in that cage? She'd fight to the death to avoid it. "No," she said hoarsely. "No, and no, and no."

Maitland looked up from the sideboard, where he was inspecting decanter labels, and raised an eyebrow. "Don't be absurd, Rachel, I'm going to have you tonight. So just be quiet and maybe you'll get pregnant quickly, simplifying matters for both of us."

She shook her head emphatically. "Never."

"You're being a fool."

She shook her head again, keeping her head high with an effort. "No matter what happens, I will never, ever, marry you."

Maitland stared at her, anger building behind his eyes. "Dammit, bitch, what the hell do you mean, saying no? You will do exactly what I say. Otherwise—"

He swung the carved crystal decanter up by its neck and smashed it down onto the table edge. It shattered, sending glittering shards across the Brussels carpet.

Rachel shrieked and jumped back, her pulse pounding. She almost tripped on her train, but managed to save herself, holding her skirt out of the way with one hand.

"Defy me and I'll break you like that crystal, you understand?" He took a step forward, and another, and another, his expression menacing.

She stepped back, trying not to look at the carpet. Her skin seemed to have completely separated from her body.

He snatched up the great vase from the center table, with its massive floral arrangement, and dashed it onto the carpet. "You disobey me and I'll turn you into dust, bitch!" he shouted, grinding his boot heel into the tumbled roses and chrysanthemums.

She threw a handful of nuts at him, fighting for time and space.

He came after her one step after another, like a hyena closing in for the kill.

Her brain raced into action, like a mill wheel spinning a river's clear waters. There were three exits in all, one of them beyond the latched kitchen door. To reach any of them, Maitland would have to be either compliant—*hah!*—or unconscious. She needed a weapon to defend herself with, although she had no idea where to find one or how to use it.

Her hips came up against something solid, the dessert sideboard with its full tea and coffee service. Automatically her hands went back to brace herself and discovered plates and cutlery. She groped, looking for something to defend herself with. Anything long and narrow. Her fingers scrabbled amongst the items, finding custard bowls, cake plates, dessert forks, sugar tongs, lemon fork . . .

Maitland loomed over her. He grabbed her, his fingers digging cruelly deep into her hips. "You goddamn bitch, I'll teach you who's master here!"

He tugged at her skirts, arching her backward.

She was all but light-headed, not entirely sure which thought was instinct or reason. Terror ran hot and fast through her veins, while ice was freezing her skin. Her right hand closed over the lemon fork.

His leg slammed between hers. He was roaring something profane and horribly explicit about her immediate future servicing him.

Rachel swung the lemon fork—as long as her hand and narrow as her thumb, its two tines sharp as an ice pick—and slashed Maitland's face down the temple and cheek to the bone, barely missing his eye.

He screamed and jerked away, clapping his hands to his face. Blood spurted out, quickly covering his face, and streaming over his neck and cheek. "Damn you, what the hell have you done?"

She flung the dripping fork away, shuddering at how living flesh had felt under her weapon.

He spun and grabbed for her again.

She jerked away and he fell onto his knees, slipping on the slimy, pulped flowers he'd destroyed.

He lunged for her ankle, his face a crimson mask. "Damn you to hell, Rachel, you'll wish you'd never been born for slashing me like this!"

Dear God in heaven, would nothing stop him?

She grabbed the nearest heavy object, the massive silver coffeepot, just as Maitland's fingers closed around her ankle. "By God, I'll take my horsewhip to you!" he vowed and started to come up on his knees.

She smashed the coffeepot down on his head. He crumpled onto the floor, his blood soaking the Brussels carpet in an obscene blossom.

Chills swept rapidly over Rachel's entire body and she backed slowly away from him. She stuffed her knuckles into her mouth and tried very, very hard not to faint.

A fist rapped at the rear door, beyond the kitchen. "Mr. Maitland, sir?"

Maitland's thugs had finally come to investigate.

Rachel gathered up her skirts and turned to run for the far door and her compartment, her heart drumming against her ribs. *Oh, dear God in heaven, please let me slip out of this Pullman unnoticed and into Omaha. No matter what it takes, let me escape into the city, where I can find someone—anyone—to help me . . .*

Lucas turned away from the depot and considered the tracks leading into the freight yard. A chill was running down his spine, sharper and deeper than the air sinking into his lungs.

Collins's private Pullman had supposedly been parked on the freight yard's edge, near the worst of the red-light district which fed on the railroad men's pay. But no one knew exactly where, since the men responsible had been so well paid that they'd immediately imbibed their wages in the closest saloon.

According to the stationmaster, Collins had half a dozen thugs with him. But a mob could rise out of Omaha's slums and overwhelm them in minutes, then loot the Pullman—and kill Mrs. Davis.

Lucas could either try to find the Pullman in the freight yard's maze of tracks, currently obscured by night and heavy fog, or go to the saloon where the men had passed out, and find the closest piece of track.

He drew his Colts and loaded another bullet into each one. They were now fully loaded, with six shots rather than the safer five. If the hammer fell for any reason, the gun would go off immediately. He needed every advantage he could get, even if it risked his life.

He headed south, moving like a prowling predator the supple wariness that his oldest friend, a half-breed Indian scout, had taught him years ago. It was a deliberate warning to all comers—and most of those watching recognized it as such.

Rachel leaned against the frozen, grimy brick wall and fought to catch her breath, the air so cold that it seemed laced with icy blades. Thanks to the low lying smoke from the railroad workshops and the commotion in the dining salon over Maitland's prone body, she'd managed to escape the private Pullman, dodging the few remaining sentries.

She panted softly, fighting to listen for pursuers—heavy boots pounding down the railroad tracks, flat Bostonian accents muttering to each other . . .

She heard nothing like that. But they could be muffled by the fog.

Foul language about card games and women poured from the buildings ahead. A woman in the shack next to her was entertaining a man carnally, obviously for money: She was insisting that he either hurry up or pay more.

Rachel shuddered, pressing her hand to her stomach, her fingertip catching on one of the jewels sewn into her corset.

Nothing Charles Dickens had ever written had prepared her for the harsh, deadly reality of this slum. She needed to escape quickly or be condemned to the same fate as that woman. Or worse.

Her stomach was flopping like a codfish on a fisherman's hook. If she had seen all of the bloodstains on her clothes, she was afraid she'd disgrace herself.

Stiffening her spine, she forced herself to move toward the street, carrying her carpetbag. She needed to make her way through this slum and into the main city. After that, she'd have to find someone who could tell her how to find the Donovan & Sons' depot.

"What the hell you mean, Annie, by movin' out on me? You been seein' somebody else?" The man's words were slurred with drink, but still vividly laced with anger and violence.

Rachel froze, barely two steps back from the street corner. Was another woman about to be beaten?

"No, Billy, I haven't," a girl's voice quavered. "But I couldn't, I just couldn't stay, Billy."

She shouldn't help her, she really shouldn't, not when Maitland's men had to be following her. Maybe the situation wasn't really immediately dangerous to the girl. She'd look the situation over quickly, before moving on.

Rachel crept forward, peering between the rapidly increasing crowd.

Billy was a narrow-eyed thug, flaunting a pair of six-guns, while Annie sported two black eyes and a face so bruised it would be a wonder if she could eat. He knocked her to the ground with one ham-sized fist. "I told you, you were mine!" he roared, standing over her, and drew back his booted foot for a kick. The reek of rum coming from him was amazing, even at this distance.

Annie promptly curled herself into an all-too-practiced ball. Rachel edged forward to help her, completely forgetting her own need to escape.

"I wouldn't do that, if I were you," another man observed, his deep voice slicing through the crowd's whispers. A very, very beautiful, masculine voice. A commanding voice, one to obey and yet take pleasure in.

Rachel froze, startled by its familiarity.

Even Billy was struck by its force. "Who the hell are you to talk to me? Annie's mine and I'll deal with her any way I want," he growled.

"No lady deserves to be beaten," the newcomer remarked. Or was it a warning?

An odd ripple in the throng, of a man half-turning aside to make a bet, propelled Rachel forward like a pea in a pea-shooter. She started to move back, shy of catching too much attention—and caught sight of the newcomer for the first time.

He was a tall man, broad-shouldered, who carried himself with a relaxed confidence that screamed of arrogance, of the utter sureness that he could accomplish anything and every-thing he chose to do. He wore a caped black wool greatcoat, high leather boots, and a broad-brimmed black felt hat, all thickly sparkled now with snow blown from the rooftops.

His thick, straight black hair just touched the base of his collar. His features were commanding and aristocratic, of the sort meant to be carved into gold coins and marveled at gen-erations later as belonging to a great conqueror. His aquiline nose, strong jaw, and high cheekbones confirmed the impres-sion of strength and power. His incredibly vivid blue-green eyes watched Billy from under the broad-brimmed planter's hat with the same icy intensity as the Missouri River used to force its way to the ocean. A wide mouth, now firmly com-pressed, was the only hint of more sensual emotions.

He seemed the very embodiment of a devil borne on the north wind, with his eyes the color of the light striking fire deep in the heart of an iceberg.

Rachel gasped, hope starting to warm her bones. She'd first seen him in a daguerreotype with other dashing young cavalry officers, their long, curved sabers held so casually ready at their sides. And he'd been the embodiment of kindness at her wedding, when he'd been the only aristocrat generous to the tradesman's granddaughter who was marrying the Boston Brahmin.

Lucas Grainger. *Thank God he was here.*

Billy glared at him. "Annie's mine!" he roared. "An' I'll do what I want wit' her."

"No. Because if you harm her, I'll kill you." Grainger's voice was deadly calm, without a hint of bluffing, despite the absence of any apparent weapon.

Was she about to see violence dealt? A whimper built in the back of her throat but didn't escape. She forced it back, recognizing Billy's threat to the broken Annie.

The crowd shifted backward. Somebody muttered a new, larger wager. Rachel allowed herself to be carried with them.

Billy stared at Grainger, clearly trying to take his measure. The ex-cavalry officer watched him, as unblinking as a cobra ready to strike. Annie never moved. Rachel held her breath, hoping somebody would show sense.

"You're only bluffin'," Billy growled and aimed a kick at Annie.

A bullet splatted into the mud beside Billy's foot. He yelped and leaped back. His hand hovered over his gun, but didn't quite touch it.

Smoke curled lazily up from Grainger's Colt's muzzle. His eyes studied Billy pitilessly. "Ready to reconsider?"

Billy looked around the throng for supporters but found none. He reluctantly came back to Grainger. "Yeah."

"I suggest you take your drinking elsewhere, in that case." There was no leeway in the offer.

The crowd almost audibly held their breaths before Billy uttered an even more drawn-out assent.

"Leave your gun."

Sullenly, Billy obeyed and turned to leave.

Grainger took a step forward toward Annie. Rachel started to draw her first deep breath in far too long.

Billy whirled and a derringer popped into his hand from his sleeve. He aimed it at Grainger, a much taller—and therefore higher—target than Annie.

Rachel screamed.

Tongues of flame stabbed through the falling snow. Billy crumpled onto his face, blood streaming out of his throat.

Rachel closed her eyes, gagging. It was the first time she'd seen violent death meted out.

A woman ran out of the crowd to Annie and they clung together, crying. All around them, the crowd departed, blatantly happy at having seen a bloody fight.

Rachel fought to control herself. She wanted desperately to restore logic to her life, not this insanity. Billy had tried to kill Grainger so the combat veteran had to save himself, since there'd been no police around.

Grainger couldn't be a thoughtless barbarian. He couldn't be, or he wouldn't have been Elias's trusted subordinate and dear friend.

She swallowed hard, wishing once again she'd had the chance to study Latin at Mount Holyoke Seminary. Life was so much simpler in a library.

"Hey, girlie. Wanna have some fun?" A man, attired in an odd assortment of sweaters, coats, and scarves against the chill and reeking of whisky, reached for her. Just behind him, two more men smirked greedily.

She flinched but drew herself up, ready to defend herself with words.

"Get out of here, boys. The night's young yet." Grainger's deep voice sounded behind her, sharp with command. Wonder of wonders in this appalling milieu, he smelled of honest scents, including leather and wood smoke.

The three cringed and edged backward. "Yes. Yes, of course. Sir."

An instant later, the only sign of their presence was the sound of their departing footsteps. Everyone else, including Annie and her friend, had also disappeared down an alley or inside a filthy building.

"Mrs. Davis? Mrs. Elias Davis?" He half-crooned her name, as if he was coaxing a skittish mare.

Rachel shuddered, facing the limits of her own abilities. If she was to stay alive and free, she needed a man's help. On this raw frontier, with people like Billy around, she'd probably be safer if Grainger was a killer.

Something deep inside her, feminine and totally illogical, simply wanted to rest against him.

She stiffened in surprise, but forced herself to smile up at him. "Mr. Grainger."

He offered her his hand, as gallantly as if they stood in the gardens at Anglesey Hall, the Davis estate.

Rachel ran her tongue over her lips, shaking a little. Cautiously, she laid her hand in his, wary of the slightest attempt to grab her.

Grainger's fingers shifted to a protective, light grasp, which barely brushed her glove. He lifted her hand and kissed it. "My pleasure to find you safe at last, Mrs. Davis."

Tears of joy touched her eyes, the agonizing relief at being treated like a lady for the first time in so very, very long. "The pleasure is entirely mine, Mr. Grainger," she managed, finding unaccustomed delight in the simple phrase when spoken to a true gentleman.

Dear heavens, she was so cold from her skin through to her bones that she was shaking suddenly. She made a small noise in the back of her throat, not even a word, and leaned toward him.

Grainger dropped her hand, she started to protest, and he wrapped his arm around her.

"I can manage, truly I can." The words were good enough but their utterance would have been better if she hadn't been trembling so very much.

"Of course you can," he soothed in a deep rumble that seemed to sink into her bones. "Please carry your carpetbag for a little while longer."

He spun on his heel and strode off at a very fast pace, so that she was compelled to almost run to keep pace. She opened her mouth to insist that she could move much more easily if he wasn't holding her—even if she wouldn't have been as warm.

Around them, the slum's sounds were slowly returning to their earlier discord—men calling for whisky, women offering themselves to men . . .

Booted footsteps pounded along the railroad tracks toward them.

Grainger simply swept her up in his arms, carpetbag included, and ran.

Chapter Four

Grainger reached a broad thoroughfare and turned to run along the boardwalk edging it, still carrying her. The street's greater width brought a frigid cold winter wind whipping along its length up from the river and driving off any casual spectators. He passed far more respectable saloons and stores, marked by barrels, crates, and stools glimpsed in snatches of lamplight.

Rachel put her arm up around his neck and nearly yanked it away when his strong shoulders and neck provided a corded nest, instead of knife-edged fragility. She'd nursed Elias for years. She knew what a man felt like—the cleanly defined bones and sinew of his collarbone and neck, which her hand could easily close around. But Grainger was different, warmly alive even through his snow-covered coat, as if his skin exhorted her fingers to seek his bare skin out. To undress him . . .

Her pulse began to beat more strongly.

"I can run," she gasped and desperately tried not to jerk away.

"Not yet." He didn't even sound winded. If anything, he was reading the storefront signs as they went past.

A tall man with dark hair touched by silver at the temples and his buffalo coat casually hanging off his shoulders, sauntered out of an alley a block ahead of them, jauntily whistling Rossini's overture to "The Barber of Seville." Perhaps he could help her and Grainger, instead of indulging in such a bravura performance.

The hated voices came harsh and fast just behind them. "There they are, boys! Don't shoot 'em; we need her alive."

She spared a glance over Grainger's shoulder and flinched. Collins's thugs were only a few paces back.

Without a moment's hesitation, the dark-haired man fell silent and raced for the saloon before them, a gaudy corner establishment.

The poltroon. Why didn't he sound the alarm and bring the law to help them?

Grainger dashed through another frozen intersection and leaped to a stretch of boardwalk. He halted in front of the corner saloon that the other man had disappeared into. There he set Rachel down, placing her behind him. "Whatever happens, stay close. Understand?"

She gulped. More violence? But she'd fought her way clear of Maitland and could hardly balk at an honorable man's defense of her. She stiffened her knees, which seemed to be trying to turn into jelly. "Yes, of course."

She peered around his arm to watch.

Four of Collins's thugs came thundering down the boardwalk and paused, their pea jackets and thick woolen caps clearly marking them as having come from a seaport. One of them chuckled, then another and another.

Rachel shivered but stayed where she was, pressed tight against Grainger's back. Why on earth was a small voice in the back of her head whispering that she might want to explore the stalwart masculine body next to her? The broad shoulders, the trim waist and hips, the strong legs.

Oh dear Lord, they were so close that she could feel every breath he took as if it were her own, resonating through her skin and into her lungs. She shivered but not from the cold.

Grainger cocked his head toward her but said nothing. His arms moved slightly, flexing in his coat. *Oh Lord, there was going to be gunplay and he might be hurt . . .*

There had to be something she could do to help. She glanced around desperately, but there was nothing there. Only benches and barrels and the great troughs that would water horses in better weather. Surely there had to be something she could at least throw. Then she spied a broom, propped against a bench only two steps away.

She smiled a little grimly. She might not know how to use a revolver but she could wield a broom—and had done so before against impertinent males, albeit of the schoolroom type. She'd grab it if she needed to.

The leader lifted his hand and the brutes fanned out across the street, settling into a pattern which would allow them to charge Grainger despite the boardwalk's railings. When they'd blocked every exit except for ducking into the saloon, the leader paced back and forth in front of the steps up to the boardwalk, all the while watching his intended prey, clearly emphasizing how neatly Grainger—and Rachel—were trapped.

"Leave now if you want to keep your skin intact," Grainger ordered calmly.

The thugs' leader hooted. A beam of light from the saloon caught his face, showing where half of his ear had been ripped away in a dockside brawl.

Rachel shuddered, recognizing him immediately. Holloway, the nastiest of Collins's men—who'd delighted in terrorizing her maids back in Boston.

He chuckled. "Did you hear that, lads? One against four and he's telling us to run?"

They laughed evilly and drew closer.

Grainger flexed his shoulders, as if preparing to move quickly.

"Now listen to me, mister," Holloway barked, stepping off his stretch of boardwalk.

Rachel whispered a silent prayer under her breath. She

shifted her weight to her other foot, preparing to make a single frantic lunge for that broom.

Grainger's hand promptly slid behind his back to block any move in that direction.

She froze, wondering how he'd known her intention when she hadn't taken a step. Never mind; should the ruffians charge him, she could still lunge for her own weapon.

"You'll hand her over now and you'll do so fast," Holloway demanded. "Otherwise, we'll carve you into scrimshaw while she watches. And it wouldn't be gentlemanly of you, would it, to put a nice lady like her through that?"

Grainger snarled, deep in his throat. "If you had any decency, you'd leave now and spare her the sight of bloodshed."

Holloway roared with laughter. "You idiot, we're going to kill you!"

Suddenly the saloon doors burst open and the heavily dressed man raced out, followed by a dozen others. They took up a station behind and flanking Grainger and Rachel, their cudgels, knives, and pistols prominently displayed. With loud screeches of overtaxed window sashes, other men pushed open the saloon's upstairs windows and cocked their firearms. All of them were yelling, "Donovan! Donovan!"

Grainger joined in the war cry, his deep voice rumbling through his back and into her bones.

It made a most infernal—and very welcome—ruckus.

Rachel gulped and began to grin. It would seem that Grainger could find friends and allies in the most unprepossessing surroundings.

The shouting finally died down and she dared to look around. Holloway was visibly furious, but still standing in the same place, his men gathered closely around him. "Gentlemen," he said sweetly, his angry expression at complete odds with his tone, "surely there's no need for a brawl in such cold weather. Let us be friends and say no more tonight."

Grainger glanced down at her. "Satisfied?"

Rachel tried to pull her wits together. Doing so would provide the opportunity to tell Grainger about the danger to William Donovan. There'd still be a threat to her from Collins, but only a husband could end that. She nodded, a bit too emphatically.

"Depart," Grainger ordered curtly.

The thugs retreated a block, every step taken grudgingly under the equally watchful eyes of Grainger's friends. Just before Collins's thugs returned to the slums, Holloway turned back. "Collins will take her back—and you'll be sorry you interfered!"

"You'll be dead if that happens," Grainger retorted in a tone so flat it sent shivers down Rachel's spine. It seemed more prophecy than threat.

Holloway made a single rude gesture and was gone. The dark-haired fellow and another man warily followed them.

Rachel's knees gave out and her vision grayed. She started to sag, faint with relief at being safe for the moment. The last thing she saw was Grainger whirling around to catch her.

Lucas laid Rachel Davis down on the settee in the *Empress*'s drawing room. A moment's work saw her bonnet removed and set aside, together with her carpetbag. *Those bastards, to reduce her to running through slums with so little!*

He shifted her gently and eased her long cape off.

He stared at the hapless beauty before him, wanting to throw a brandy snifter against the wall.

How the hell was he to deal with her?

Of average height with slim, sweet curves, she reposed on the settee like a fantasy from his oldest dreams. Her features were as delicately etched as any Roman cameo, making her every man's dream of womanly perfection.

Rachel was his only female friend; God knew any conversation with his sister Hortense was best confined to recitations of her social engagements. Rachel also trusted him as a friend, as evidenced by years of correspondence on subjects ranging from politics to flowers.

At least she was breathing steadily, albeit shallowly. Her pulse was fast, her color pale, against the deep blue upholstery.

Cursing the thugs who'd reduced her to this, he unbuttoned her tunic—moving quickly and surely down her front and careful to keep his fingers from lingering too long in any one spot.

The poor darling had been chased by ruffians who wanted to kidnap her and haul her back to an obviously appalling hell, which had almost certainly been created by Albert Collins.

At least he was almost certain the bloodstains on her dress weren't hers. But when he thought of what she must have been through . . .

He growled automatically, his fingers tightening in her cape. Its fine wool snagged under his callused fingers, a mute reminder of her quality. He smoothed it out—easing her clothing as he could not soothe her now unconscious mind— and stood up.

She still hadn't moved, except to take those barely perceptible breaths.

He dragged himself away and carefully draped her cloak over a sitting chair to dry.

If he'd been at an assignation with her, he'd hang up her cloak exactly the same way. But when he'd turn back to her, she wouldn't flutter—no, those golden eyes would be warm with welcome and eagerness for the coming hours.

His heart immediately skidded into a faster beat. He flung his hands out, snarling at his unruly flesh. Dammit, when would his body learn that she, like every other respectable woman, was not for him?

He shrugged off his coat, dropping it on the nearest chair, and skimmed his hat onto an upper rack.

Lucas paced as best he could in the confined aisle, reminding himself that he needed to have himself under control before Braden appeared.

She drew a shuddering breath.

He spun on his heel to look at her—but before he could reach her side, she fell silent again. Surely her color was a trifle better?

For her sake, he must be the complete gentleman. Mrs. Elias Davis deserved the utmost consideration and chivalry from every man who saw her, starting with himself. He'd warn the Donovan & Sons' men, although he doubted they'd need the words. As frontiersmen, their respect for good women was bone deep.

He shoved a hand through his hair, forcing the heavy mane back.

No, the difficulty was likely to be his. He needed to keep telling himself that she was off-limits as his former commander's widow, as she'd been since he met her at their wedding.

Not that he'd ever flirted with a woman of his own class, of course. But it was so damned easy to be enticed by glossy chestnut hair and clear amber eyes, wide-set under winged eyebrows that looked a man straight in the face and smiled without simpering. Lord, how he'd envied Davis!

Her marriage had been difficult, with Davis an invalid. Having Collins as her trustee must have been like passing through the nine circles of hell. Well, he'd make sure that bastard never got his hands on her again.

His patience shredded further. Maybe strong coffee would help her.

He spun and strode toward the kitchen, his heavy boots striking solidly through the carpet.

Mrs. Davis moaned and flung her arm up over her eyes.

Lucas immediately came to a stop beside her, cursing his impatience for disturbing her. "Mrs. Davis?"

Rachel shifted again against the tufted, velvet upholstery, trying to understand where she was. Collins's hired Pullman didn't have finely upholstered furniture like this, without any spikes and sags in the horsehair stuffing. Collins's Pullman's gas lighting had eternally fizzed and sparked, telltale signs of dirty lines and lamps, yet another scar from hard use by multiple previous renters.

But the *Empress*, as an engraved brass plate above the door proclaimed her, had all the elegance of a rich man's private library. Elias and his father would have exclaimed over the superb Circassian walnut used for the woodwork. It was heavily carved, of course, but in a Georgian style which was far simpler than what she would have expected to find on a legendary family's conveyance. The curtains were deep blue, as was the upholstery, with a superb Brussels carpet covering the floor. Settees were scattered between big, comfortable sitting chairs, while spittoons and small tables were regularly placed for guests' convenience. Brilliantly polished lamps hung from the ceiling, casting a golden glow over the scene.

In all too many ways, the *Empress* was more attractive to her than Anglesey Hall, Elias's home, had ever been.

"Mrs. Davis?" the deep, kind voice asked again. Definitely *not* Collins or Maitland.

She turned her head and looked directly at her companion, rather than the walls and ceiling. "Mr. Grainger?"

He smiled at her, his harshly masculine features almost cracking in the attempt to be gentle. He was crouching beside her hip, careful not to crowd her. His blue-green eyes truly did look remarkably like jewels from this close. "How do you feel? Are you hurt anywhere, Mrs. Davis?"

"Hurt? Why, no, I don't think so, Mr. Grainger. A little tired perhaps." She tried to sit up, struggling against the awkwardness of her position and her clothing. A full bustle and train didn't help. In fact, the effort made her want to curse—or cry. Or do anything that would return her to her old, simple life back in Boston before she'd married Elias.

Flexing his fingers and shifting slightly on his feet, Grainger stood by for a few moments before speaking again. "May I help you, Mrs. Davis?"

Rachel gulped back the foolish, threatening tears. Surely she'd do better, if she was given just a little more time to recover. "Thank you."

He scooped her up in his arms—didn't he believe in ever allowing a lady to stand on her own two feet?—and quickly, efficiently tweaked her heavy hoops and bustle into a neat ripple, not an untidy jumble. Then he rearranged her skirts into a smooth waterfall over the settee. Finally he settled her into a half-sitting, half-reclining position, comfortably supported against the settee's arm.

Grainger stood back to study his handiwork. "Are you comfortable now?"

She sighed, recognizing that he had done a better job than she could have, given her unsteadiness. She was so tired that she was simply grateful for his expertise, instead of curious as to how he'd acquired it. "Yes, thank you."

"Would you care for some coffee? There's always a fresh pot of that available. Or Braden, my steward, can brew you some tea."

Rachel flinched, picturing a proper tea tray with its lemon wedges and lemon fork. "No!"

Grainger's eyes narrowed, his expression immediately turning deeply concerned. "No?"

She gathered herself, reaching for self-discipline. She didn't have to jump at shadows, not here, not in Grainger's private Pullman. "I mean, it's hardly necessary for your steward to make anything special for me. Coffee will do very well, thank you."

He searched her face for a moment before he nodded. "Good. I'll ask him to bring something to eat, too. I didn't have a chance to dine earlier this evening. Perhaps you'd care to join me."

Agreement was easier to this suggestion. Surely her present shakiness was due as much to the lack of a good meal, as it was to the stresses of the past hour.

Grainger departed down the aisle toward the kitchen, in the easy, narrow-hipped glide of an expert horseman. The sitting chairs framed him perfectly—the broad shoulders, roped in muscle, that could barely squeeze between them. The powerful legs that had made such quick work of racing up that hill in the freezing cold—and now looked capable of dancing all night.

Or slipping into a lady's boudoir, whispered her treacherous loins.

She blinked, completely taken aback by the dangerous surge of heat floating through her. It had been years since she'd looked at a man and considered his carnal potential. In fact, she'd have to admit that the last male she'd studied in that fashion had been Bobby Thompson, age eighteen, when she'd been sixteen.

While she'd grown to enjoy Elias's attentions, they weren't why she'd married him. Of course—to be entirely honest—given the amount of nursing Elias had needed, she hadn't often had the opportunity to consider him from a purely carnal perspective.

She shook her head before rubbing her face, trying to force sanity into her idiotic body. Marriage was a desperate necessity, if she wasn't to be returned to Collins's company. An affair, no matter how enjoyable, wouldn't help her in the least. She'd set aside her childhood dreams of studying Latin to resolve this threat. Surely, a frivolity could be forgotten, too.

No, first she had to warn Grainger about the threat to Donovan. After that, she had to find herself a husband—without thinking about Grainger's possible bedroom skills, given Elias's jokes about his friend's predilection for always having a mistress close at hand. Of course, that sort of arrangement wasn't surprising, given his family's reputation.

She couldn't possibly dream about being a woman who'd be warmed against that big body, kissed into near mindlessness, stroked and pleasured by those big, skillful hands into ecstasy. Why, if he lifted her up against his heart to kiss her while his hand sought out her breast inside her evening gown's neckline . . .

She trembled, startled by fantasies such as she'd never allowed herself to be lost in before.

The kitchen door swung open and Grainger returned, carrying a laden tray.

Lucas's eyes flickered over Mrs. Davis. Her eyes had lost much of that flat stare and her cheeks were gaining color. Dammit, he wished he had the time to go back and kill Collins, for having put so much terror into her face.

The old anger surged up again, making him aware of his dirk. He broke stride for a moment, but quickly regained control. She was safe here. And if Collins had the idiocy to come searching for her, Lucas would take the greatest delight in teaching him better treatment of women. He grinned privately at some of the options he'd learned for teaching brutes and moved forward. "I brought simple food, ma'am. Ham sandwiches, beans, coffee."

He set the tray down on the table next to her. She smiled shyly up at him and his pulse skipped a ridiculous beat. It had barely steadied by the time he was settled into a chair facing her and they were both munching on sandwiches, washed down with cups of fresh coffee.

She ate rapidly at first then slowed, until she was almost picking at the excellent meat and bread.

Lucas observed her covertly but said nothing, allowing her to eat in peace. Judging by the tight lines around her mouth, it had been far too long since she'd been allowed to relax.

She laid down an uneaten piece of her sandwich and he came fully alert, unaccustomed to anyone leaving food untouched on the *Empress*. "Are you finished? Would you care for a piece of jam cake? It's Lawson's—the cook's—specialty."

She smiled at him, a bit tremulously but quite sweetly.

His lungs seized. No woman had ever given him that look before.

"Jam cake? I haven't had any of that since we had to let all of Elias's old servants go after his death, including Cook."

Lucas frowned and set his own plate down. Why the devil would she have needed to fire Davis's servants? "What do you mean?"

She propped her chin on her hand, gazing into a past whose shadows concealed no joys. "Collins used every possible threat he could to force me into an engagement with his son," she said softly.

Lucas came to his feet in a rush, unable to sit still, willing to meet even an old danger with violence. "He did what? What made him think he could get away with that?"

The deep lines around her mouth tightened, as if etched in vinegar and salt tears. "We had no private friends of sufficient power or wealth to challenge him. The other trustees cared only for public appearances, their legal duties as trustees, and their personal interests in the estate—which covered the library, the art, the gardens, and the horses. The grooms and the gardeners were safe but nobody else. I begged the trustees for help but—" Her voice roughened and she took refuge in her coffee.

"The negligent slugs!" He began to pace, picturing how those well-dressed, oily men must have looked down their noses at any suggestion they'd take action on behalf of the lower orders. His fingers flexed, automatically reaching for his Colts. "What next?

"Collins learned very quickly that I would do a great deal to protect the household servants—except marry his son." Her tone was flat, almost conversational.

What an appallingly deadly game of cat and mouse she'd been forced to play. "Did you run the Davis household? Did he have the opportunity to make demands?"

"Yes, I nominally gave the orders. But he could cause a good deal of—mischief, since he controlled the accounts." A pulse throbbed in her temple and her fingers clenched on the delicate silverware in her hand, until her knuckles turned white.

Lucas froze, brought on alert. He waited to learn just how harshly he'd need to mete out justice.

"One day, he announced that all the indoors servants would be paid two dollars a month until Maitland was given the key to the housemaids' quarters."

She rose to her feet, as if even sitting still left her besmirched by memories.

Lucas's beloved dirk slipped into his hand, ready for use. "The devil he did! Did he honestly think he could use Davis's house as a brothel?"

"I countered that by sending them all off on year-long vacations." A wicked smile blossomed on her face, a startling match for such purity. "With excellent references, of course."

His head jerked back in surprise, then he bowed from his waist in homage, quickly returning his dirk to its sheath. "That was cunning of you! Sherman himself would have been outfoxed by such tactics."

She smiled, a bit wryly, and began to pace, her train's ruffles swirling. "Collins was furious, since he'd meant to use the Davis mansion as his own."

Lucas searched her face, hearing more echoes of a battle fought long and hard. "What happened next?"

"He turned on Mother and my sister." Her expression stilled, obscuring any signs of the enchanting plotter. "After a few weeks, he shanghaied us to his family's estate in the Elizabeth Islands. He said we'd stay there until we rotted or I married Maitland."

Lucas slammed his fist against the paneling. "Wouldn't someone help you?"

Her mouth tightened for a moment before she hid the unusual display of umbrage. "No, not even then."

"And the other trustees were all baa'ing like sheep under the Collins crook, I suppose, while they enjoyed the use of the Davis stable and artwork!"

Rachel Davis choked—thankfully, with near-hysterical laughter, not disgust.

He bit back a string of curses before he could reply to her. "How are your mother and sister now?"

"Safely on their way to London, thank God." Relief brightened her countenance. "I diverted Collins's attention at Jersey City long enough to allow them to escape their guards and board a ferry for Manhattan. According to Maitland, they caught a packet for London. Knowing they're out of harm's way has been my only comfort these last two days."

She had managed to bamboozle Collins and his array of hardened sailors? Amazing. He'd have to make sure she never faced such dangers again.

"Well done, Mrs. Davis. I'm sure the Lord will watch over them for the remainder of their journey. I'll cable my London man of affairs to meet them."

"Thank you. They should be happy in Oxford with my father's friends."

She paused for a moment, straightening the tassels on one of the curtains. He waited, every sense alert for trouble.

"I must thank you for rescuing me, from the slum and from Collins's men. If it hadn't been for you, I know I'd be dead—or worse—by now." She smiled brilliantly, her eyes sweeping over him as if he was some sort of knight in shining armor.

Surely she couldn't think that of him.

"My pleasure, but it truly is what any decent man would do." His jaw tightened at how poorly the men of Boston had behaved toward her before he continued. "I'm deeply sorry you had to endure such trials in order to escape," he continued, forcing his hands not to double-check his Colts. Or better yet—his beloved dirk. She needed comfort more than he needed to kill Collins. "I have been following you since Chicago, in hopes of helping you. Please believe that as Major Davis's widow, you command my *full* support in whatever you want."

She chuckled rather weakly. "Thank you, Mr. Grainger. But I'm afraid the only step that will keep me from returning to Mr. Collins's custody is marriage."

Lucas gaped at her, caught totally off guard. "Marriage? What do you mean? I thought you inherited the Davis fortune outright, with the trust created for its management until you remarried."

She laughed more believably this time, a little color returning to her cheeks. "No, nothing like that. Father Davis left his fortune to Elias, then to Elias *and my* children after that."

She cocked an eyebrow at him and waited.

He puzzled over the unusual phrasing for a moment. "*And yours?* Do you mean that the pattern of inheritance was to Elias Davis first, then his children, and finally your children?"

"Exactly." She added fresh coffee to her cup, her hand not nearly as steady as her tone.

"And since he died childless, everything goes to your children."

"My *legitimate* children."

"Good Lord, Collins must have been after you day and night to marry that son of his, in order to beget grandchildren!"

She flinched, sending the cup rattling over the saucer, and started to set it down.

Completely forgetting the need to be gentle around her, Lucas gripped her wrist. "Mrs. Davis, they won't take you back, I swear. Donovan & Sons' men are patrolling the area around this railroad car now. You're safe here."

"Maitland Collins tried to force his attentions on me this evening."

A growl vibrated deep within Lucas's throat and his hand wrapped around his knife.

"I successfully—but bloodily—defended myself. I believe he still lives." She swallowed hard, her pulse drumming in her throat. "According to the trust's terms, Mr. Collins is the principal trustee and controls all the money and properties, subject only to the other trustees. If he goes to a court, it will send me back to him. Can you stand against that?"

He smiled at her, deliberately baring his teeth. "It would give me great pleasure to do so."

She gaped. "Mr. Grainger, you cannot be serious!"

He shrugged, unrepentant. He probably didn't have enough cash for all of the necessary bribes, but he could certainly make it very painful for the bastard. "Entirely."

She closed her eyes and said firmly, "I will forget you said that. I'm concerned that your methods might be extremely illegal."

His mouth twitched, but he remained silent.

Her eyes swept over him.

He frowned for a moment, before banishing it. Had she studied him, as a woman considers a man she finds attractive? Surely not—and yet, he could have sworn her gaze had lingered overly long below his face. His cock stirred.

"Even so, I must remarry and quickly," Rachel announced.

Marriage to someone else? Well, he'd always known it would happen one day. But it seemed more wrenching now that he'd carried her and known the softness of her in his arms, and the sweet smell of her in his nose.

"There is no time for a protracted struggle against Collins, here in Omaha. It is vital that he be immediately cut off from all revenues, especially as my trustee."

Lucas at once came fully alert, recognizing her sharpened tone. "Why is it so urgent?"

"He means to trap William Donovan at the Bluebird Mine and kill him."

"*Murder* Donovan? Why, that bast—toadstool!"

She nodded agreement. "But if he's no longer my trustee—"

His mind was racing, considering the implications—and half-aware that her presence might be so distracting as to overset his logic "Then he can't give orders to the men at the Bluebird Mine in your name."

Her pacing brought her less than a foot from him. She stopped with a small gasp and pivoted, swishing her train out of his way. Did she glance too long at him over her shoulder? But if so, she wasn't behaving like a woman who knew how to flirt.

"Yes. Elias bought the mine several years ago from an old friend, who needed to raise cash. He also sold an interest to Donovan, as part of a bigger deal."

"So Humphreys, the mine's manager, has always answered to Boston."

She sank down onto the settee by the coffee tray. "Exactly. I'll need to tell him personally that I've remarried so he won't help Collins in any way."

Every protective instinct in Lucas revolted. "No! You won't go anywhere near the Bluebird, not if there's about to be a murder attempt."

She raised a haughty eyebrow. *Ah, that was more like the woman he was acquainted with—who enjoyed challenging his mind, not his loins.*

He relaxed, ready for a pleasant round of debate.

"Mr. Grainger, it's critical that an innocent man's life be saved. That's far more important than any polite folderol about not sending women into danger. I'm certain that once Mr. Humphreys understands I've remarried, he won't assist Mr. Collins, and all will be well."

A Nevada mine supervisor fall into line like a sheep when she crooked her finger? Appalled at her optimism, Lucas opened his mouth to roar objections, but she was still talking.

"No, what I need your help for is to find another husband. Immediately—before Mr. Collins can take legal steps to regain my custody."

Lucas frowned. Rachel Davis and another man—in her wedding bed? Someone certain to be honorable, polite, and respectful even in the bedroom.

He growled, deep in his throat, and began to stride up and down the carpet.

Like hell anyone else was climbing into her bed, if she was willing to accept a marriage of convenience!

But marry her himself?

He swallowed hard.

She was right: The best way to protect Donovan's life, given Collins's malice, was for her to marry. He owed Donovan a blood debt for helping him avenge Ambrosia that his life alone would not repay—but his honor would. Marrying Rachel would even the scales.

Did his old vow never to marry carry any weight against saving Donovan's life?

He grimaced and spun on his heel. No.

Dear God, if she ripped him apart the way Ambrosia had . . .

But Rachel was his friend. She wasn't looking for love, just protection and companionship. They could build a solid union together on that basis.

But in marrying her, there'd be the necessity of siring children. For the first time in his life, he'd have to hope that his seed would set fruit. Fruit that could grow to become a little child, vibrant and alive, beautiful, intelligent, happy to see him. A true family, in other words, and his oldest dream.

He began to smile.

A child, laughing, running and playing, vulnerable . . .

The oldest nightmare blasted through his skull, of black hair and sodden blue skirts rippling in the waves.

He froze in his tracks but forced himself to move, driving the vision back with plans. Cowering had never helped against that terror.

He'd have to watch his child very carefully to make sure it never came to any harm. He'd do anything—anything in the damn world—to keep it safe.

Lucas turned back to face Rachel Davis, allowing himself to consider her as his wife. She looked enticing as hell seated there, delicately nibbling on a ham sandwich.

"Tonight?" he ventured, startled by how fast some of the visions crowded into his brain and heated his blood. She was such an elegant lady, resembling the goddess of wisdom far more than Venus.

She nodded, looking a little pale, and peeped at him from under her lashes. "If possible. An honorable man, of course."

"Certainly," he managed, his thoughts whirling inside his head. "Let me think about it a little more."

He'd always sworn never to take a wife, certain that his overwhelming carnal urges would lead him to dishonor his marriage vows by taking a succession of lovers. As both of his parents, all of his father's siblings, and three of his grandparents had. And blatantly enough that he'd been well aware of their behavior before he'd turned twelve. He was more than willing to enjoy sensual pleasures—but not at the price of dishonor.

If he married Rachel Davis, he'd have to keep his vows and be faithful to her alone for the rest of his days. Oh, the delights he could enjoy with her. To finally be able to explore the wonders of her sweet breasts, or kiss his way down that elegant spine . . .

He shot her a sideways glance, noting how her slender fingers curled around the bread. If he did this, he'd have her in his bed for the rest of his life.

Besides, what did any of that matter against the need to protect her from Collins? The pig had genuine power in Boston, given his centuries-old family and their shipping line, but he'd have a harder time standing against the Graingers.

Besides, it would also infuriate his family if he married a woman who came from a less than aristocratic family, even if she did bring a fortune with her.

He started to grin. They'd always seen him only as a breeding machine. Well, he'd be siring children for his purposes, and Donovan's, in this match, not for theirs. Marvelous.

"Will you marry me, Mrs. Davis?" he asked briskly. "Tonight? I'm sure we can find a minister here in town."

She dropped her sandwich, almost upsetting her coffee cup. "You? Isn't there anyone else?"

His mouth twisted at her clearly unflattering opinion of him. It had been years since he'd been put in his place so effectively. "Not that I can find within the next few hours."

She blushed and clumsily blotted the table with her napkin. "Please forgive me if I offended you but, but I always thought you'd never marry anyone. Why me? Why now?"

"Your situation has made me reconsider my objections to the institution of marriage."

Her jaw set. "No, that's not enough. We're good friends. Let that continue to be our relationship."

Why the devil was she objecting so strongly? "Collins will be here in a few hours."

Terror flashed into her eyes. "No!" She controlled herself with a visible effort and shifted ground to something more reasonable, while still guarding her expression. "You've told me nothing of your reasons."

Dammit, would she always make him think and speak of things he'd prefer not to?

He gave her logic, but not all of it. She was no flighty female to be swayed by nonsense wrapped up in fanciful sentiment. "I am here and you already know me as your friend. I have the money and family connections to defeat Collins. Your husband was my first commander and Donovan has saved my life. Unless you have someone else in mind—"

He paused but she said nothing, her expression unreadable. If she'd look at him, if he could feel her eyes rest on him again, he'd be more confident.

"I submit myself to you as the best candidate available. Rachel—"

Her eyes met his openly, clearly startled by the intimacy of a first name. He desperately needed to capture her, the brilliant mind mated to the fiery core that had fought to keep Elias alive for so very long.

"I swear I'll do my utmost to keep you and our children safe and happy. And to protect your mother and sister, wherever they are, as well." God help him, he meant it, too.

She reached across the small table and took his hand, a single tear trembling on her eyelash. Her fingernails briefly cut into his palm and the slight pain brought him back to life. "Thank you—Lucas. I'd be honored to marry you and I pray this marriage will work."

Her voice was very husky.

He lifted her left hand and kissed her finger where his ring would rest, shoving his terrors back into the darkness.

Collins leaped up the steps into the vestibule and stormed into the private Pullman, Holloway following close behind. The once elegant dining salon was now a disgrace with flowers and coffee ground into the carpet, cups and plates tumbled against the teapot on the sideboard, and a superb crystal decanter's broken base peeking out from under a chair. He ignored all of that, as well as the hired servants rushing frantically back and forth with hot water and clean cloths under his sailors' distrustful glares.

"Where is he? Where's my boy?" he demanded in a voice he hardly recognized.

His men fell back, leaving a path to the settee.

Maitland lay stretched across it, a bloody towel wrapped around his head. Nothing could be seen of his face and he was utterly unmoving. He was covered in blood as far as his shoulders and it still stained his hands as if he'd fought until the last against his attacker. He reeked of rum, as though someone had poured it over him.

Collins groaned, an animalistic sound. *Great God, if Maitland died, his own world would end.* Maitland was everything, had been everything since the day he was born and his mother had died. Every hope for the future, every plan, was wrapped up in his son.

Holloway flinched but remained silent.

Steeling himself for the worst, Collins reached for the improvised bandage and peeled it back. He swallowed hard and did not flinch from his son's time of need. He'd taken ships through pirate-infested South Seas waters and brawled along more than one foreign dock. He was more than familiar with facial wounds. But this one?

Maitland had been jabbed, almost sliced, beside his left eye, tearing his skin until even a bit of bone was visible. Blood smeared his skin and clung to his lashes. The blow had been long and jagged, and the resulting scar would be a fearful one.

Rachel Davis must have plotted long and hard how to trick Maitland, in order to cause such a wound.

It would be a miracle if Maitland kept his eye or his sight. His face's left side might permanently drift toward the floor, the skin sagging without any muscles to support it. He might have difficulties eating or talking or . . .

He might take an infection and die . . .

And, dammit, Rachel Davis deserved to be destroyed for having caused even the least of these ills!

Collins gently smoothed the towel back into position, cursing under his breath when Maitland twitched—but didn't have the strength to wake up.

He glanced over his shoulder. "A military surgeon was staying at the Cozzens Hotel. Fetch him here; I'll only have the best for Maitland."

"Yes, sir." Holloway glanced at one of his men, who promptly turned to leave.

"Give him an ice bath before he enters. I want him sober as a judge before he touches my son. Scrub him from the waist up in carbolic soap, like a supercilious French surgeon. I'll not have him anything less than shipshape."

The man's mouth opened and closed, but he was wise enough not to voice his questions. One quick glance at Holloway, who nodded curtly, and the fellow disappeared.

As if he, Albert Collins of Boston, gave a damn about the Army's opinions when Maitland's life was at stake!

"Holloway."

"Sir?"

"Where is Mrs. Davis now?"

The other men froze. Holloway, to give his best man full credit, barely hesitated. "Mrs. Davis, sir, is presently with Mr. Lucas Grainger at the Grainger family's private Pullman."

Collins jerked erect, yanking his hand away from Maitland. "What the devil? With a *Grainger?*"

Maitland moaned.

Collins promptly gentled his voice, cursing himself privately. "Hush, son, hush. All will be well."

Especially after I lay my hands on that hell-born slut!

"I have two men watching Grainger's railroad car. They won't go anywhere without our knowledge," Holloway assured him.

Collins shot him a glance, careful to keep his hands steady and gentle on his son. "Excellent."

He was going to take the greatest pleasure in watching Rachel Davis's slow, painful death—after she'd been bred like the vicious bitch she was.

Chapter Five

"Are you certain you wish to marry Mr. Grainger?" Reverend Anderson asked quietly. "If not, you are welcome to remain here with my wife and me until we can arrange your reunion with your family."

He and his wife, both sweet-faced and all too observant, had been conducting evening services at their small church when Rachel and Grainger had arrived in search of a minister. The small congregation of hard-working people had wholeheartedly welcomed a wedding celebration. Her grandfather would have felt at home with this church and its members, so totally unlike the enormous edifice with its supercilious congregants where she'd married Elias.

Mrs. Anderson had quickly taken Rachel into the parsonage for some final, feminine touches to Rachel's outfit. Thankfully, Braden, Lucas's steward, had already worked miracles by sponging out the last dirt and bloodstains. Lucas was waiting for her just outside the door, clearly ready to make his vows.

She was about to marry into a family of notorious adulterers. She also knew from Elias that Lucas had usually kept a mistress close at hand to satisfy his lusts, even on military posts where such arrangements were difficult to manage.

While Lucas was her friend, he was also her last choice as

a husband—because how could she be sure that he wouldn't behave like the rest of his family?

Yet what choice did she truly have? Collins could appear any minute with a court order to drag her back. She had to marry *now*, if she was to protect Mr. Donovan. Lucas was the only man who stood ready and wouldn't be crushed by Collins.

She'd feel so much more certain if she could talk this over with her mother. But that wasn't possible—and logic told her that this was the only road to take.

Still, she simply couldn't believe that he'd told her everything. And yet, did she have the leisure to explore his motives in detail? No.

Given that, Rachel knew what her answer to Reverend Anderson was, no matter how much her overstretched nerves vibrated.

She quelled a half-hysterical chuckle. How could she explain to them that she feared a reunion with her legal guardian more than anything else on this earth? "Thank you, Reverend, but I truly want to marry Mr. Grainger."

Mrs. Anderson glanced over at her husband. "Are you finished with the formalities yet, dear? Can't you tell from the way he watches her that he's not just marrying her for a woman to do the cooking and cleaning?"

Lucas need a wife for *housekeeping*? A chirp of laughter escaped Rachel before she could control herself.

Reverend Anderson studied her expression for a moment and nodded approvingly. "Yes, you two should do very well together. I'd never marry a woman who was being forced into it, of course. But I've always hesitated to give the church's blessing to a union of pure convenience, either. But you're not that, not if you're smiling at the thought."

Rachel's eyebrows flew up, but she didn't explain the true joke.

"I'll go to the piano now, dear," Mrs. Anderson said

briskly. "When you hear me play 'Jesu, Joy of Man's Desiring,' come in."

"Thank you, Mrs. Anderson." His reasons might be unknown, she might dread the future—but marriage to him would keep her out of Collins's hands and help save Mr. Donovan's life. That had to be enough—even if her heart did skip a surprising beat whenever he touched her.

The small woman with the twinkling eyes amid the wrinkled face leaned up to kiss her on the cheek. "You'll do very well together, child," she said softly. "He'll always protect you and you'll teach him to laugh."

Rachel blinked but, before she could say anything, Mrs. Anderson was gone, the door whispering shut behind her. The reverend looked over at Rachel, his brown eyes warm. "If you change your mind—"

She shook her head.

He closed his sentence with a flick of his fingers and went on, "Then I'd best make sure your impatient groom hasn't torn down my church to see what's standing between him and your marriage."

Rachel nodded, her throat a little tight. Their concern for a stranger made this feel far more like a true wedding than she'd expected.

After what seemed like only a minute later, the piano glided into Bach's graceful phrases and Rachel stepped into the church, shaking a little.

Lucas immediately spun to face her, his eyes searching her face.

She hesitated for an instant, assessing him for the last time as a free woman. As the one who'd share his bed that night and for the rest of her days.

His raven black hair gleamed under the gaslights, rippling as if it invited her to run her fingers through it. Unlike more fashionable men, his jaw was clean shaven, blatantly taunting the world with its strength and contempt for conventional mores. And his mouth, that had been so harshly controlled earlier, was softer now, more openly sensual—and incredibly more tempting.

"Rachel?" he asked, his deep, beautiful voice as alluring as any caress.

She lifted her hand to trace his lips, possibly even explore those high cheekbones . . .

Someone shifted in the pew, making the wood creak.

Rachel promptly adapted her gesture and firmly slipped her hand through the crook of his arm, using a possessiveness meant to reassure him—or herself.

Surely she couldn't have been about to fondle her fiancé in public. No fiancé could be so attractive, so virile as to inspire such wanton behavior. Possessiveness was acceptable in public, but not desire.

A very masculine smile of anticipation curved his mouth, but he said nothing.

She'd seen its like before on Elias's face, when he'd had one of his good days and was eagerly anticipating the coming night. She flushed at the memories and glanced away from Lucas.

He patted her hand. Mrs. Anderson, who'd been playing the same few bars over and over again, emphatically began the melody from the beginning. Lucas took a step forward and Rachel moved with him, walking toward the altar and her wedding night.

Their walk down the aisle seemed all too brief, given how her pulse thrummed at his touch.

The church was almost full and everyone looked quite pleased, in complete contrast to her first wedding when the attendees had watched her for the slightest signs of fumbling or other ill-bred behavior. All the original congregants had stayed and been supplemented by the Donovan & Sons' men who'd come with Lucas and her from his private railroad car. Only her mother's and sister's dear faces beaming approval of her choice would have made it better.

She tried not to think about the sentries standing guard outside, lest Collins's men return in force.

This marriage had to succeed, even after she was rid of Collins, no matter what Lucas's true motives were.

"Dearly beloved," Reverend Anderson began, when they'd come to a stop in front of him.

Rachel forced herself to pay attention to every one of his words, to every detail of Lucas's expression. This was her husband, the man she was binding herself to for the rest of her life. The man she hoped to make a child with tonight.

Oh dear God in heaven, have mercy on us . . .

She gave her vows firmly and clearly. "I, Rachel, take thee, Lucas, to be my husband . . ."

His voice, on the other hand, was a little rough, but still understandable. His eyes were focused on her and quite determined.

She had no idea how he'd contrived to find it—but he slid a gold ring on her finger, which fit perfectly. She blinked back a very sentimental tear and vowed to be the best possible helpmeet to him, especially when she saw his matching gold band. It was so very, very rare for a man to wear a wedding ring.

"You may now kiss the bride, Mr. Grainger," announced Reverend Anderson.

Lucas promptly leaned down and kissed her on the mouth, one hand resting lightly on her elbow. It was a decorous salute at first and she responded chastely. But that didn't seem enough, not for the man who'd rescued her. She slid her free hand up his arm and opened her mouth slightly to him, indicating her willingness to be a true wife. His tongue promptly brushed her lips lightly, sensually, teasingly.

She sighed, quickly remembering the pleasures of simply enjoying a man's touch. Her head fell back, easing the angle for him, and her fingers stroked his forearm. A slow surge of heat bloomed within her, pulsing softly every time she touched him.

He rumbled approval deep in his throat and opened his mouth further, his tongue coming forward for even more play.

Somewhere someone cheered.

Lucas's head snapped up. Rachel blushed but managed to hold her head high, startled by their audience's reaction— and her own need to ignore it, so she could return to kissing her husband.

She hoped his reasons for marrying her were solid and worth fighting for, so their union would have a hope of surviving.

William Donovan automatically braced himself against the *Astoria*'s heavy roll and enjoyed Carter's praise of his ten-year-old son. Somehow the next generation of Carters promised to be taller, stronger, and cleverer than any other young gentlemen currently causing trouble for their teachers in San Francisco.

Even standing here in the lee of the *Astoria*'s superstructure, the bitter north wind threatened to snatch his bowler away and hurl it into the ocean. It was undoubtedly foolish—but he couldn't stop trying to listen for any other passengers coming up on deck.

It was after dinner, the sun had set, and no one onboard could see just how close they were to the mouth of the Columbia River with its notoriously rough water. "That seven-shouldered horror," Lewis and Clark had called it, referring to dangers like the twenty-foot high waves all too common in a winter storm like this one.

William simply prayed that the storm didn't worsen with Alaska's savage fury to give it strength—or that his beloved, all-too-independent wife didn't take it into her head to leave their cabin to help someone else. Viola, descended from generations of seafarers, was happily sure-footed, no matter what the weather. But every time William glimpsed her moonbeam-bright hair or delicate frame coming down a passageway or crossing the deck—and never once grasping a safety line!—his heart would stop beating and he'd pray to the Virgin Mary that his darling would be spared for him just a little while longer.

On this rough afternoon, a handful of other passengers were also standing in this little niche, some trying to gauge the storm's strength by the frothy, white spray blowing off the wave tops. Others were trying to smoke pipes or cigars, an arduous task in this gale.

The *Astoria* pitched, slamming one of the other passengers across the niche.

William lunged for him, grabbing the fellow's arm before he could lose his footing.

The *Astoria* righted herself with a lurch. The man found his feet, one hand clutching the safety line, his eyes wild and staring, even in the dim light. He muttered something and yanked away from William, then dived for the door that led back inside.

William silently watched him go, doubting he'd see him outside again unless there was a flat calm. An unlikely occurrence on this route, at this time of year. After returning to his previous location and grasping the safety line again, William gave Carter a quick apology and resumed their previous conversation—and his private worries about his wife.

Keeping guard over Viola would be easier if Jenkins, his new telegrapher, had been able to spell him rather than keeping to his cabin, supposedly because of seasickness not whisky.

Ah, well, he was fussing like a hen with one chick. Viola had assured him that she'd remain with the other women— probably so she could play with the children.

The *Astoria* labored to the top of yet another wave, hung there for a moment as if allowing every soul onboard to fully understand just how fragile the craft was in comparison to the ocean's power, then careened down its backside like a sinner rushing toward hell. Water tumbled over the deck in a fury of spray and howling wind, but withdrew sullenly.

In the distance, wood slammed against wood, echoing through the ship to William. His skin chilled, even where no ocean spray had touched it.

His head snapped around and he stepped forward quickly. Someone was coming out of the private cabins, from where the women and children were.

William swung around and looked out of the niche onto the main deck, shielding his eyes against the pounding spray blowing back from the ship's bow. Safety lines crisscrossed the open expanse. But the mountainous seas could easily toss someone above the ropes or knock them flat, and sweep them overboard—especially if a section of railing was destroyed.

Who'd come on deck?

A sturdy ten-year-old boy was running toward the bow, dodging under the ropes and chased by a slight woman wearing a cape. The boy was unfamiliar but the lady . . .

Every cell in William's body screamed the alarm. Carter threw away his cigar.

"Father!" shouted the lad and waved at them.

"Good Lord, that's my boy!" exclaimed Carter and bolted out of the niche toward his motherless child.

The woman's hood blew back, exposing a lock of pale hair, which was quickly soaked. Viola, William's wife and undoubtedly the only one onboard who'd been fast enough to follow Carter's imp when he'd run off to find his father.

Another great wall of water began to rise behind them.

Time slowed. If he breathed at all, William didn't know it. Business deals, life itself—nothing mattered, next to reaching his lady before the next wave crashed over the deck.

The *Astoria*'s engine whined and she wavered, before she started to careen down another wave. She rolled and the child lurched sideways into Viola.

William's beloved wife slipped on the slick deck and lost her footing. The boy went screaming in the opposite direction.

William bellowed a war cry, ancient and Irish and written for another ocean, and hurled himself over the ropes. Hauling himself along them—like the sailors rushing to help— would have taken far too long. Carter was running on the diagonal, heading for where the ship's roll would send his son.

Water gathered itself beyond the railing, touched by spectral silver, and reached toward the sky.

Viola slid toward the railing. Slight as she was, she could slip between two of those bars, especially if the heavy seas tore out just one piece of wood. But, praise God, she wasn't paralyzed with fear. She managed to grab one of the safety lines as it went past, her face straining with effort under the almost blinding sheets of rain.

She stopped with a jerk, sending her body swinging around— and her legs heading straight toward the railing.

The *Astoria* pitched and rolled. Viola couldn't hold on firmly. She started to slip, closer and closer to the roiling Pacific Ocean. To the widow-maker formed by the Columbia's mouth.

William hurtled over a rope and caught her with one hand. His heart in his throat, he wrapped his other arm around the safety line and pulled her close to his heart. If the ocean wanted either of them, it would have to take them both.

The wave broke over the deck in a fury of salt and water, driving into his lungs, all the way through his clothes and his skin, pounding up from the deck. It could have lasted five minutes, it could have lasted five hours. All William truly knew was that Viola—his beloved fairy queen—was as much a part of him as his own bones.

The *Astoria*'s engine groaned and her wheel ground into the boiling cauldron. She began to labor up another wave and the water retreated sullenly.

William gasped and looked down at the breath of his life, desperate to see if she'd survived.

Slender fingers touched his face, shaking a bit. He kissed them, telling her he was alive, too.

Strong hands pulled them away from the safety line. "Come on, Sir! We've got to get you two inside before the next wave breaks. Mr. Carter's taking his son down below now."

William brought Viola up to her feet carefully and headed toward the cabin, his arm locked firmly around her, bracing himself against the wind to protect her. There was no way in hell that he'd let her out of his sight for the rest of the voyage.

Rachel walked down the hotel corridor beside Lucas, her gloved hand tucked in his arm, and tried to think of something safe to say. A bit of polite conversation to take her mind off what would happen next—consummating her marriage to Lucas Grainger!—or something seductive that the worldly women he knew might utter. But nothing occurred to her.

Her body's reactions were even more startling. Her leather gloves were sturdy, designed for Boston's worst winters, and her hand rested on his thick winter coat. She couldn't possibly feel anything unique to him, any more than what she'd noticed of his servant or Reverend Anderson.

So why did her pulse insist on racing as if a towering ocean wave was about to sweep her off her feet? Or why did her breasts tighten against her corset with every breath she drew, trembling at his scent? And as for the fashion in which frissons danced over her skin every time she caught a new detail of his person—such as how the snowflakes melting on his coat emphasized the width of his shoulders. Or how deftly he'd held the hotel door to bring her in from the cold. And, as for the way her eyes kept returning to the shape of his mouth, as if begging to taste a kiss . . .

She bit her lip and told herself firmly she was being silly. She was as acutely aware of him—of his strong arm under her fingers, his leg brushing against her skirt and setting her ruffles swaying as they walked side by side—as if they were lying beside each other on an embroidered coverlet, rather than walking alone together.

Theirs was a marriage of convenience, not one of passion. Lucas would be courteous in their wedding bed, as befitted a gentleman and her friend. She should pray for gentleness and not hope for passion.

This was no time for her brain to flit like an agitated canary between the absolute certainty that Lucas was nothing like the invalid Elias—and eager anticipation of exactly how he'd demonstrate the differences to her. Why, Elias's bullet-riddled shoulder had rarely allowed him to do anything as simple as escorting her in the conventional manner, with his arm bent and her hand resting on his, for more than a minute or two. Yet Lucas acted as if he could brace himself on his elbows and tumble her many times during a single night, a most incredible feat of strength.

If Lucas did that, surely his hair would sweep forward onto his brow. His mouth would be bruised from having kissed her long and often. And his eyes would grow heavy-lidded, giving him a look of carnal anticipation . . .

She flushed at the unexpected vision. A much stronger surge than with dear Elias, who'd often given her joy in the bedroom but never so greatly that she couldn't think about how to pleasure him, while conserving his limited strength.

Startled, she forced down her body's instinctive reaction to Lucas, demanding that logic play an equal part as it always had before. She needed to start planning now for the coming night with Lucas, in order to involve her brain, not her senses. As his wife, she had to make sure Lucas enjoyed himself, not greedily focus on her carnal fantasies.

Metal turned softly in a lock and she snapped back to the present, embarrassed at having lost track of her surroundings.

"Rachel, my dear." His deep voice was quiet and alluring. She looked up at him inquiringly.

"Are you certain you're still willing to go through with this tonight? We could wait."

She blushed and silently shook her head.

"Very well, if you're quite certain." He stroked a single finger down the side of her face, finishing at her throat.

Instinctively, she tilted her head to catch more of his almost insubstantial touch. A bubble of heat ran from her neck down to her womb, making her gasp.

His mouth curved, softening that harsh face under the dark hat.

He traced her lips with his finger, lingering over every curve as if they'd been sculpted by Michelangelo.

Her eyelids fell and her knees weakened. She couldn't have stepped away, even if her mother had been there to yank her away. Was he trying to create a romantic wedding night for them, in utter contrast to their marriage negotiations?

"Lucas, anyone can see us here," she whispered reluctantly, all too conscious of the long corridor with its multitude of doorways.

"Who cares? We're married."

Who cares? She gaped at him.

Before she could correct his disregard for society's rules, he swept her up in his arms with one arm around her shoulders and the other under her knees. She squeaked, clutching at any portion of him she could reach. He chuckled softly and bent his head, gliding his tongue gently over her lips.

She started to protest—the public place, the embrace, their passionate display . . .

He deepened the kiss, teasing her lips and tongue.

Rachel moaned softly, involuntarily. Warmth shimmered enticingly through her, like a golden filament linking her mouth and breasts and loins. She wrapped her arm around his neck and tried to move closer, her mouth shaping to welcome his.

He growled approvingly, softly, deep in his throat—and kicked the door shut behind them, taking them into a softly lit hotel room. His tongue swirled deeper into her mouth, exploring the different textures of her, enticing her tongue to dance, while he slid her slowly down his body until her feet touched the floor.

When he finally lifted his head, she was dazed and pliable. He cupped his hand under her cheek and turned her to face the room. Her mumbled protest died when she saw the fantasy spread before her.

Potpourri had been scattered throughout, bringing the rich scent of summer roses to the room. Candles stood tall on every surface, ready to replace harsh gaslight with their truer, softer light. A covered silver tray held foodstuffs of some sort, while a bottle of champagne rested in an ice bucket.

She tilted her head back and stared up at him. "How did you manage all this?"

He chuckled softly. "It's our wedding, remember, Rachel? I wanted—and I hoped you might enjoy—more than simply standing up in a clerk's office. I gave Mitchell a list of everything desired and he found it, including the church and our rings."

"I'll have to thank him tomorrow." She turned back to him. "You've somehow given me a proper wedding. Thank you." She leaned up to kiss him on the cheek but he captured her mouth with his, leaving her senses swimming.

When she came up for air, she was seated on the bed and Lucas was lighting all the candles, with the gaslight turned off. The warm glow transformed the simple room into a magical palace, rich with fantastical scents.

He opened the champagne and came back to her, carrying two glasses. She accepted one, twining her arm around his a little shyly. At least their sensual attraction should make this wedding night easier and hopefully the marriage to come, as well. Perhaps it might even keep him faithful for a time.

"To our new family," he saluted and drank, the strong muscles in his throat moving deeply.

She smiled at that toast and swallowed her wine, letting

the bubbles slide their way down her throat. Surely a home and family with Lucas would be splendid. God willing, they were the center of his motives for marrying her. "Lucas . . ."

His eyes, seen from this close, were turning more green than blue.

He stroked the lip of his champagne glass over her mouth. Her eyelids drooped and her mouth half-opened for the caress.

"Yes, Rachel?" he breathed against her cheek.

It was an effort to open her eyes and remember her question. "May I have some more champagne, please?"

He was watching her lips move as if he wanted to eat her. He tossed his hat aside, sending it spinning onto a coat hook. "If you kiss me again."

His words seemed to pour themselves into her veins, as intoxicating as the finest French champagne. Every inch of her flesh hummed with eagerness for him.

A lock of hair spilled over his forehead, an unusual sign of dishevelment for him. She longed to push it back and run her fingers through his thick mane. A half-smile teased his lips, softening those stern features until a dimple almost appeared.

Taking all of her courage, she slid one hand up into his magnificent hair and kissed him, her blood sparkling like the wine. Her fingers stroked his scalp, the silk of his hair falling over her wrist.

He whispered against her ear, his warm breath fanning her cheek. "It's time for our private feast. Oysters? Cheese? Chocolate?"

He caressed her again, the barest movement of his fingertips against her jaw, his hooded gaze scorching. "Or another taste of my wife?"

She blinked and ran her tongue over her lips, even as her brain tried to come back to life. They'd never discussed what he liked to do in the bedroom. "Lucas, perhaps we could talk a little—"

He raised a disbelieving eyebrow. "Talk? Now? When we can do this instead?"

His lips claimed hers again. Unable to disagree with his logic, Rachel moaned and arched against him, her mouth opening farther, her tongue twining with his. His kisses' rhythm swirled through her, washing away all consciousness of anything else. Her pulse began to throb softly, regularly to the same beat. Deep within her core, a soft, rich fire shimmered into life, magically linked to his lips and her breasts.

He left her mouth, to her groaned disappointment, and tasted her face, kissing her cheeks, nuzzling her forehead, delicately nibbling her nose. "You're a passionate woman, Mrs. Grainger, and a very sweet one. I need to taste every inch of you."

"No!" She tugged his head back to where it had been. He chuckled, a rough male sound of anticipation, and claimed her more thoroughly this time, aggressively plunging his tongue deep into her mouth.

She answered him hungrily and pressed against him, her bones melting with eagerness for more. Her mind's logic was losing control over her anatomy.

Her eyelids were heavy when he stopped and she had to force them open. Somehow he'd managed to take off his long frock coat and vest without attracting her attention. The sight of him in shirtsleeves, a strong pulse beating in his throat, rendered her almost speechless with hunger. His chest moving up and down, as he'd surge in and out in her . . .

"Shall I suckle your fingers?" The look in his eyes was both devilish and highly anticipatory.

For the first time in her life, her throat was almost too dry to speak. But she managed a brief nod.

He peeled her gloves off and kissed her fingers, one by one, slowly pulling on them with his mouth. She shuddered, tremors running through her until she could barely stand. What would similar caresses to other places do to her?

She forced herself to give voice to her duty. "Lucas, what do you want me to do for you?"

"For me, Rachel?" He shot her a disbelieving look and boldly cupped his magnificently rampant cock through his trousers. "Enjoy yourself, my dear."

"But I should . . ."

He pressed a kiss into each of her palms. "Writhe in pleasure across the bed?"

"Oh, Lucas . . ." She closed her eyes, unable to voice the images his words brought to mind, given how her body melted with hunger for them.

He chuckled, in a harsh, deep rumble that was closer to a lion's eager growl. She shuddered, her hips lifting toward him.

"Rachel, you'd tempt an archangel," he muttered, his eyes glittering with hunger. Breathing harshly, like a horse in the middle of a hard-fought race, he tossed her mantle across a chair and unbuttoned her simple jacket quickly. He kissed and licked every inch of newly discovered skin, making her tremble even more. By the time it fell from her shoulders, she was writhing against him, begging shamelessly for more of his touch. Her skin was as flushed as if she'd been standing next to a bonfire. Liquid heat was building deep in her core, in time with the drugging rhythm of his kisses. Rational thought was a ridiculous impossibility, yet . . .

Her brain barely gathered itself to notice when he told her to step out of her skirt, since she was so enthralled by his attentions to her shoulders and arms. Her bustle and petticoats disappeared in even less time, since he'd discovered magical places on her neck where a single kiss—or nibble!—could make her throw her head back and moan in agony, desperate for another intoxicating taste of his mouth.

"We should talk," she gasped.

"Not now, Rachel," he growled and went back to courting her neck, his hips rocking against hers through his trousers.

Her hands restlessly sought and clung to his head. Her fingers pulled him closer, while small, needy sounds crept from her throat. Her hands could barely grasp his broad shoulders. His arms were hard bands of muscles under the crisply starched shirt.

She writhed against her husband, rubbing her aching breasts against his chest, while passion's drumbeat thrummed stronger and faster through her veins. Her skin was tight and hot, as if ready to burst from desperation. She wanted more of him, more than his kisses, more than his hands, enough to satisfy the liquid lust dripping onto her thighs.

His big hands slid down over her hips and gathered her rump to him.

Rachel gasped at the totally unfamiliar caress and how easily he'd accomplished it.

"That's my good girl," he crooned.

He kneaded her derrière, sending shockwaves of delight deep into her core. Her swollen pearl pulsed, sending more cream gliding over her thighs. Her head fell back, offering herself for more; she was utterly unable to do anything else.

He growled softly, triumphantly, and tipped her up onto the bed on her back. She landed gently, her legs sprawled in welcome. Her breath caught in her throat at the naked hunger on his face.

Slowly, deliberately, she widened her legs, flushing at her own temerity—and startled at her own carnal passion. She'd never been so sensually desperate.

His eyes glittered, looking almost entirely green in the candlelight. One of his big, callused hands wrapped around her leg just above her boot and slowly stroked it. "My beautiful golden lady is on fire," he purred.

Involuntarily, her eyes closed to savor the delicious contrasts between his strength, the caress' gentleness, and his skin's roughness. Frissons ran up the insides of her thighs from his hand to her folds, tightening and swelling her pearl. She moaned and closed her legs around his fingers.

His left hand repeated the caress on her other leg, making

her wriggle in sheer pleasure. His right eased higher, playing with her. Her pearl pulsed again and again. She was on fire, barely able to breathe, fully surrendered to him.

His blunt finger found her intimate flesh through the slit in her drawers, played with her folds, and fondled her pearl.

She gasped, tossing her head across the pillows, heedless of her hairstyle, and thrust herself against his finger, seeking the familiar delights of a man's hands. Elias had been so very skillful at sending her into raptures this way.

Lucas chuckled rather roughly and stroked her again, circling her entrance. She was so very wet that his finger slipped in easily. She groaned in satisfaction and arched, driving herself down upon him.

He shifted, rearranging her legs, and bent over. An instant later, he nuzzled her intimate folds and licked her pearl, swirling his tongue over her like an exotic delicacy. She gasped helplessly and bucked against him.

"Sweet, very sweet," he muttered. "But you'd look better half-insane with lust."

The prospect sent spears of anticipation blazing through her. Climax was threading through her veins, its pulses building in her loins, the rhythms driving her irresistibly on.

He gathered her hips up in his hands, kneading her rump in those most delectable spots. She writhed again, moaning Lucas's name, and threw a leg over his shoulders. Anything for more stimulation.

His fingers played with her rump and hips, but always came back to her entrance. First one finger, then two, stretched her.

But he wouldn't let her climax. He stripped down, his shaft rampant with eagerness and sweat gleaming over his banded muscles. But always, always—his mouth and his big hands taught her how to lust.

Soon she was more breathless than before, even more desperate for a taste of him. Her heart was pounding in her ears so loudly she couldn't think and her hands were frantically searching out his every shape and texture.

A third finger entered her and she stilled briefly, faintly surprised at how much he'd stretched her. But he teased her pearl again, making her hips clench and rock more and more. The rich, dark currents of orgasm were centered on his mouth and his hand, pulsing hard, building fast.

She bucked against him when he finally lifted her hips to meet his shaft, his hands unsteady and his breathing harsh. She wrapped her arms and legs around him, pulling him deep inside her, and met him thrust for thrust, eager to claim every bit of carnal satisfaction he'd promised. His scent filled her and his strength enveloped her, while his strokes plunged into her again and again. Rapture spun closer and closer.

He reached down between them and gently rubbed her pearl.

Instantly she climaxed, sobbing his name as her world exploded and reformed, washing her away in crimson and gold. He followed her in the same moment, groaning her name, his hot seed filling her womb with the chance of a child.

Sleep crept up all too easily afterward, given Rachel's complete satiation and how protectively Lucas cuddled her against his chest, his breathing stirring her hair. She yawned and twined her legs more comfortably between his, her eyelids drooping.

Next time, she'd have to ask him where he'd like her to kiss his body first. He'd never answered any of her questions. In fact, he'd never talked at all about how to enjoy each other—only made sure they'd done so. And it had been so delicious.

She smiled, her eyes closing completely. There was a reason why she needed to talk to him, but she couldn't think of it now.

Ten seconds later, she was fast asleep.

Chapter Six

Lucas paused in the shadows outside the hotel. He'd have been happier in bed with Rachel. He'd left her sleeping peacefully with a note explaining he'd left to check on the *Empress*, in case she woke while he was gone. After the stresses and excitements of the previous hours—and a very delightful consummation of their vows—she was unlikely to stir.

Unfortunately, this place was where his instincts insisted he should be. He glanced around, more than just his eyes alert. It was too damn quiet here, with everything speaking of a well-ordered street, not the stillness of an attack waiting to happen.

Where the hell was Collins? That bastard should be planning something, to regain Rachel and as punishment for the younger Collins's wounds. God forbid he should go after the *Empress*. Made of wood and furnished with heavy silks, she'd go up like a bonfire.

He stepped out into the moonlight, broken by clouds passing before the moon. An instant later, his sentry gave him the all-clear and Lucas loped toward the station and the *Empress*.

He paused a block away to consider the scene. Everything looked as it should—the well-tended private Pullman, the station in the background with its lights glimmering amid the smoky fog from the rail yard, and the slums only a few blocks away next to the rail yard. Now that it was past midnight, only the slums and the rail yard were vibrant, but even they were more subdued than in daylight.

Oddly, the slums were quieter than they should be at this hour. He'd have thought that at least one of the saloons would have a piano blaring out a tune, but there were only a few soft melodies to be heard.

Lucas slipped into the shadows and went forward more cautiously.

A cluster of bobbing torches, like a great beast, surged forward out of the slums toward the *Empress.*

"Now, boys!" shouted a Bostonian. Dammit, it was Collins's bully boy, Holloway. "Remember—a hundred dollars in gold if you bring me the woman, unharmed."

They didn't know Rachel was at the hotel? He'd known a spy hadn't followed them from the wedding. But Collins must have been very distracted not to have reconnoitered the *Empress* more thoroughly.

A hungry roar answered him and the mob charged.

Lucas hurled himself into the fight, dirk drawn. A feint, a slash, and a stab killed the villain who'd meant to knife one of Donovan & Sons' best farriers. With the fallen ruffian's torch in one hand and his dirk in the other, he began the true—and very bloody—fight, with blood, burns, and broken bones to count score by.

But the bastards just kept coming and pushing his men back toward the *Empress.* The torches' heat was intense, blinding his eyes and searing his face—a bitter contrast to the icy ground they fought on. If one of those torches reached the Pullman, she'd catch fire since there was no firefighting when the water barrels were frozen.

A torch sailed overhead, tumbling in great arcs to land barely a foot short of the *Empress.* Braden and Lawson, conspicuous in their livery, immediately pounced and doused it.

Lucas shoved a ruffian into the one who'd thrown it. They

both went down, tripping their fellows. But more appeared, like rats.

Dammit, how many men had Collins bought?

A growl went up from behind the *Empress*, which turned into a full-throated roar. A phalanx of Union Pacific mechanics, switchmen, and other workers swung into sight, heavy tools over their shoulders.

The slum rats hesitated, shifting from foot to foot.

The phalanx advanced farther and began to tap their tools on the palms of their callused hands, demonstrating easy mastery of the deadly pieces of iron and wood.

The slum rats turned and fled back to their warrens, carrying their wounded, hastened by the winners' taunts.

Lucas watched them go, allowing himself a smile. The war wasn't won, but Collins would think twice before he tried another brazen attack against Lucas's railroad car.

A little later, Lucas silently slipped back into his hotel room, holding the latch up to avoid even the slightest click, and purred at what he'd come back to.

Rachel slept on, undisturbed, a single stray beam of moonlight bathing her pure profile. She was naked now, thank God, and her mouth was slightly swollen, drawing attention to its sensual outline. The image, in fact, of everything he wanted.

Good Lord, how that woman could kiss! He should have known that Davis's blatant satisfaction with his marriage was due to more than Rachel's intelligence and skill as a nurse. Lucas could have spent hours last night enjoying her taste and textures—and the way her tongue danced with his! Only her hips undulating against him had made him depart to explore her breasts and thighs and . . .

He'd find no hardships in conceiving a child with her, especially given her complete delight in carnal activities.

She muttered something and rolled over, displaying a bare shoulder and arm that could have graced a temple atop

Athens' Acropolis. His mouth dried, aching with the need to kiss and lick every smooth inch.

Two seconds later, he'd unceremoniously hung his coat on a hook and was jerking off his boots. He shoved his suspenders down his arms and unbuttoned his trousers with fingers that were far too clumsy for a man of his experience.

His drawers caught on his swollen cock when he first tried to pull them off. Cursing under his breath, he eased the fine linen away and a cool breath of air kissed his cockhead. Fire and ice lanced into his gut and his heart. His cock surged, pre-come gliding down in a heated stream. Oh yes, he'd be in Rachel's arms again soon . . .

He stroked himself slowly, using his foreskin and the sandalwood-scented oil Mitchell had thoughtfully provided to polish his shaft, his eyes shut to focus on and increase the sensations. Fireflies of pleasure floated into Lucas's groin and through his body, speeding his pulse and his breathing. It felt so delectable, perhaps he should simply stand here and prepare himself while watching her, then go to bed with her.

Another blast of cold rocketed across his ankles from under his door. He hopped, damning all hotels who couldn't keep drafts out of their rooms.

Or perhaps he should simply stop being a triumphant fool and warm himself up in Rachel's bed.

He glanced over at her. Her back was turned to him—still begging for a kiss!—so she shouldn't notice if he was rampant, as long as he didn't touch her.

He used his shirt to quickly rub the snow out of his hair, and inserted himself smoothly into the bed. He settled where he could see the clean furrow of her back and her elegant shoulder, his cock now happily warm. Only a few inches separated them now, the covers locking them in an intimate cocoon, while the hotel's sounds were blurred and distant beyond the room's walls.

Damn, she smelled good—all female without any cloyingly sweet perfumes and a trace of his musk to mark her. His skin prickled with sensual awareness, as if every inch of skin, every muscle and nerve, wanted more of her in their own ways. His chest tightened, making breathing difficult and turning his nipples into hard centers of desperation.

She mumbled something and moved back against him, wiggling her rump against his crotch and settling herself against him from shoulder to knee. It was the unconscious, confident move of a well-loved wife, not that of a whore who can make more money in other activities than sleeping with a man and therefore seldom does so.

Caught by total surprise, Lucas groaned with pure pleasure. His balls were tucked between his legs and the underside of her rump, while his rampant cock fit snugly between his belly and the narrow crack separating the twin globes of her rear. They were so tightly pressed together that the slightest movement by either of them could result in his foreskin's capture and his subsequent masturbation.

He closed his eyes in pure bliss, absorbing how perfectly they fitted together. Blood rushed into his cock, setting its veins throbbing and making him even more incredibly sensitive.

Rachel wriggled again, much harder this time, not quite pulling away from him. Her rump rubbed over his cock.

His breath caught in his throat. His left hand, which had just been slipping around to cup her breast, froze.

She rubbed herself against him again—and dragged his foreskin up his cock.

Lucas gasped, the most incredible tendrils of pleasure rippling through his spine and into his nipples. Nothing else he'd ever done—and he'd always made every effort to seek out new forms of sexual delight whenever possible—had ever felt as enjoyable as the results of her untutored movements. "Oh, dear God in heaven, Rachel . . ."

"Are you awake?" Mercifully she sounded alert.

He chuckled rather brokenly and gently wrapped his arms around her. "Of course I am."

He cupped her breast in his left hand and began to delicately draw circles on her soft skin with a single finger.

She writhed again, but not as much, and laid her head
back against his right shoulder. "You've been outside," she
observed and rested her hand on his wrist, gently encouraging his attentions.

"Hmm." He willingly fondled her breasts, glad she was so
eager. The pressure of her rump against him was enough to
drive a saint insane, their sweat acting together with his pre-
come to lubricate his cock and make his foreskin move faster.
Hell, it felt like the most subtle, sustained hand job he'd ever
had, sending shards of lust through his body every time she
shifted.

His right hand fanned over her belly in a pattern of soft caresses, designed to carry his fingers south to her delectable intimate flesh. *Surely you must feel some of the same excitement
I do* . . .

She sighed and relaxed subtly against him, stroking his left
hand. He gently rubbed and squeezed her breast, making her
groan and arch back against him—and driving her hips into
his.

His cock hardened further and his pulse slammed.

Rachel gasped. "Lucas . . ."

Good; she definitely sounded very willing.

She wriggled again, making his foreskin slide even farther
and faster, up and down his cock. He slipped a single finger
between her legs and started teasing her pearl.

"Lucas, you feel bigger against me—oh, my!—in this position than you did last night. Did I have all of that—ah!—inside me then, or are you bigger now?"

He stilled, caught just as he was about to delve for the
source of the cream glossing her thighs.

An old jealousy awoke, burning the most primal sphere.
Lucas had shown her more carnal pleasure, but Davis had
held her heart. That must be why she'd hesitated so long before she'd agreed to marry him.

What the hell was he to do?

He could burn himself into her memory, stamp her with his possession, every time they made love. It would have to be enough.

His fingers ruffled her inner folds. He nuzzled her hair and courted her breasts more assiduously. "Yes, you did, darling Rachel," he purred against her ear, "and you'll enjoy it just as much the next time."

He caught her earlobe between his teeth and sucked it gently.

She moaned softly, arching her neck to offer herself for the caress.

Damn, she was lovely with passion's flush gliding over her creamy skin. She moved so easily and spontaneously, too, as graceful as a young doe running across a meadow.

She stroked her hand down his thigh, the only caress she could consciously provide. She tried to roll over to face him but he stopped her, slipping a single finger into her. "No. I'm enjoying myself; aren't you?"

He circled it slowly inside her, exploring how tight she was. His hips rocked forward desperately, urged on by his throbbing cock.

"I can't see your face," she protested hoarsely, shifting against his hand, rubbing her derrière against his cock. It somehow managed to swell even more, until it was a single pounding ache that demanded everything from his thighs, hips, and spine. His balls tucked themselves up against their roots, hot and frantic for release.

He ignored her demurral, slipped a second finger into her in response, and began to slowly pump her. Conversation was for parlors and dining rooms, not times like this.

Rachel groaned and yielded, as clearly as she had the night before. Cream flowed over his hand, marking her willingness and easing his way.

"That's it, that's my girl," he crooned encouragement. His lungs were tight, barely able to power the pulses building in his loins, as his body fought his brain's command to wait for her.

"Ah, Lucas, please . . ." Her breath caught in her throat when his third finger fucked her. Her hips pushed back against his, fully matching his hand's rhythm.

Thank God.

He lifted her leg, opening her to him, and shifted.

She uttered a raw, questioning sound of feminine desperation and tried to roll to face him.

His cock slid down her back, leaving its frustrating nest against her rump, and slipped between her thighs. He cupped her mound with his hand, controlling her, and fondled her pearl again.

She was closer to the verge than he'd expected: She cried out in rapture, spasms rippling through her intimate flesh.

He twisted against her and his cock slid inside her. Last night, with her, had been the first time his cock had ever felt all the wonders of a woman's interior without the barrier of a condom. It had been everything and more than he'd dreamed of—and he'd immediately lost all control. Surely he could do better this time, for both of their sakes.

She was hot and wet, slick and rapturous, delicate muscles embracing his cock. Perfection.

Her channel clenched his cock, dragging it deeper and deeper, caressing it. He threw back his head and groaned, his hips rocking against her.

Her orgasmic waves started to slow, just as he set his hand on her.

Take your time, Lucas. You know how to show her the stars again . . .

He gritted his teeth and fought for both of them. He moved slowly and steadily inside her, his free hand circling her pearl, his impending climax darkening his vision.

Her body started to pulse around his and she grabbed his hand, kneading it like a cat.

Finally! He allowed himself to move faster, still holding

her against him spoon fashion and savoring the access to her. Joy of joys, the only sounds coming out of her mouth now were his name.

He growled his triumph at the thought, all restraints falling away. He bucked once, twice—and climaxed, fire bright waves of pleasure tumbling him over and over, as thoroughly as he washed her womb with his seed. As completely as Rachel intimately locked her body around him, pulsing with delight, and sobbed his name.

Afterward, he rolled her over to face him. "Rachel, darling, I promise you that next time, we'll look each other in the eye."

She looked at him blearily. "Tyrant. You're not truly sorry for taking me from behind, are you?"

He tried to conceal his all-too-satisfied grin. "Are you?"

She harrumphed. "Undoubtedly a tyrant. No, not really." She flung her arm around his waist and abandoned herself to slumber, her head resting trustfully against his shoulder.

Lucas smiled wryly at the title and he pulled her closer, their skin clinging together. He frowned at the sensation: There was more involved than sweat. His seed. His seed's stickiness linked them.

The skin on the nape of his neck stood up.

For the second time in his life, he'd tried to make a baby— another little one who might die as a result of his folly . . .

He blanched, ice-cold terror seizing him like a grizzly's claws. He almost shoved away from Rachel to demand that she douche.

Outside on the street below, someone whistled "Kathleen Mavoureen," often chosen as a password by Donovan & Sons' men. The sentries were keeping watch, lest Collins try to attack Rachel again. And the only safety for her was breeding a child to inherit the Davis fortune and break Collins's rights as a trustee. Lucas had married her and he'd sworn to protect her, which meant giving her that child. Plus, the only way for him to have a family was with her.

He rested his hand over her belly, where their child could be growing even now.

I swear to you, little one, that I will protect your mother with my life. I have learned my lesson. I will not fail you either, no matter what it costs me.

He swallowed hard and forced himself to relax, muscle by muscle.

Fog hung heavy and dank through the railroad yard, barely lightened by the dawn. A locomotive's engine chugged patiently, while metal clanked and rattled, marking a train being made up. Another locomotive's whistle blew from far away, echoing over the river.

Collins waited beside the tracks, refusing to pace. Maitland climbed slowly down from their hired private railroad car, jerking his collar up as high as possible to cover his bandages.

Seeing that, Collins growled deep in his throat and ran his thumb over his old dirk inside his pocket. Death was too good for the bitch who'd nearly taken his son's eye, who'd definitely destroyed his only child's good looks. The long, jagged wound ran from the corner of his left eye across his cheek almost to his mouth and had ripped open some of the skin around his eye.

The military surgeon had done his best to stitch Maitland up but had flatly stated that the scar would likely never become inconspicuous. Any infection would certainly cost Maitland's vision in that eye and could quickly take his life.

Within minutes after he'd thanked the surgeon and shown him the door, Collins had started sharpening his father's— and grandfather's—dirk. Rachel Davis needed to be taught a lesson. As soon as she was back under his control, he'd use his dirk to draw a matching line in her flesh so she'd know who was master.

"I thought the t–train didn't leave until eleven," Maitland commented, taking up position beside his father.

Collins's lips tightened. Maitland was mumbling, due to having stitches so close to his mouth and the laudanum the surgeon had used to incapacitate him. *Damn, damn, damn that bitch!*

He forced back his anger and displayed only a father's strength. "The main body doesn't. But we're leaving with this freight so we'll catch the work train. That's the snow-plow, which precedes the passenger train to clear the tracks. We should be at least an hour ahead."

Maitland's one good eye gleamed. "Enough to cause mischief."

"Or worse," Collins agreed. "I'm sure Humphreys will arrange everything at the Bluebird exactly as we'd like. We're lucky that Donovan irked him from the outset with his insistence on accurate bookkeeping.

Maitland nodded. "C–cable instructions to him from the train about what to do."

They shared a look of vicious anticipation over those possibilities.

He had to deal with the upstart Irishman first, not Rachel Davis—more's the pity. It was a damnable shame that the attack on her bower in the Grainger family's private Pullman had failed and cost him too many of his best men, especially since he'd learned she was actually at the great private hotel. Now he no longer had the resources to challenge Grainger openly for possession of the bitch, dammit.

But Donovan had the ability to haul him into court for fraud or bring down the wrath of the California banking crowd and their very powerful allies on his head. No matter what, he had to destroy him first, then the bitch.

"Are you sure Donovan won't know anything's untoward?"

Ah, Maitland must be starting to feel a little better, if his brain was beginning to consider implications such as those.

"His ship shouldn't dock in San Francisco for several more days. Even after that, I've bribed his telegrapher not to pass on anything that says much about us. So Donovan should go directly from the ship to the train, and on to that mine in Nevada without suspecting any foul play."

"You bribed a rich man's personal telegrapher on the opposite side of the country? Well done, Father, very well done!"

Collins allowed himself a brief smirk.

Their locomotive's steam engine steadied and began to beat more strongly.

"I believe our transport is ready. Breakfast should be ready, as well. Shall we board and depart this sorry excuse for a city, my son?"

Maitland nodded. "When we go home, let's t–travel by sea, as befits Collinses, and avoid this cesspool," he suggested, his tone striving for idleness.

Collins's heart twisted. Dammit, his son should sound just as sure of himself as he had a week ago, before Rachel Davis had turned on him! He had to swallow hard before he could answer. "Of course, we can travel by sea," he agreed. "A family's triumph should always be celebrated in the manner most suited to its traditions."

The early morning sun had just brightened the lobby when Rachel sailed down the stairs on Lucas's arm and encountered a dozen, quickly veiled stares. They were undoubtedly curious about the Easterners who'd arrived separately in town and married quickly.

Lucas growled softly under his breath and glared around the room, visibly daring any male present to embarrass her in any fashion. Startled blinks and coughs were his answer, plus some quickly concealed smiles from the few ladies present. But everyone returned to their prior occupations, ostensibly paying no heed to Rachel and Lucas.

She flicked a sideways glance at him, silently pondering his motives. Was he on edge this morning, to have warned off men whose only crime was a little curiosity about strangers? Was there more danger than he'd warned her of? Or could he have a more personal reason?

At least he'd given her a long, hot bath and massage so she could walk without hobbling like an old crone. It had been a year since she'd slept with Elias and, even then, her flesh had never been left so completely sated afterward. If Lucas hadn't tended her so tenderly, thoroughly—and skillfully—she would have limped through the hotel, displaying her crippled state in a most embarrassing fashion.

A dark-haired man opened the front door for them, his buffalo coat as good as a sign proclaiming his identity.

"Good morning, ma'am, Grainger," Mitchell greeted them in his deep Virginia drawl, as helpful now as when he'd rescued them from Collins's thugs. "There's a cab waiting at this end of the porch."

The cold air outside almost snatched Rachel's breath away, so very much drier than Boston's sea-laden winds. Lucas promptly tucked her closer to him and covered her hands with his, lending her some of his warmth. She was absurdly grateful for his assistance, however courteous its roots. It was more difficult to accept close proximity to his guns, though.

It was so early that few people were to be seen, most delivering supplies on the frozen roads. A handful of shopkeepers, well bundled against the cold, were sweeping the boardwalks in front of their stores and setting out a few samples of their wares. A single pedestrian, clearly the worse for wear, was making a very slow and wavering progress up the hill toward the hotel.

Lucas surveyed them all efficiently and warily, while moving her briskly down the porch. Rachel went with him, perplexed by his unorthodox reaction to an ordinary street scene.

When he cocked his head back to study the skyline, she opened her mouth to question him, but Mitchell spoke first. "Our men have the high ground, but there's little need to worry about snipers. Collins departed earlier this morning."

Lucas stared at him, somehow managing to hold his tongue until they were all seated inside the cab and headed toward the railroad depot. "How? The passenger train doesn't leave until almost noon."

"He hitched his private railroad car onto a freight train."

Disbelief ran through Rachel. "But those are very slow, required to stand aside every time a passenger train wishes to come through."

Mitchell shrugged. "It doesn't make much sense to me, either, because it's unlikely he'd hold his lead for long."

"How long?" Lucas demanded. He had his arm wrapped around her and was using his body to protect her from the worst of the carriage's jolts. He'd also tucked the cab's buffalo robe over her lap. "You've been helping Gillespie ship freight across the Rockies. What do you think?"

"Given the trains' schedules and the weather? A day if the weather holds."

"Which would let him reach Cheyenne first, maybe Laramie," Lucas said slowly. "Allowing him to connect to the work train, with the snowplow."

"While we travel with the main section, a few miles back," Mitchell agreed.

There was a distinctly unhappy silence.

"What are you talking about? Doesn't the passenger train always have a snowplow directly connected to it?" Rachel asked, trying to understand the western trains' composition.

Lucas glanced down at her, his features far harsher than they'd been earlier in their hotel bedroom. "No, the Union Pacific always runs their big east-west passenger train in three sections during the winter. First, there's a work train with a snowplow and a barracks full of men to shovel snow."

"About an hour later comes the main section, with the first-class passengers. Six hours or so after that, there's the emigrant train," Mitchell completed the description.

Rachel nodded, mentally contrasting the difference in quarters. First-class passengers would travel in the equivalent of the finest hotels, or better. But emigrant trains were as bad, or worse, than the crowded, squalid tenements that had burned in Boston a few months ago. "Shouldn't that be enough to get through any sort of weather?"

"Yes, *if* there's a snowplow and *if* the three sections stay close together," Lucas agreed.

"That's ridiculous," she exclaimed, forgetting all about the cab's frigid temperature. "Of course, there'd have to be a snowplow. The transcontinental railroad is one of the wonders of the world."

Her husband snickered and tucked the cab's buffalo robe a little higher around her. "Besides coping with the weather, the railroad is also a moneymaking creation for a set of greedy men, who don't always hire intelligent, efficient subordinates."

"What do you mean?"

"To begin with, a winter gale can cover railroad tracks in snow within minutes, forcing any passenger train to stop no matter how close it is to the work train," Mitchell drawled.

"Plus, there's only one snowplow for all of Wyoming," Lucas continued the litany of dangers. "Last year, the superintendent took it apart for most of the winter, just to see how it worked."

She gaped at him.

"And work trains have been known to continue traveling west, if separated from their passenger train—without trying to rejoin it," he added.

"Dear Lord," she said faintly. "We could be stranded."

"During what's been a very bad winter, with constantly diminishing stores of food." Lucas's tone was very mild, while his broad-brimmed hat hid much of his expression. "It's a dangerous time of year to travel, my dear."

"In that case, gentlemen, we'd best join our train quickly," she said briskly. "We want to be ready when the main section pulls out."

"Who's the supervisor in Laramie, Mitchell?" Lucas asked crisply.

"Kincaid—but after last winter, he's taken leave for the months of January and February."

Lucas snorted in disgust. "Typical of him. What about his deputy?"

"Leventhorpe is always ready to provide excellent service to the last man who pays him the highest price," Mitchell said flatly, adding after a moment, "but only in gold. As a Southerner, he'll have nothing to do with bank drafts or greenbacks."

"Are you sure he isn't a Yankee, if he's so obstinate? Well, cable him and see if you can reach an agreement as one Southerner to another."

"Very well."

"And cable Little, back in Denver. Ask him to go to Cheyenne and learn what he can of Collins."

"Lowell will probably join him, just simply to escape boredom."

Lucas groaned. "Well, Little probably has a better chance of keeping Lowell out of mischief than anyone else, especially if those two stay away from civilization. Perhaps they can temporarily join the shoveling gang, to get aboard that work train."

"I'll send that cable now, sir." Mitchell rapped on the ceiling. The cab pulled up and he was gone, after a polite farewell.

"It would be easier if we could warn Donovan, directly," Lucas mused a minute later.

"Why not?"

"He's sailing back from Seattle to San Francisco."

She pulled a face. "We don't have any proof that Collins has done anything wrong yet, either. So the law won't help us."

"We're on our own," Lucas agreed. "But perhaps we don't need to strike at Collins directly."

"What do you mean?"

"As your husband, I can be a trustee, correct?"

She cocked her head, startled by the suggestion, and slowly started to grin. Oh, the joy of having Lucas on the board, blocking Collins's every nefarious move and possibly even becoming the principal trustee. What she wouldn't give to see Collins's face when he found out! "Certainly you could."

"So I'll cable my father and tell him to file suit."

Tell him? To file *suit*? Lucas was about to order his father to go to court? Rachel tried hard to imagine herself instructing her own father to do any such thing, or Father Davis meekly obeying Elias's orders. She had to try twice before she could say anything. "Are you sure he'll listen to you?"

"Of course he will, once he understands how much money the family stands to make."

Rachel frowned, hoping the cab's dim interior hid her expression. Enriching himself was the only reason for helping his son, not love?

And why had Lucas married her? He sounded very dismissive of mercenary motives.

"Are there any other reasons you could mention?"

"None that he'd listen to." Lucas's tone of voice didn't encourage additional questions.

Rachel winced, hating the idea of how many times Lucas must have tried—and failed—to gain his father's blessing. But he was the only one Lucas had and she didn't want her husband hurt any more. To give his father orders sounded a guarantee for a fight, if the Grainger blood ran true.

"Hmm," she said noncommittally, deliberately trying to reduce Lucas's evident emotional tension. "But the situation is different now, since you're a married man and he now has prospects of becoming a grandfather."

"What are you driving at?" At least now Lucas only sounded testy, instead of dictatorial.

She sent up a prayer that a little bit of feminine diplomacy would work in this situation. "Perhaps if you asked him politely to undertake this on behalf of his future grandson? I have noticed that very few *older* men can resist the mention of seeing themselves well-established in future generations."

Please notice, Lucas, that I called him older, *implying a contrast to you as the* younger *generation.* She kept her face serene and waited.

"Are you asking me to be diplomatic on your behalf?" He was so surprised, he sounded as if he'd swallowed a frog. "You've never met him, after all. He could greatly dislike you."

She bridled. "He's your father, Lucas," she retorted, "and the grandfather of our children. He deserves our courtesy and I will teach our children to respect him, as their grandfather."

"Good Lord." Evidently stunned, her husband fell silent.

The carriage slowed, its wheels rolling over the gravel which probably marked the approach to the depot.

"Very well," Lucas said abruptly. "I'll ask him politely— but I'm doing it solely as a wedding present for you. I don't expect it to work."

She blinked at his reasoning, but decided to be gracious. "Thank you, dear."

"You're very welcome, wife. I expect to send the cable of my choice, couched as arrogantly as I please, the second time around."

She frowned but accepted his hand and stepped down from the cab. "You could be wrong," she pointed out stubbornly.

"I doubt it. I've fought him all my life." He stroked a finger down her cheek. "Don't worry about old dragons like him, dear. I'll keep you safe."

He offered her his arm, which she accepted automatically, before she could find words to tell him that she wasn't worried about being attacked by his father, not with him around to protect her.

The sun had now risen enough that the coal smoke-tainted fog had burned away, leaving only billowing sheets and wisps, instead of its previous, impenetrable blankness. Seen in the crisp, winter sunlight, the depot was a simple one-story, wooden structure, set amidst a sea of railroad tracks running east and west, as well as south to the railroad yard. The railroad yard was a mass of swarming men and machines, as industrious and clever as any beehive. To the north and west, shops and saloons marched up the bluff, their upper stories overlooking the depot and rail yard.

Every vista was so much clearer than it had been last night when Rachel had run for her life from Collins's private railroad car, parked on the edge of the railroad yard.

But the Grainger family's private Pullman was just as warmly welcoming as it had been the night before. Its wooden sides were varnished a crisp yellow and the trim painted a brilliant blue. Beautifully carved letters above a laurel wreath proclaimed it the *Empress,* an appellation that perfectly suited its beauty and elegance, and heartwarming scents of good food coming from the kitchen.

In front of the steps leading to the vestibule stood a man of average height and imposing presence: Braden, the Grainger family's steward, his blue and gold livery matching the *Empress*'s colors. He possessed an abundance of white hair, crisp mustache and beard, and the piercing blue gaze of the British sergeant he'd once been.

Rachel would have wagered Anglesey Hall that he was totally loyal to the Grainger family and to Lucas, just as the Davis family retainers had been to Elias.

She smiled at him, relieved to be near someone whose motives she understood, unlike her husband. "Good morning, Braden."

"Welcome aboard, Mrs. Grainger, Lieutenant Grainger. If I may be so bold as to offer you both my most sincere congratulations?" He bowed politely, his face shifting into a smile of equal formality.

"Thank you, Braden," Lucas returned briskly and Rachel echoed him.

Braden stepped aside, letting them precede him into the *Empress*. "Mrs. Grainger's wardrobe arrived a short time ago."

Rachel spun around, holding onto the railing. "My wardrobe?"

Lucas bowed slightly to her, looking a bit uncertain. "I asked Mitchell to buy the best available from the city's dressmakers."

"Numerous items have arrived, Mrs. Grainger. I'd estimate them to fill at least one trunk," Braden offered.

She leaned over and kissed her husband on the cheek. "Thank you, Lucas. You are very, very kind."

He stiffened, clearly startled, before relaxing. "My pleasure, Rachel."

Rachel smiled, relieved by his indulgence and yet still just a little uncomfortable.

Only a few hundred feet away, towered the great iron and stone railroad bridge linking Iowa and Nebraska, across which the passenger trains would travel to leave for Nevada and California. Beneath it, ice covered the mighty Missouri River, cracking and groaning as it fought to reach the ocean—and sounding as unsettled and unpredictable as her marriage.

Chapter Seven

The great train sped west over the prairie like an arrow, the railroad track bed so smooth and the *Empress* so well balanced that not a drop of coffee in Lucas's cup spilled. Its whistle wailed, long and loud, and another one answered it. With a whoosh and a roar, the two trains passed each other, smokestacks blasting clouds of smoke into the sky and their locomotives' great wheels pounding relentlessly onward.

The elegant railroad car had joined the daily east-west train's main section, holding the first-class passengers, while the emigrant train was six hours behind it. Collins and the freight train were still almost five hours ahead.

Displaying all the graciousness of his Virginia upbringing—and common sense—Mitchell had somehow managed to obtain another private Pullman from the Union Pacific's yards in Omaha. It was a business car, designed principally for men's use, and traveled directly ahead of the *Empress*, carrying him and the other Donovan & Sons' men who'd be guarding Rachel. There were only a handful of them now, since Donovan & Sons was always shorthanded in the winter when the seasonal workers were gone. Lucas hoped yet again that his friends could join them in Cheyenne.

The *Empress* followed the floor plan of most private Pullmans. The drawing room was in the rear, filling the entire car's width. Next to it stood the telegrapher's small private office, with a desk and bunk. The master stateroom came next, as large as many houses' bedrooms with its immense bed, not surprising since both of Lucas's parents had used the *Empress* for assignations. There were also two smaller staterooms, both equipped with bunks. Rachel's luggage was currently stowed in one of them, allowing her privacy. The connecting corridor ran along the railroad car's left side, providing the maximum amount of quiet for the car's occupants.

The beautiful dining room boasted of its intricately carved woods, multiplied over and over again by mirrors, especially the great mirrored pass-through to the kitchen. There Lawson, a culinary genius—born in Charleston and trained in Paris—created masterpieces in an ingeniously designed, but very cramped space. Last was the larger than average crew quarters.

To Lucas's total lack of surprise, Mitchell and the other men had already persuaded Lawson that the Union Pacific cook assigned to their private Pullman was a sorry lout, incapable of even soaking hardtack. They ate aboard the *Empress* now, albeit at different times from him and Rachel.

Rachel Davis—no, Rachel Davis *Grainger*—had propped her chin on both hands, while she considered the chessboard laid out on the drawing room table. Her golden eyes had darkened to amber under the straight line of her eyebrows and her chestnut hair was arranged in a complicated set of braids, which allowed her to clearly see the game's pattern and him to admire the elegant line of her neck. She'd changed into a simple green cashmere dress, which buttoned down the front and neatly outlined her graceful figure. Mitchell's nighttime raid on Omaha's dressmakers had produced some exemplary results, albeit not in great quantity.

Barely looking at the chess game before him, Lucas moved his king's knight as he'd planned a half-dozen moves ago. He didn't want to beat Rachel too quickly or too easily.

The *Empress*'s legends arose from the refinement of its fittings, the superb quality of the crew, and the depth of its stores. Lucas prayed that the last two factors wouldn't be tested on this run. A typical kitchen carried food for a dozen days, for the typical cross-country journey of less than a week. But during a hard winter, many trains took longer to travel the thousand miles west to Ogden. Last year's bitter weather had slowed one train's passage to thirty-six days and forced its passengers onto starvation rations.

Lucas had ordered Braden to fill the other unused staterooms with food. It wasn't fancy stuff, but it would keep them alive, especially if Rachel was carrying a child.

He pictured the stateroom-turned-storeroom one more time in his mind's eye. Was there anywhere else they could stow some more food? Braden had filled both of the bunks and stowed crates underneath, as well as half of the room itself. Perhaps another box in that corner by the far wall? Or the entire room? No, probably not. They could live comfortably now for forty-five days.

Outside, the endless plains whizzed past, covered in a sea of white and marked by an occasional tree. Three feet of snow, lifted by yesterday's howling winds into drifts of six feet or more, had turned the flat prairie into a deadly cold sea. Every ten miles, he could glimpse the stations where a few dozen soldiers guarded the railroad against Indians, each station as distant in a blizzard as Chicago or New York.

He took a drink of his rich coffee and set it down, savoring his warm surroundings and his companion.

He eyed her dress's buttons, calculating how long it would take to undo them . . . No, he'd promised her they'd play chess until dinner. Unless she changed her mind, of course, and he was hopeful enough of that outcome that he'd just shaved. He calculated he'd best do so three times a day, if he wished frequently to enjoy—and protect—her delicate skin from whisker burn.

Perhaps he should have her portrait painted like this, rather than in a more conventional pose. An intimate private portrait for his office; he'd need to establish a permanent base soon, now that there'd be a child to rear.

Rachel's hand shot out, her ruffled sleeve falling back to reveal her slender wrist, and brought her white queen lunging down the board. "Checkmate," she announced and sat back, as erect as any monarch.

What? Lucas stared down at his all-too-few ebony chessmen scattered across the black-and-white squares. Only a few seconds' study convinced him of the accuracy of her summation. Dammit, she'd rolled him up as neatly as Grant had taken Vicksburg and faster than many top players in private clubs.

He began to laugh at his own overconfidence, thankful the Donovan & Sons' men were playing poker in their business car and hadn't witnessed his defeat.

"Congratulations, Rachel." He held out his hand.

"Thank you." She shook it, smiling. "But you're a very fine player; you almost had me boxed in several times, especially at the beginning."

He winced slightly and began to reset the pieces. That would teach him to think about quartermasters' stores when he played chess with her.

She poured herself a fresh cup of coffee and gazed out the window, a blissful smile toying with her mouth. "Isn't this the most beautiful place in the world?"

Lucas froze, his hands full of chessmen, and stared out the window. No, it was still the same endlessly flat expanse of snow.

His gaze shot to Rachel's face suspiciously. Was she teasing him? No—she seemed damn near as rapturous as she had last night in the bedroom. He'd learned early how to judge when whores were counterfeiting similar expressions and he frankly didn't believe she had the experience to do so. So she had to be telling the truth: She thought Nebraska was truly lovely—in the dead of winter.

"When I stand on a station's platform, I can see for miles in every direction," she went on dreamily. "And I know that I can travel anywhere I want—north or south, east or west—and as free as a dove. All I have to do is board a train or stage, and go."

Lucas stared at her, his blood chilling. Had she no idea of what she might be getting into? The truly unpredictable weather, which could be summer in the morning and the depths of winter by nightfall? If anything happened to her or their child . . .

He managed to clear his suddenly very tight throat. "And somehow manage to find decent meals on a regular basis . . ." he suggested, trying to make a joke out of the notoriously bad cooking on stage routes.

She giggled and glanced back at him. "True. We can't stop in any event, since we have to proceed to Nevada immediately," she agreed. "Even so, everything here is so much more spacious than the tight confines of Collins's Ledge. That's why whenever we come to a depot, I want to disembark and throw my arms wide and embrace all of it. As I've done every stop since we left Omaha."

She smiled beatifically upon him, took another sip of her drink, and went back to gazing out the window, humming softly.

Lucas gulped down the rest of his coffee, wishing he dared refill to it with whisky. Dammit, was she truly planning to stand outside at every stop, no matter what the weather? Since the locomotive needed to frequently refill its cistern, it stopped every thirty-five miles or so. Would he have to watch her dancing with the elements every hour or so? In temperatures that would freeze her beautiful hand to the *Empress*, should she happen to brush against it without gloves? Not if he could help it!

What should he do?

He could persuade her not to go outside.

Win an argument against her nimble mind in a direct confrontation? His mouth twisted wryly. He suspected he'd be glad if her tact allowed him to usually win their *public* arguments.

He went back to resetting the chessmen, frowning. He couldn't prevent her from going outside, since that would mean locking her up onboard the *Empress*. Imprisonment would be an act of foulness, befitting that brute Collins—or desperation.

Maybe he could distract her instead . . .

Or if he kept her in their stateroom as much as possible? She was a very uninhibited, passionate lady, thank God. She wasn't showing any shyness or stiffness after last night's frolics, so he could take her back to bed and try several more times to conceive a child. If she still wanted to go outside after that, some long bouts of pleasuring her with his mouth and hands should leave her exhausted and inclined to fall asleep.

He purred, imagining her sated, boneless body sprawled over his chest with her slender fingers twined around his, and quickly set the last pawns into place.

"Mrs. Grainger?" he invited, wiping his face of everything except polite inquiry. "I believe the first move is yours."

She shook herself slightly and turned back to face him, still smiling softly. His heart thudded against in his chest. *Damn, she was beautiful—a modern goddess of home and hearth.*

"Lucas, that's the first time you've called me 'Mrs. Grainger.' "

He lifted his cup to her, deliberately ignoring the sudden rush of heat into his chest. "And here's to many more such salutations, Mrs. Grainger."

She blushed slightly and brought her pawn forward.

He answered her move quickly, determined to end the game as soon as possible. This shouldn't take too long, especially now that he was determined to concentrate.

Half an hour later, he was calculating the tenth in a series of moves that should check Rachel's king—but probably wouldn't bring checkmate—when the train's whistle blew, a brusque note which announced a brief watering stop.

Rachel promptly thrust her chair back.

His hand shot out and grabbed her wrist. Was this his chance to lure her back to their stateroom? "What about the game?"

She gaped at him. "I, ah—"

"You promised to play straight through until dinner. No mention was made of interruptions, such as disembarking for a watering stop. Are you forfeiting the game?"

She hesitated and threw a helpless glance at the window. The sun was setting rapidly now, shooting sparks of light off the snow and forming rainbows from the ice crystals hanging from tree branches.

At another time, Lucas might have admitted the scene was handsome, but not now. "Are you forfeiting the game?" he repeated, more softly.

She looked back at the board, then up at him and nodded. "Yes. You'd have won in a dozen moves anyway."

A *dozen?* He tried to pretend he'd known the solution all along.

The locomotive blew out steam and the brakes screeched. The train began to slow.

She held out her hand and he lifted it to his lips. "Dear wife." He lingered over the kiss, nuzzling her fingers and her knuckles.

She trembled, her eyes growing huge in her previously serene face.

Very pleased with the effects of a little flirtation, Lucas pressed a kiss into the palm of her hand and stood up, lifting her with him.

She gripped the back of her chair, visibly trying to regain her composure. "Lucas, do you know what town this is?"

Poor darling, when would she learn that two people didn't always have to make conversation? He retrieved their coats from the other side of the drawing room. "Someplace close to Grand Island, I think."

He wrapped her simple mantle around her, for the first layer of protection. "But it's only a dirtwater town, established solely to provide water for the locomotives," he added.

She knitted her brows at the explanation, accepting her heavy mittens. "They build towns for that purpose?"

"Certainly they do." He briskly fastened his coat and tossed a scarf around his neck. "In parts of Nevada and Utah, the Central Pacific Railroad has even built towns *and* hauled in water for them to give the trains."

She shook her head. "It truly is a Great American Desert."

He kissed her cheek and wrapped her thick, shaggy buffalo coat around her. At least this would keep her warm and stop any wind from touching her.

But if the breeze touched any bits of exposed skin . . . He'd have to watch her closely for frostbite.

The coat's rich, dark brown framed Rachel's face, its soft fur brushing against her smooth skin and making her look even more delectable.

Lucas leaned down and nuzzled her cheek. "You can see the station from here," he suggested softly.

She hummed and tilted her head to one side, her hand coming up to caress him. "But then I couldn't tell exactly how much space it has around it, could I?"

Drat her logical mind. Lucas reluctantly muttered agreement and continued to kiss her, even as the train rumbled to a stop, its iron wheels screeching.

He was disciplined enough to take her outside immediately, however reluctantly. A watering stop was so brief that there was little time to spare, if she was to see anything. But he went down first and handed her down the narrow, ice-covered steps very carefully.

Outside, Mitchell and another Donovan & Sons' man were pacing around the platform, warily regarding the scene beyond. Nearby a handful of chimneys spouting smoke rose above small frame houses. Lucas would be surprised if this town's entire population amounted to two dozen.

Wind brushed his face with its sharp, cold claws, eager to harm the unwary and reminding him of more storms to come—a younger brother of yesterday's gale but still dangerous in its own right.

He pulled his scarf up higher, leaving only a little skin around his eyes exposed underneath his fur cap, and glanced over at Rachel.

She opened her arms, as if to embrace the entire scene, and turned around slowly, her expression ecstatic. The wind ruffled her fur cap, slowly sliding it back from her face. "Beautiful," she sighed. "Simply beautiful."

His heart plummeted into his boots. *Dear God in heaven, what would he do if she caught pneumonia?*

He wrapped his arm around her and pulled her in front of him. He rocked her against him, slowly spinning them both around, until the wind beat against his back. Body warmth, that was it—give her body warmth, the best medicine of all against cold.

"Lovely," he agreed, "lovely beyond compare." He quickly smoothed her cap back into position over her braids, protecting her delicate ears and hiding her face from the deadly wind.

"Lucas!" she protested, sounding as if she was blushing not infuriated.

He paused, surprised, and went along with her assumption of a flirtation. "Shouldn't I proclaim my wife's beauty?"

"You can hardly compare a woman to a landscape."

"Why not? Shakespeare said something about a summer day and his lover. But you're far more golden and passionate than his dark lady."

"Lucas!"

He'd wager if he could see her face, she truly would be blushing. He didn't dare grin. "Can you feel any wind now, my dear?"

"No, of course not. You're blocking it—for which I thank you."

He lowered his voice. "It's my pleasure—especially if it keeps you warm. I enjoy thinking of you hot, perhaps melting *under* your clothes."

There was a moment's silence, broken only by the gurgling water as it tumbled into their locomotive's cistern. Mitchell and the other man were on the opposite side of the station's platform, their conversation obscured by the wind and distance.

Lucas wished to high heavens that he could see Rachel's face to gauge her thinking.

Her voice was very soft when she answered. "Yes, I'm quite *hot*—and I hope you are, too. Perhaps when we return onboard we can see to each other's, ah, comfort before dinner."

"An excellent idea." He rubbed his chin against the top of her head, the closest he could come to a caress in this weather. She moved closer to him, until her bustle started to slide up out of the way against her back, bringing her hips closer to his through their heavy clothing.

He rumbled wordless approval and cradled her, not entirely sorry moments later to see the station attendant close off the water valve.

"All aboard!" cried the conductor.

"Come, my dear, it's time to return to the *Empress*."

He swung her up into the *Empress*'s vestibule, totally avoiding the icy stairs, and followed her immediately. An instant later, he saw Mitchell and the other board their car. No trouble here from Collins, not that he honestly expected it before the Rockies.

The train's whistle blew, marking their departure.

Inside the *Empress*'s drawing room, Braden was pulling the blinds and closing the curtains.

Rachel blinked at him, her breasts heaving and her mind spinning. The world seemed to have become a different place with every color brighter and every scent richer. The curtains were now a brilliant cobalt blue, instead of a dull navy blue. Surely she could not be smelling fresh roses and cedar, instead of faint traces of those living scents. No cinders in here, of course, unlike common passenger cars.

The train's whistle blew, its bell ringing continuously. The big wheels clanked and began to turn, their heavy rhythm pounding slowly, deeply through her feet and into her bones. Heaven help her, it rolled into her core . . .

Activities that had been so straightforward once had now taken on a new meaning. Had she really made an assignation with a man, even if he was her husband? Could his servant be screening the room to ensure their privacy?

How could she be so sensually self-assured as to even consider doing so? This was very different from studying Latin declensions.

Well, at least Braden was protective.

"Thank you, Braden," she murmured, keeping her head high, even as her core throbbed in time with the *Empress*'s wheels . . .

"My pleasure, ma'am. Will there be anything else?"

Lucas calmly dropped his hat, gloves, and coat onto a settee. He silently came up behind her and nudged her toward the corridor with one hand on the small of her back, his carnal intentions as unmistakable as if he'd shouted them.

She definitely blushed. "No, thank you, Braden. We'll call you if we need anything."

"Very well, ma'am." No smile touched his face, which would have been very improper, but somehow she sensed his complete approval. He bowed slightly as they went past.

Lucas promptly wrapped his arm around her waist and kissed the top of her head. Her body promptly purred its enthusiasm and melted. Heaven help her, he seemed virile enough to make her pregnant within a day. No matter what he hoped to gain from this marriage, whatever happened in the future—she had to accept and trust how all her five senses thrilled to his touch.

"Are you still warm?" he whispered.

"I believe I'm very hot—although that could be my attire," she returned, trying for a light tone.

He chuckled and pushed open their stateroom door. "We'll have to investigate that very quickly. It would never do to have my wife languish from heat prostration."

Her blush deepened, as she recognized what she'd just invited.

She glanced around their stateroom, trying to decide where to go. The main stateroom was an opulent nest, deliberately designed to look as much as possible like a medieval knight's bedchamber. Heavily carved mahogany paneling and furniture were accented by oriental carpets, rather than the more modern Brussels carpets. The lamps on the wall were shaped like torches with great globes and long handles, while the single lamp hanging from the ceiling resembled Aladdin's lamp—as if the medieval knight had brought back trophies from the Crusades. The big bed, with its four posters, could easily hold two people in comfort and there was also enough space to walk easily around the furniture, rather than eternally dodging other occupants. Even the small stove in the corner, which had come from the Russian railroad system, was an ornate oriental affair. The overall effect was surprisingly hedonistic and comfortable at the same time.

If she hadn't known that it was Lucas's father's private Pullman, Rachel would have concluded that the *Empress* had been built as a love nest.

She came up against the bed and turned around, ready to ask Lucas what he wanted her to do.

Lucas unfastened her buffalo coat and tossed it aside carelessly, close to the stove.

Rachel stiffened, appalled by possible damage to the fur, and started to protest. His brilliant gaze caught her, his eyes hooded but oh, so very hungry.

She stopped, the first syllable hanging in her throat, and stared back at him, utterly unable to move. The heat that she'd teased him about, on that small railroad platform, twisted through her spine and into her veins like a match to kindling.

He was watching her as if she alone would satisfy him. As if she was the most delightful, seductive woman he'd ever hoped to find.

Her breath caught in her throat. Her? Scrawny, brown-haired Rachel?

She ran her tongue over her suddenly dry lips. He avidly studied every millimeter of movement.

Oh my. Her core tightened, sending a jolt of heat into her breasts.

He took one step forward, then another.

Dear heavens, every step brought his scent closer to her, spreading the heat through her body. If she'd tried to lift a finger, turn, take a step—she couldn't have done so.

He lifted her hands and began to take off her gloves. Every time he uncovered a finger, he kissed it.

She stared at him, her eyes enormous. The simple caresses seemed to be ricocheting to places deep inside her that she hadn't known existed, weakening her knees. The spirals of fire and hunger reached into her toes and her fingers. "Lucas," she breathed, "shouldn't you kiss . . ."

He glanced up at her from over her knuckles. "Your fingertip, dear? What an excellent idea."

He sucked it into his mouth, gently scraping his teeth over it.

Rachel felt the tug all the way to her womb. She moaned and grabbed for his shoulder with her other hand. "Dear heavens, Lucas!"

His smile was full of masculine anticipation. "You have nine more fingers, Rachel," he pointed out, "and I'm not sure I'm done with the first."

He licked her finger again, increasing her sensitivity, and sucked. Her knuckles turned white where she gripped him and she spread her legs for balance. By the time he took her jacket off, she was begging for more than kisses.

He dropped her jacket onto the floor and unfastened her

skirt, his hands fumbling slightly. Moments later, her petticoats followed it onto the pile with her cloak, leaving her standing in her corset, chemise, drawers, stockings, and boots. She blushed, ducking her head since she had no veil of hair to hide behind.

"Dear God in heaven, you're beautiful," he whispered.

Rachel's head jerked up in surprise and she stared at him. He truly was watching her avidly, his chest rising and falling as if he'd been racing the train.

A slow smile bloomed on her face, matching the liquid fire in her core. "Lucas, sweetheart . . ."

"What?" He wasn't looking at her face. She eyed the great bulge behind his fly and a secret, feminine smile touched her lips. Surely an experienced woman would know how to tease her lover into removing his clothes.

"You're still wearing things that could scratch my skin." She tried to pout; wasn't that what flirts did?

His head shot up, sweeping an adorable lock of hair back off his brow. "Damn, I'm sorry, Rachel."

He managed to very quickly remove his jacket, with its few buttons. He yanked his boots off and threw them into the corner beside the stove.

Rachel propped one foot up on the small footstool and stretched, pretending she wasn't watching him. If she looked directly at him, she was very much afraid that she'd leap on him in a most improper fashion. She closed her eyes and hissed in the near pain of frustration, rubbing slow circles over her stomach and wishing desperately that she could fondle herself more intimately, given the tendrils of lust curling between her breasts and her core.

He growled and fumbled at his shirt, with its infinity of small buttons and tight cuffs. He kept stealing glances at her, which she glimpsed in the mirror over the dressing table.

Was he growing more excited because they weren't facing each other, with their eyes open? Was the same eagerness driving her?

She daringly fondled her breasts, as she would if she was alone. "I'm definitely melting, Lucas," she murmured, trying to remember the words he'd used for flirtation.

He cursed and yanked his cuff open, sending buttons flying. He shoved his suspenders and whipped his shirt over his head off his shoulders.

It was her first sight of him, naked to the waist. Forgetting all pretense of disinterest, she spun around and looked her fill at her magnificent male animal

She'd already known he was strong, because of how he'd carried her through Omaha. But had she truly realized how clean-limbed he was, how superbly his smooth sweeps of muscle worked with sharp lines of bone and sinew to form such a potent, barely leashed strength? Even his stomach was ridged as though it too was banded with muscle. Blue veins twisted and rippled across his creamy skin like foreign artwork. He was as primal and irresistible as the train itself, carrying her ever onward to an unknown destination.

He was breathing hard, his chest rising and falling quickly under the neat, thick dark mat of hair as he watched her. Dark coppery nipples gleamed amidst it, looking tight and hard. Did he enjoy love play there, as she did? He'd never spoken of his likes, nor truly allowed her time to discover them.

A great silver slash ran across his left arm and a half dozen puckered scars marked bullet wounds gained through service to his country. Dear heavens, he was even more masculine and attractive when seen in the light, than in the dark.

She choked, unable to breathe or voice her hunger. Surely he burned, too, given the flush darkening his chest.

Her nipples pebbled hard against her corset, desperate to rub against him.

He pulled her into his arms. "You're tumbling me into your bed."

Her tongue ran over her lips. "Wonderful."

"Witch," he said feelingly and tipped her up onto the bed. An instant later, he'd stripped off his trousers and joined her.

He leaned over her. "Minx. You passionate darling—and *my* wife, thank God."

He kissed her and she responded immediately, giving herself completely to the enticing caress. His clever fingers found their way to her breasts, fondling and tweaking, insidiously courting her. The combined sensations overwhelmed her senses and she finally pulled her head back, unable to catch her breath against her corset's constriction.

Lucas rumbled approval and dropped his ebony head. If his fingers were clever, his mouth was devilish in its ability to incite her into madness.

Her northern devil, with his eyes like the blue-green fires in a block of ice's heart. Outside, everything was frozen but here, everything was on fire.

Her core was burning for him, cream melting onto her thighs for him. Her most intimate flesh was rich and full, infinitely sensitive in readiness. She couldn't think clearly past the need to feel him more deeply.

She gripped his shoulders and back, pulling him closer. Once she scratched him—but he growled her name and went back to loving her with redoubled passion.

Waves were hurtling through her blood, demanding fulfillment.

His blunt finger sought her pearl and she willingly opened for him, eager for more of his touch. He toyed with her folds, teasing her, until she thought she'd go insane. Her hips rocked back and forth, desperately seeking him.

And then—there he was, wonder of wonders, kneeling between her legs, gathering her up by the derrière to prepare her.

Rachel was almost blind with lust, but she threw one leg up around his hip—and almost died for the infinite delight of feeling Lucas pressed against her thigh.

She was so burning hot and wet that he came completely into her on his first thrust. He lay solidly against her, his heart sounding as loud as any steam engine. He wrapped his arms around her to steady her and she instinctively wrapped her other leg around his hips. A moment later, he began to move.

He rode her hard, fire ripping through them both. The waves of lust were too great, too close to the surface, too easily transferred between them to be long denied.

She clawed his back, silently demanding completion. He came immediately, shouting her name in shock. The hot pulses deep inside her triggered a startling climax, tumbling her into it as if it had been days since she'd experienced release, orgasmic waves shaking her spine.

And always, jet after jet of his rich, hot seed filled her womb. Somehow, this time he was deeper than ever before.

Afterward, all she could do was lay on top of him and try to catch her breath, while he gently petted her back. The fact that she was still wearing most of her underclothes was quite unimportant in comparison.

"Damnation, but I'm a lucky man," Lucas muttered and tossed the light, embroidered coverlet over her.

"Hmm?" She probably needed to eat something but that would mean leaving his arms. No.

"Having a wife who's eager to make love with me."

Rachel blinked and briefly stopped trying to wrap some of his chest hair around her little finger. He was so wonderfully furry there.

They'd been friends for more than five years. She might not know all the reasons why he'd married her, but she had managed to lure him into bed for their mutual pleasure. With that ability, his ring on her finger, and his child under her heart—her place in his life should be very solid.

Even if he might one day take another mistress . . .

She smiled and smoothed out the little lock of hair. "And

I'm the luckiest woman in the world—having a husband who's eager to give me pleasure."

Lucas rumbled approvingly, deep in his throat, and pulled her up his body for another kiss.

The train's whistle blew long and low. The *Empress*'s great iron wheels screamed softly, warning of a stop.

Lucas nibbled on her nose. "Dinner time. Do you want to disembark and eat in Grand Island?"

Rachel jerked her head back and shot him an appalled look. "Are you joking? After tasting lunch, I've been waiting all day for Lawson's first dinner."

"In that case, we should rise and dress." He didn't move.

"Could Braden serve us in here?" What a hedonistic evening that would be . . .

A wicked smile played over her husband's lips. "Of course he would. I'll ring for him."

He stretched out his arm but couldn't reach the bell pull without disturbing her. Rachel sniffed, trying to sound disgruntled, giggled, and slid off her husband.

He lightly swatted her rump, making her jump. "Silly wife," he teased her.

Their train blew its whistle once again, the wheels screeching to a stop and steam hissing up past the windows.

Another train's whistle sounded very, very close.

They both froze, listening hard to the unusual sound.

Rachel frowned. "That sounds like it intends to stop here, too, Lucas."

He sat up, frowning. "I wonder . . ."

She watched him with growing alarm. "What do you mean?"

Harsh lines appeared beside his mouth, deeper than when he'd faced down Holloway and Collins's thugs for her outside the saloon.

The other train's whistle blew again, very close, signaling its stop.

The other train's wheels started to screech.

Lucas threw back the covers and stood up. The lines beside his mouth were white now and a muscle ticked in his jaw. "It sounds like a Baldwin from the Pennsylvania Railroad, one of those used for private trains."

He poured water from the jug on the stove into the big bowl and began to sponge himself off quickly, looking as though he was considering a dozen revolting options. She was hardly surprised that he didn't use the tub in the small private bathroom.

"A private *train*?" Rachel sat up. "Who do you think it is?"

"My father." He caught sight of her face through the mirror and spun to face her. "I'm not ashamed of you, dear—never, never think that!"

An ugly fear died before it had ever been truly born. She managed a tremulous smile for him.

The other train's wheels screeched loudly, sounding as if it would stop on the track beside the *Empress*.

Lucas slapped the paneling, his expression shifting back into wariness and rage. "Damn, I hope I'm wrong and it's someone else."

Braden had laid out dinner clothes for both of them, which Rachel had thought far too formal for a train in the middle of Nebraska, even if Mitchell had somehow managed to acquire a superb Parisian evening gown for her.

Now Lucas began to jerk on the finely made raiment with scant regard for its quality. He even dug out pearl studs and an elegant diamond stickpin to wear with his black frock coat, immaculate white linen, and charcoal gray trousers. It was the attire a man would wear for the opera or dinner at the White House, certainly not for a comfortable gathering *en famille*.

She opened her mouth and closed it with a snap. For once in her life, she didn't ask any of the questions trembling on the tip of her tongue. Elias had told her nothing of Lucas's relationship with his family, although he'd known much about their social and financial importance. Lucas wasn't talking and she gave him the quiet he needed.

An impatient halloo sounded outside just as he finished. A woman's voice called for Braden.

A muscle ticked in Lucas's jaw. "Damn."

"Who?" she whispered.

"Mother." The single word sounded like another man's name for all of the four Furies.

He leaned over and kissed Rachel gently on her forehead. "Wait here for me, dear. There's no need for you, too, to face her malice."

Malice? Flabbergasted, she opened then closed her mouth, unable to think of a response to a son who'd use that word for his mother's actions.

He left without another word, striding out of the stateroom like a cavalry officer going into battle.

Rachel promptly scrambled out of bed. Like hell—as Elias would have said—would she permit her husband to face any sort of appalling social scene alone and unaided. But if he felt this called for pearl studs and a diamond stickpin, she would need something more than her very simple dinner dress. Thankfully, she'd smuggled some of Elias's more ostentatious gifts of jewelry with her from Boston.

What else would she need?

She surveyed herself in the mirror.

Her braids and corset had survived Lucas's lovemaking— more or less. She'd have to wash up, of course.

She also looked exactly like what she was: A newly-married wife, who was deeply confident of her husband's attentions. That was armor well worth having in any confrontation with another female, even his mother.

She yanked the bell pull, hoping Lawson and perhaps some of the Union Pacific porters from next door were helping Braden cope with the current upheaval. She'd need every bit of Braden's genius to reach the drawing room quickly.

*   *   *

Lucas faced his parents across the drawing room, praying Rachel would have the good sense to stay in the stateroom and out of the line of fire. Any scene, however unpleasant, would be worth it, as long as her social position remained solid.

To his surprise, he felt more relaxed than usual around his mother.

In contrast to his father's autocratic stature, Aurelia Grainger stood slightly less than average height and had retained the soft curves of a young matron. Her once-blond hair had seamlessly transmuted into silver, but her classic features and translucent skin allowed her to pass for a woman of less than half her age. She always wore either full or half mourning, depending on the occasion, and always in the latest Paris fashion. While his father was a power among the East's great railroad and banking boardrooms, a word from his mother could make eastern society's most rarefied circles tremble.

She was wearing an evening dress made in Paris and styled in full mourning's deep black, with what his sister called her dowager's jewels of pearls and diamonds. She obviously wanted to gain the maximum amount of sympathy during this conversation, probably to burden him with guilt.

"Welcome aboard, sir, Mother. Would you care for something to drink?" He wouldn't invite them to join him for dinner unless forced. "Coffee, tea, or wine?"

T.L. shifted slightly, an unusual admission of discomfort. Mother, however, pushed forward regardless—as usual. She'd been the Grainger matriarch since the day she married T.L., almost thirty-five years ago, and thus ruled her surroundings. "We'll take wine, of course."

Lucas glanced at the Union Pacific steward, who nodded and withdrew, his expression impassive and his arms overflowing with fur-trimmed coats. Where the devil was Braden? Probably helping Lawson in the kitchen, who'd need every bit of assistance to cope with these guests' expectations.

"Please sit down," Lucas invited.

Mother shook out yards of ornate black silk ruffles and pleats, sat down on the central settee, and arranged her skirts and train in the most imposing fashion possible. *All hail the queen,* was what her children had always called that move.

What blistering lecture did she plan this time? Surely the Old Man had said everything possible in Chicago.

T.L. took up his station beside her, his hand on the back of her settee—in the perfect position to back or even increase her demands.

Lucas moved to face them, also resting his hand on the back of a carved settee. Damned if he'd look like he was still a schoolboy, waiting to be whipped.

Silence fell within the *Empress.* Outside, the faint sounds of a few hundred people competing to eat within a few minutes at the station could be heard.

Lucas's jaw tightened before he offered the first conversational gambit, his duty as host. "I hope you had a pleasant journey. The weather's been quite gentle the past day or two."

"The wind was bad on the first day—" the Old Man began, accepting the need for social chitchat. After all, he was one of the country's great bankers and had been through many difficult negotiations.

But Mother broke in. "We're not here to discuss the weather, as we all know. So let's discuss substantive matters instead."

Ah, that was the mother he knew: Brusque, dictatorial, and self-centered. Lucas lifted an eyebrow and waited.

She surveyed him like a disdainful butcher. "I understand you refused to marry the Tallmadge chit."

Lucas stiffened. Dammit, when would she accept that she had no right to order him into marriage, let alone for this reason?

"You must understand that it's your duty to do so, in order to provide another daughter named Martha to the Grainger family."

How many hundreds—thousands?—of times had he heard

this demand for restitution before? Since he'd first grown old enough to attend a cotillion and be introduced to respectable females as an eligible *parti*. Nothing else about him mattered to her anymore, except as an avenue to replace the lost child.

His fingers clenched but he managed not to grip the settee, especially when he wanted to lunge at her. He'd try to behave like an adult, even if his mother insisted on treating him as a child, whose every action could be ordered according to her whim. He was the spare to Tom's heir, bred for family necessity not love.

"No, I don't understand that at all," he said carefully. "Another woman named Martha would be exactly that—another woman, not the sister I once knew."

"She'd be a daughter for me—someone to go shopping with and share the latest gossip with, as only a daughter can be trusted. And unlike Hortense, who has always whined too much to listen to anyone else."

A muscle ticked in Lucas's jaw. No, family life was something he'd glimpsed with Rachel—something strong and warm, something chosen by its members, that was strengthened every day. "If you want a daughter, adopt one. You have contributed generously to many orphanages and I'm sure one would help you."

He watched his mother warily; they'd never spoken so openly on this topic before.

Her mouth tightened. "You're responsible for the solution, since you caused the tragedy."

"It happened twenty years ago," he said quietly, "and all of us have changed. No, I will not marry simply to introduce a woman named Martha into the family."

His mother swelled, looking like a puff adder getting ready to strike. Her mouth opened, words clearly taking form to strike.

"Good evening, my dear," Rachel's gentle alto voice swept through the room like sweet summer rain.

Lucas spun to face her and his jaw dropped. Behind him,

he heard his father, ever a connoisseur of feminine beauty, whistle very softly.

He'd taken to his stateroom a well loved but simply dressed wife. He beheld a ravishingly beautiful society matron in a stunning Parisian evening dress, with rubies and diamonds blazing at her throat and ears. Only her complicated braids remained from earlier, but even they were now adorned by glittering jewels. A queen would have been proud to call her friend.

Nothing in her demeanor showed that she'd heard any of his mother's demands.

She'd also just trumped his mother's attire of dowager's black. Even the family matriarch would have to take Mrs. Lucas Grainger seriously.

"My darling Rachel." Lucas went quickly forward to her, kissed her cheek, and brought her forward on his arm, always keeping his hand protectively over hers.

Rachel wanted to tell him that he was the one who needed help, not her, but settled for gently patting him.

"Mother, Father, allow me to introduce you to my wife Rachel."

"Your wife!" His mother came out of her settee in a rush, rather like a vicious kitchen dog who'd been deprived of a bone.

"Rachel, my parents, Thomas and Aurelia Grainger."

Rachel swept her mother-in-law a curtsy, keeping her face composed. "Mrs. Grainger, Mr. Grainger."

So this was Lucas's nightmare. Aurelia Grainger was probably sometimes called handsome, although her face was contorted and ugly at the moment. She'd certainly made some extremely selfish demands of a grown son.

The older man gripped his wife's hand very hard, making her stand still.

"Impossible!" the elder Mrs. Grainger protested. "You weren't married to her three days ago."

"No, we wed yesterday." Lucas's jaw set, visibly daring them to argue.

"Then you'll annul it immediately," T.L. snapped. "If I'd believed that cable you sent, instead of dismissing it as folderol, I'd have already told you so."

Rachel blinked at her father-in-law's demand. Aurelia Grainger had already shown her colors but she'd hoped for common sense from the head of the household.

"You'll have to find another way to obtain the Tallmadge money," Lucas snapped. "Besides, Rachel's children will inherit the Davis Trust. Given that and what I provide, the *San Francisco branch* of the Grainger family will be well funded."

Lucas's father had wanted his son to marry for money? Of all the selfish, blind reasons! Worse, did he think that Lucas was a witless boy? Had he paid no attention to Lucas's character and deeds these past ten years?

"San Francisco branch?" T.L. queried, sounding startled.

"Yes. I will never live in Philadelphia again."

"It's your home!"

"No, it is not—nor has it been for years," Lucas snapped back.

"What about visits?"

"Rarely and only for Tom's sake." Lucas clearly saw little need to grace his decision with elegant words.

Aurelia was studying Rachel, eyes narrowed suspiciously. "Rachel Davis?"

"Yes, ma'am." Rachel waited warily, her face calm. She'd faced the most supercilious circles in Boston society before. But she didn't want to offend Lucas's mother in front of him.

T.L. hissed out a breath. "The bookseller's granddaughter. Good Lord, Lucas, couldn't you have done . . ."

"If you insult my wife, sir," his son purred in a deadly soft voice, "I will take the greatest delight in throwing you off this train—when we are halfway between stations. Need I say more?"

The two men measured each other, almost as if they were in a pugilist's ring. Finally T.L. flicked his fingers, looking as if a pit had opened at his feet that he needed to judge how to bridge.

"Do you know what sort of man you married, girl?" Aurelia demanded, her voice dripping vitriol.

Rachel's gaze snapped back to her. "Ma'am?"

"He's a murderer." She uttered the words with all the conviction of a town crier.

Rachel shook her head. Good heavens, her husband hadn't been joking about malice. "Not Lucas."

He shifted convulsively beside her and she tightened her grip on him, refusing to be moved. This confrontation—with his mother, for whatever reason—was why she'd come to support him.

"For twenty years I've mourned what he did." Aurelia's voice dropped to a lament that would have done credit to King Lear. "Look at me, still wearing black! But not him— he's built a happy life, all the while refusing to listen to our counsel."

Rachel tried to defuse the scene by offering some indisputable facts, couched as diplomatically as possible. "Twenty years ago, ma'am, Lucas was a child of only seven or eight years old. Nothing he could have done . . ."

"He murdered his sister, Martha." Aurelia Grainger unpinned a mourning locket and thrust it at the younger woman.

Rachel would have been more comfortable handling a scorpion.

"She was my mother's namesake, a perfect angel sent among us by heaven above," her mother-in-law said softly, producing a lace-trimmed, black handkerchief, "and she drowned because of *him*."

"She was a hoyden, who would obey nobody!" Lucas burst out. "She'd just gotten another governess fired. Don't tell me she hadn't because she was bragging about it."

"Lucas . . ." his father growled.

His son whipped around to face him. "No, this has to be

said. We have all been silent too long. Martha was eight years old, yet she'd had four governesses in that last year."

Rachel flinched, the locket nearly falling out of her fingers. Having raced after Mercy many times, she could vividly imagine what scrapes Martha must have gotten into.

"Lucas, you're reminding me of that dreadful day . . ."

"Am I wrong?"

His mother glared at him, but didn't argue.

"That's why you left her with *me* at the lake, because everyone else had either failed before or refused to keep her out of trouble. I was only seven so I couldn't refuse and I was taller than she was. I'd never failed because I was too young to have been entrusted with her before."

T.L. gasped.

Rachel's gaze shot to him. He'd gone very pale under his tan.

"Mother was only going to be gone for a few minutes, to have tea with Mrs. Wilson. Tom was fishing and Hortense was playing croquet with school friends. But Mother knew Martha would walk across that fallen log because she always did what people had forbidden her to do," Lucas accused his mother.

"I did not," Aurelia snapped.

"But that morning, the log was wet, there was a river underneath, and Martha's skirts dragged her under," Lucas went on, his deep voice the sound of a judge's wrath. "Her governess had always told her to 'be careful, next time you'll slip and drown.' Well, that time it did happen. But I'm damned if I'll take the blame for the rest of my life."

"Oh, dear Lord, I hadn't known all the details before," T.L. whispered. It was a prayer, not blasphemy.

The mourning locket fell open in Rachel's hand and she glanced down. A smiling face looked up at her, full of quicksilver merriment and deviltry. A child who'd have disobeyed every command given her and laughed at the consequences, not an angel meant to move sweetly and quietly at her mother's side.

Tears filled her eyes, blurring the childish features and their likeness to Lucas. She closed the locket, making sure the latch was tightly fastened.

"You're wrong," Aurelia cried. "Wrong!"

Lucas's features could have been carved out of granite, for all the compromise they offered. Deep brackets were etched from his nose to his mouth, lined in white. His eyes were as coldly blue as light glinting off a revolver's muzzle.

"Perhaps. But I won't fail my children, as you failed her. I'll always guard and protect them to the utmost, no matter it costs me—because that's what Martha's death taught me."

Chapter Eight

It was a few hours after dawn and the air was harshly cold, carrying the raw bite of deep winter at more than seven thousand feet above sea level. The wind was laden with sagebrush, backed by the tang of snow and ice from the distant mountains.

Every writer called it the finest grazing land in this part of the continent, a place of flat, open plains full of running antelope. Yet it stood only one hundred fifty miles from the Continental Divide and Utah's brutal mountains. Collins strongly suspected that, given the heavy clouds hanging above the mountains, snow would start falling within a few more hours.

All around him, clouds of steam, touched with sparks and cinders, rose from the great wooden machine shop and roundhouse. Workmen pounded with massive sledgehammers as they labored over the great locomotives and their attendant equipment, all designed to take passenger trains safely to and from Utah and Nebraska. A massive woodshed flanked the roundhouse on one side, while an equally enormous coal shed flanked it on the other, ready to feed the great locomotives' appetites for fuel.

Dozens of laborers, traveling aboard the work train to shovel snow, piled into the station house, intent on eating a hot meal made to their taste, rather than the Union Pacific's budget. Two of them, at opposite extremes of life—a half-breed, sinewy and weather-beaten by the years, and a rawboned young man—came last out of the work train's barracks. They chose to devour their scant rations standing in the sun near the woodshed, rather than with the other laborers—and downwind of the supervisor's office.

Collins leaped up the stairs to the office and heartily shook hands with Leventhorpe, the Union Pacific's assistant supervisor at Laramie.

"A pleasure to meet you again after all these years, my dear Alexander," he exclaimed, genuinely delighted. "I do hope the lumbago isn't treating your father too poorly this year?"

The well-dressed man beamed. "Not at all, not at all. The hot baths you recommended have worked wonders for him. Indeed, he hasn't been so free of pain in years—even if he did have to go north, into Yankee territory, to find it."

Collins slapped him on the back and they laughed companionably together. Savannah's Leventhorpe family had always found it amusing that one of their most profitable business partners was the very northernmost Collins shipping line. Collins had sponsored his third son into a Yankee college, where he'd gained enough mathematics to earn an excellent series of jobs with the railroads. The two families had stayed in touch, of course, although little business had been conducted during the past few years, given the War's ravages.

Maitland came slowly up beside his father. His wound had swelled considerably until he could barely speak and only eat bread soaked in milk. His head was wrapped more in bandages than scarves. He was in agonizing pain but had refused all laudanum, claiming it dulled his mind.

Collins swallowed another instinctive demand to send his son back to their private Pullman. "Alexander, may I present my son, Maitland?"

His son bowed slightly, mumbling something polite.

An appalled expression washed over Leventhorpe's face, quickly disciplined into a gentleman's civility.

Hope burned deep in Collins's heart. *God willing, if he played on Leventhorpe's desire to avenge Maitland, he'd have an ally here.*

"A pleasure to meet you, Maitland," Leventhorpe responded, with only the slightest hesitation. "My father will be very glad to hear I've made the acquaintance of the next generation of Collinses."

Maitland bowed again, more deeply.

Collins's lips thinned. His boy always did have such perfect manners in public. *Damn the bitch for ruining his chances of becoming a great name in society!*

"What can I do for you, Collins? I admit that it's a surprise to see you here, so far from any ocean." Leventhorpe's gaze slipped briefly back to Maitland before he brought himself under control.

"As I mentioned in my cable, we're traveling to Nevada on business," Collins began smoothly. "It's urgent stuff, so we must stay with the work train and cannot linger here as we'd like. Please convey my sincere regrets to your wife."

Leventhorpe nodded. "She'll be sorry to have missed you."

"Given the season and the harsh weather so far, I was hoping you could show us something of your equipment and preparations, to assure us of safe passage over the high mountains."

"My pleasure." Leventhorpe turned away from the station and started walking toward the roundhouse. "But if you're traveling with the work train, we only have a few minutes. What are you particularly interested in?"

Collins could almost feel his dirk slipping into his hand. *Now to arrange the bitch's downfall!*

"I understand you have another snowplow, kept here to ensure the safety of the passenger trains."

Leventhorpe frowned slightly. "Indeed we do."

"A backup, in effect, to travel directly with one of the passenger sections?"

"Yes, or replace the work train's snowplow, if it's damaged."

"Excellent, excellent. I am delighted to hear that the Union Pacific is so well managed."

He stopped a few paces away from the roundhouse, near the woodshed. Hats over their faces, the half-breed and his young friend were drowsing in a patch of sunlight, leaning against a wall and just out of earshot.

Young Leventhorpe was studying Collins very closely now. Of course, he'd be aware of how often the Union Pacific's efficiency had been compared to the Central Pacific's and found wanting—especially after last winter. "What are you thinking of?"

Collins met his eyes directly, allowing his jovial mask to drop. "A prudent man would make certain that this snowplow was always in the best possible condition, in order to guarantee that those passengers always traveled safely. Correct?"

Leventhorpe nodded curtly.

"It's a minor curiosity that the individual responsible for my son's, ah, difficulties in speaking is traveling on the section immediately following this work train," Collins finished softly.

The other man's eyes narrowed. "The devil you say!"

"Hell, yes," Maitland agreed, somehow managing to be intelligible.

Leventhorpe clasped his hands behind his back and turned to stare toward the east—and the individual's train. He paced beside the track, occasionally pausing to survey the machine shop.

Collins contained his impatience, watching the very properly dressed man who just might get that bitch much delayed.

Leventhorpe turned back to them, his expression impassive behind his spectacular mustache.

"You are entirely correct: This snowplow must be treated with the utmost care. This winter has been long and hard and the plow should be thoroughly serviced immediately, which will take at least a week." His Georgia accent was very deep, in an amazing contrast to his words' decisiveness. "It will not be available to travel with any passenger train in the meantime."

Maitland started to say something hot and approving, but Collins elbowed his son hard in the ribs. He gravely inclined his head to the master of this enterprise. "Well done, sir, well done. Your grandfather would have been very proud of you, showing simultaneous appreciation for both human life and your employer's property."

They smiled at each other in perfect understanding.

The work train's whistle blew the signal for departure. Dozens of men tumbled out of the station and began to trot toward her. The half-breed and his young friend slowly straightened up and returned to the work train, tugging scarves up until their faces were warm and invisible.

Rachel lifted her head and tried to see over her husband's chest to the clock. "Shouldn't we be in Cheyenne soon?"

He didn't move a muscle. "Another five minutes or so."

She squeaked and started to sit up in bed. "But we can see the Rockies from here!"

He yawned. "One mountain, not even an entire range."

She leaned on her elbow and looked down at him. "It must be covered in snow."

"Probably—but so are the prairies."

"Are there forests, too?"

"The Black Hills, which are straight ahead to the west, have pine forests."

"We can look at those. Aren't there animals other than prairie dogs?

He shrugged. "Lots of antelopes, which make good steaks. Personally, I'd rather observe my wife."

He ran a possessive—and highly flirtatious—hand over her derrière.

She gawked at him and somehow refrained from asking, *Even after all of last night and this morning?*

Aurelia Grainger had gone into noisy hysterics after Lucas's bitter accusations and his father had immediately taken her off the *Empress*. Lucas had snatched Rachel into his arms, holding her so tightly as to almost crush her, and swept her into their stateroom for a bout of frantic lovemaking.

They still hadn't left it.

They'd spent the rest of the evening in their bed, alternately making love, sleeping, snacking on Lawson's delicious offerings—and never conversing. Lucas hadn't said a word of explanation about his parents or his childhood.

Her heart had broken for him a thousand times whenever she'd thought of the agony he must have gone through, blaming himself for his sister's death, slowly realizing that he couldn't have prevented it, growing into today's strong man—and, all the while, being continually tortured by his mother's accusations and his father's demands. She wondered if they'd ever, once, simply asked him to lead a moral life and let him define how to do so. But she was almost certain they'd never listened to him, only harangued or ordered him.

She hadn't the heart to raise a single question, only to let him do as he pleased—and give him everything he asked for.

He cocked an eye at her. "Do you truly want to get dressed, Mrs. Grainger? Put on all those clothes and go out into the cold?"

She hesitated. "What do you have in mind?" she inquired, very cautiously.

He rubbed the back of his forefinger very lightly up and down the center of her chest between her collarbone and her breasts. In some ways, it was a perfectly proper caress. In other respects, it sent the most amazing shivers all the way down to her toes, making her want to toss her head back. "What do you have in mind?" she repeated, with a definite tremor in her voice.

"Play a game in here, instead."

"Game?"

"Rachel, sweetheart, it occurs to me that if you're going to inquire so much about the local scenery, I should receive a reward for giving you so many answers."

She frowned, torn between wanting to smack him—for placing conditions on a simple discussion!—or pull him closer. "What do you mean?"

"I'll tie you up—very gently so you won't be hurt. While I do exactly what I want with you, you can ask me any question you want."

Something inside her promptly purred and wanted to hurl herself at him. She froze, caught off guard by her own reactions.

"Do you object to that?"

She considered, then shook her head vigorously. "Not by you, not in the bedroom. I'm sure you'd never hurt me."

He looked as if she'd given him all the keys of the kingdom. "Thank you for your trust."

She smiled at him a little crookedly and went back to thinking hard.

Was this some silly bedroom game about orders and obedience? Given the lack of trust that he'd experienced while growing up, did he need her to prove her trust in him, here and now? If so, it seemed easy enough, especially if doing so made him happier.

What harm could there be in agreeing? As long as she talked, he'd answer—and heaven knows, she'd always been able to talk for a long time. It would give her the opportunity to teach him how to converse in the bedchamber. It was also, as ever with Lucas, guaranteed to be extremely enjoyable.

She tilted her head back and smiled up at him. "Very well, my dear."

"The next station after Cheyenne is Hazard, then Otto and Granite Canyon, about twenty miles away," Lucas said briskly. "Stand up, darling."

She gulped and did exactly what he'd told her, ripples running through her skin. How could those simple, matter-of-fact words have had such a profound effect on her? If she tried to stand up, she honestly thought her knees would buckle under her.

"Beautiful," he whispered and kissed the corner of her mouth. "Remember you can ask questions all the time."

Questions? Oh yes, to teach Lucas about civilized behavior, like conversation in the bedroom. "What does the scenery look like at Granite, ah, Granite Canyon?"

"We'll have risen six hundred feet—very quickly, too. The snowfall's heavy enough that the locals build snow fences from limestone dikes, as well as strong timber."

There was a disturbing bit of information there, but she didn't have the energy to find it.

"Now lie down on the center of the bed, please."

His soft command sent a surge of lust through her, shaking her to the core. She obeyed him all too easily and lay down on her back.

He produced a very soft cashmere stole and wound it around her wrists. He tied it to the center of the headboard, securing it around a deeply hooked carving. She could have easily freed herself. But it seemed very, very ridiculous to think about escape techniques when she was watching hunger for her build in Lucas's eyes.

He stretched, as totally immodest as ever. She watched him avidly, his male beauty firing her heat like the sound of the train rumbling through his bedroom.

Trains . . . Traveling. She hadn't asked any questions for a few moments. It would be far harder to do so once he touched her again, especially if he did so with his talented mouth.

She closed her eyes and tried frantically to think. But about what?

She rubbed her legs against each other, wishing she could free her hands and pleasure herself. Her hips twisted against the embroidered cotton coverlet.

She'd never yet been able to give him oral attentions . . .

She started to open one eye but forced herself to stop. Who knew when she'd have this chance again?

"Is Granite Canyon the highest point on the railroad?" *Thank God, there was nothing in the bargain about her voice being crystal clear.*

"No, Sherman follows thirteen miles later, the highest point on any railroad in the world."

He wrapped his mouth around one of her nipples, through her chemise, and suckled her. The warm, wet tug of his mouth sent a fiery jolt from her nipple through her spine and into her core.

Rachel bucked hard against him, crying out his name.

He kneaded her gently and licked her again, pleasuring her as if the silk wasn't there.

She moaned and writhed under him. She tried to think of another question for him. But conversation seemed very trivial when her nipple was being transformed into an exquisitely taut center of sensation under his mouth.

His skillful fingers circled her other breast, bringing it into the same circle of delight.

He lapped at her, used his teeth and his fingers to send shards of lust dancing across her skin and into her bones. Explored a thousand different avenues to excite her, always willing to repeat the ones that delighted her.

Logic slipped out of reach.

She couldn't have said why she breathed, when her lungs existed to push her breasts up toward his mouth for more attention. Her skin was hot, crackling with desperation—yet her core was melting with liquid fire. Cream slipped onto her thighs and she rubbed them together.

He whispered her name against her throat.

She lifted herself against him, begging for more of his touch, begging for fulfillment.

Her body clenched, pulsing from her breasts to her core. Fire lanced through her veins, bringing her nipples erect.

Lucas's hand swept up her thigh and fondled her folds.

Rapture hung so agonizingly close. "Lucas, please, soon, please . . ."

He lifted her leg and came into her, with a skillful twist of his hips. Her intimate folds, exquisitely trapped between his shaft and her leg, sent a ravenous jolt of pleasure up her spine.

"Lucas, oh yes . . ."

Then he rolled, turning her to face him, though she was still tied to the bed. He thrust, slowly, his face a mask of concentrated lust.

Dear heavens, he was big and perfect. Another hungry surge shot through her.

Her channel wrapped itself around him. He was her husband and he'd be the father of her children. Anything he wanted, she'd give him. She writhed against him, desperate for rapture, aching for his seed.

His shaft came back into her, velvet soft skin, fiery hot, granite hard—an infinity of sensations against her pearl, a microcosm in itself.

"Lucas!"

He thrust slowly, drawing out every moment of entering and pulling out only to return. Giving her every aching pulse of agonizing tenderness, infinite cherishing.

Her breath matched every move of his, her pulse beating with his. Even the deep, heavy throb of oncoming rapture in her hips and thighs matched how his hips rocked against hers.

He thrust in more deeply and fondled her pearl. "Come for me now, Rachel!"

She spun into ecstasy, spiraling through a web of light. Her channel clenched him, hard, milking him rhythmically.

He growled and climaxed, his body matching her waves of pleasure with rich, hot floods of his seed.

Afterward, he took the scarf off her wrists with a single quick twist and cuddled her, still lying side by side, facing her.

Rachel laid her head back down on his shoulder and tried not to sigh. If only Lucas's lovemaking didn't feel like the actions of a man determined never to show his own heart.

Somewhere it had to be daylight, bright and shining as an afternoon should be. But not here, high in the Black Hills, where the snow had been falling ever since they left Cheyenne. She could no longer see the open prairies, stretching for uncounted miles in every direction.

It was most especially not true, when traveling through endless wooden snowsheds. This was like moving through a covered bridge where it was possible only occasionally to glimpse the outside world. Black snowdrifts built up inside and out, filthy from cinders. Even the train's normal sounds were muffled inside, so that the tracks' continual clackety-clack became more of a dull kerthump-kerthump and the whistle was an occasional whoosh, rather than the great, echoing wail. The train was jolting, too, much more than on the flat prairies.

Imprisonment on Collins's Ledge had been easier. There, all she'd had to do was look out a window and see the wide Atlantic. Now, the world existed only a few feet beyond the *Empress* in any direction and was drawing closer, as the snow built up next to the tracks inside the snowshed.

There were rumors of heavier storms in the Utah mountains ahead, strong enough to slow the previous days' trains.

Lucas had gone forward to the UPRR Pullman car, saying something about inspecting everyone's firearms. While Elias had once shown her how to use his cavalry revolver, she had no desire to be around a drawing room of men playing with revolvers, knives, and rifles.

She could almost rethink that decision now, except for the difficulty of passing from railroad car to railroad car in this appalling weather.

She drummed her fingers on the drawing room table, watching the dim light flicker through the snowshed's timbers. She definitely needed to stay outside at the next watering stop, no matter what Lucas said about her chances of catching lung fever.

The *Empress* had a small library, its volumes chosen more for their binding's beauty than their literary merit. Perhaps if she read one, she might drift into Morpheus's arms and stop thinking about the walls of snow closing around her.

The cellar walls were icy cold, as dark and unyielding as a blizzard's bowels. Even the floor below her was solid and the ceiling was less than an arm's length above her head. If she took a deep breath, she'd choke on the dank air.

Rachel stretched out her arms, searching, searching for an escape. Behind her, to the left or the right. Anywhere.

Maitland tossed his torch from one hand to the other, the hissing flames reflected in his red-rimmed eyes. "Go ahead— run. You know how much I like it when girls run."

She shrank back against the wall, certain there was another choice. Instantly, the wet went through her dress and into her skin.

She jumped.

Maitland laughed and swung the torch toward her in a great arc.

Rachel screamed and screamed and screamed . . .

"Rachel, darling! Sweetheart, please wake up." Lucas was shaking her very gently by her shoulders. A single soft lamp showed that they were in their stateroom, in their wondrous bed.

Rachel threw herself at him.

He grunted in surprise and hugged her, quickly wrapping

the embroidered silk coverlet around her shoulders. He patted her a little awkwardly.

She gave a little chirrup of relief and burrowed closer, sniffling.

Thank God his first instinct was to give affection. Perhaps as compensation for his hellish childhood.

"Are you crying?" He sounded horrified.

She swallowed hard. "Of–of course not."

"Okay." He didn't sound convinced. He leaned out of the bed and she clung fiercely. "Relax, sweetheart, relax. I'm here, I'm not leaving you."

He stroked her hair and she tried to obey. But the cellar's cold was too ingrained in her bones; only his warmth was keeping it away.

He settled back into the bed. "Here you are." He pressed a handkerchief into her hand.

"Oh . . ." She sighed, warmth blooming in her heart. He'd been taking care of her, as he always did. She sniffled happily and blew her nose, then settled back against him as closely as possible.

Her man.

Lucas looked down at his wife. She didn't appear to be going back to sleep, after what had obviously been one hell of a nightmare. What the devil should he do now?

He might have asked advice about other kinds of problems. But marital? Even if he'd been inclined to discuss those issues, the only person whose example he was likely to follow was thousands of miles away.

"Do you want to try to sleep some more?" he asked cautiously.

She jolted into his chest, as if propelled by springs.

"Woof!" "No!" they exclaimed simultaneously.

He snickered at himself, wishing he dared rub his ribs. "Very well, dear. We won't try to do that."

Now what? Talk—in the bedroom? Well, he wouldn't

make love to her, not when she'd been so scared. So, conversation it would have to be.

"Would you like to talk? Or just hold each other?"

She gasped softly.

Lucas frowned but waited for her answer.

"Both, perhaps?" she requested tentatively.

He blinked, totally unsure of how to execute the combination. "Uh, very well. What would you like to discuss?"

She shifted positions, settling her head on his shoulder. Her braid spilled down his arm, tickling his ribs and hip.

He watched her with a certain appalled fascination, well aware that he was being judged by very unfamiliar standards.

She cocked her head hopefully, gazing up at him. "Something simple. Perhaps how Mr. Donovan saved your life?"

His jaw dropped. That story? Best to start with the most respectable facts. "I first met William Donovan seven years ago, in Kansas during the first winter after the War. He owns Donovan & Sons, one of the great western freighting houses."

These simple statements somehow made Rachel beam. "Go on," she encouraged, twining her fingers companionably with his.

"Donovan & Sons specializes in the delivery of high-risk freight to high-risk places and there weren't many places more high risk than Kansas during those years. There were many times when his men's deliveries of bullets and beans were the difference between life and death for us."

"Most admirable!"

Now the tale became more risqué. He hesitated.

"And?"

"We encountered each other more than once, while relaxing in the, ah, sporting districts."

She cocked her head. "Was he married?"

"No, not at that time."

"Then I don't know why you're hesitating to tell me that

you both diverted yourself with soiled doves and the like. Isn't that what you mean?"

He went on quickly before she could ask him for more details of his activities. "Correct. We both enjoyed ladies of the evening and agreed on their treatment, which was always in accordance with the highest standards."

Something in his voice must have given him away, because this time she simply rubbed his arm when he paused.

"I kept a mistress for a time."

"Did you care for her?" Her voice was very small.

He answered flatly. "I thought I loved her."

"Oh, my. I'm sorry."

All he could do was nod and go on. "One day, my enemies killed her."

"I'm so very sorry, Lucas."

Lucas gripped her hand hard. Only two people had ever offered him sympathy for Ambrosia's death—Donovan and now his wife. He went on, the words coming harsh and faster. "I knew who had killed her, but there was no evidence that would stand up in court. Rather than shoot her murderers down like the dogs they were . . ."

"And become a murderer yourself." Rachel nodded approvingly.

Lucas's mouth twisted. Nothing so honorable—but he wouldn't risk destroying her good opinion of him by saying so. He briskly picked up the thread. "I chose to challenge them to a duel, knowing their South Carolina upbringing would demand they accept."

"You'd need a second for that. Donovan?"

Her fine mind was at work again.

"Exactly. Nobody else would have stood up with me, both because of why I fought and who I fought. During the duel, my enemies fought foul and Donovan saved my life. It was a very close fight."

"I'm glad he did," Rachel agreed contentedly. "Otherwise,

I wouldn't have you now. You said he wasn't married back then. Is his situation different now?"

He chuckled softly at her romantic turn of thought. "Yes, he has a wife now. You should heartily approve of Viola Lindsay Donovan, who was a miner's widow before she married him. They're a very loving couple and cannot abide being separated." His tone gentled on the last phrases.

Rachel's voice was very soft. "Are both of them your good friends?"

Lucas nodded fondly. "Yes, both of them, although I don't understand them."

"I shall look forward to meeting them."

She settled down against him, showing no signs of continuing the conversation.

He thought he should be relieved, but suspected he'd missed a feminine undercurrent.

T.L. strode into his wife's hotel room and jerked his head at her longtime maid. No fool, Madeleine dropped a curtsy and left immediately, although it had been years since he'd entered his wife's rooms after teatime.

Aurelia spun around in her chair to stare at him. She was beautifully dressed in a silk and lace confection that showcased her still elegant figure. Pity she'd never seen her body as anything but a weapon. "What are you thinking of, T.L.? She was brushing my hair!"

T.L. held up a pair of cable forms, covered in feminine handwriting. "Recognize these?"

She stared blankly for a moment before a horrified look briefly passed over her face. She concealed it quickly with an innocent mask, but the damage was done.

"Yes, I thought I recognized your turn of phrase, madam."

She flung herself up out of her seat to face him. "I did not write those cables."

"Don't lie to me, Aurelia, it will get you nowhere. Did you

think I wouldn't know your handwriting after all these years?"

She hesitated. He almost laughed to see her trying to think of a way to turn this confrontation to her advantage.

Now to remind her of the ground rules.

"Remember, Aurelia: All family disputes are fought in private, as you've been warned before. If you take them outside, to the papers—as you attempted to do in this case—the rest of your life will be spent outside the family circle. At the house in Wilmington."

"Wilmington!" Her horror couldn't have been greater than if he'd said Istanbul.

He waited, not reminding her of that city's virtues, such as its short distance from Philadelphia and her supposedly well-loved grandchildren.

She sulked, pacing around the room.

At least she didn't try to use her famous blue eyes on him. That ploy hadn't worked in decades, not since he'd realized that his true importance in her life was as her bankbook and her social foundation—never as an exciting attraction to her senses. He had no right to regret the lack of anything more, since he hadn't asked for it.

But he was damned if he'd let anyone he loved suffer for her stubbornness. He might not have demonstrated that very well before to Lucas, but he could—and would—change. He had to, if he wanted to see his second son again.

Dammit, if he'd realized before what had really happened before Martha died, instead of being blinded by his own guilt, he would have behaved differently. He wouldn't have focused all his drive on making sure that nothing like that ever happened again, on making Lucas the perfect son, always living where his father could watch him. No, he'd have known that Lucas was Uncle Barnabas's image, destined to make his own way in life—and to do so very well indeed.

God willing, it wasn't too late. He'd already started his campaign for Lucas's trust by sending his best lawyers to hound the hypocritical devils on the Davis Trust's board.

She stopped and faced him. "Very well," she said sullenly. "I will not discuss my son's wedding, marriage, or wife with any newspaper again."

"I'm glad you finally see sense," T.L. purred.

She looked as though she wanted to spit at him. "Now will you leave?"

"No. You will not interfere with Lucas in any other way at any other time."

She gaped at him. "Are you saying that you approve of his marriage to that—that servant?"

"Lucas's wife is a respectable woman who has moved in Boston's finest circles with honor. She comes with a far greater dowry than the Tallmadge chit and, by all accounts, will be an excellent mother to our grandchildren. I see no reason, whatsoever, to object. In fact, I will do my best to see him seated as principal trustee of the Davis trust."

"Have you gone insane to change your mind like this?"

"Most important, Lucas is a grown man and he has chosen her. I will support him in this matter, as in all others. I have tried to be a good father by making him follow in my footsteps. He refused and has successfully made his own way. It's time to recognize his success and follow its direction."

"He's a murderer and a failure!" Her voice rose to a shriek.

"He was set an impossible task for a child. Does the lack lie in him—or in the taskmaster for the error of judgment? In another arena, as a man of affairs, I would punish the taskmaster."

"T.L.!"

She hurled herself at him and he shook her off furiously.

This wasn't the first time he'd have liked to wring her neck. But it was certainly the first time he'd contemplated how to dispose of her body. He bit back his rage, wishing yet again he hadn't been stupid enough to marry the first pretty face who came with a great family name.

"Let me be extremely clear, Aurelia: You will make no further attempts to bring another daughter named Martha into our house through marriage, whether with Lucas or Tom. If you wish to have one, let us discuss adoption."

Aurelia was crying, the tears running almost silently down her face. She produced a handkerchief from her sleeve and blew her nose. "No, it must be through the blood. Martha was my darling, my showpiece. People always spoke so highly of me as a mother after seeing her."

She might believe only blood mattered, but Lucas had forced him to realize his son had a choice who he'd accept as family. If T.L. wanted to be included, he would have to earn it.

"Then it will not happen because I will not have our—my, if you wish to disclaim all relationship—son's life destroyed to change what cannot be undone."

Her shoulders were bent and her face hidden by the enormous piece of lace and silk, while great racking sobs shook her body. More of her anger was probably genuine than she'd like to admit. He hadn't seen her cry this much since he'd forced her to live according to a budget.

"Do you understand, Aurelia?" he repeated. Implied understandings were of no use with her.

"Yes." The answer was muffled but unmistakable.

He turned to leave.

She blew her nose loudly. "What will you do now?" she called.

He turned, one hand on the door, surprised by her unusual display of curiosity in anything other than herself. "If I am to see him again, he must make the first move—which means I must support him now to my utmost as one grown man to another. What he needs is a snowplow, but they're worth their weight in gold. If I can, I'll send him one—but only Divine Providence can guarantee that it will arrive in time to aid him."

Chapter Nine

Rachel and Lucas stood by one of the drawing room's windows, watching the train pull into the big Army fort. The earlier snowfall had eased, allowing them a clear view of the broad Laramie Plains, the omnipresent sagebrush now only lumps under a blanket of snow.

Lucas hadn't served here while he was in the Army, although he'd passed through. Had he seen it with his mistress? Had she laughed and flirted with him? Had he adored her?

Did it matter if the woman's ghost watched Rachel's marriage, given his passion in the bedroom?

At least she had fewer worries about his future fidelity, if he'd been in love with his mistress. Guarding against romance would be easier than frequent bouts of unbridled lust for any comely female.

"At least we're almost at Laramie." Lucas started to button his jacket. "We should be able to find out the snowplow's health, one way or another."

Rachel was glad to return to flesh and blood realities. "Mitchell hasn't been able to learn anything?"

"No, which implies whatever's holding Leventhorpe is tighter than Lee's gray wolves, since both he and Mitchell served in the Army of Northern Virginia. Only blood kin or the like can account for that."

She winced. "Which means there's little chance of turning him."

"Next to none. We've already tried gold and he's not reachable by blackmail."

The train blew its whistle loudly, an earsplitting wail. Its wheels backed, screeching a protest, and came slowly to a stop. Lucas looked out onto the platform—and frowned slightly. "Scouts are back already."

His expression had turned fiercely contemplative, as if he was pondering a hundred options, few of them pleasant.

"Should I be glad?" Rachel asked cautiously.

He glanced down at her, a little wryly. "It's always better to go on campaign well informed about the enemy, no matter how painful the resulting adjustments must be."

She nodded slowly, reminded yet again of just how very successful he'd been as a cavalry commander. In addition to being determined and cunning, he was also intelligent and ruthless enough to change himself whenever needed. A very deadly opponent indeed.

"Wait here, Rachel, and I'll bring them in. You'll be warmer here, out of the wind."

He was gone in an instant, leaving her no chance to protest that she could have snatched up her coat and gone with him.

Lucas returned a minute later with two men, both black-haired and dressed in rough clothing that had seen hard usage.

One was tall and strongly built, his hat and broad shoulders almost scraping the door's boundaries. He had much Indian blood in him, given his strong features and black eyes, yet something about the lightness of his skin stamped him as a half-breed, rather than a full-blood.

The other was a rawboned young man, with alert blue-gray eyes and raven hair that flopped into his face when he removed his hat. He moved with an agility around the *Empress*'s fine furniture and crystal that belied his coltish frame.

He might one day be startlingly handsome, although never pretty.

They both looked like men to trust with one's bottom dollar, although she didn't think they'd fit neatly into a ballroom.

Lucas performed the introductions quickly. The big halfbreed proved to be called Little, which seemed very unsuitable, while the younger man was called Lowell.

They both looked exhausted, cold, and hungry, but their manners were excellent.

Mitchell and the other Donovan & Sons' men joined them, marked by a round of understated masculine greetings.

Rachel glanced at Braden in a silent command, who nodded and disappeared. She relaxed, satisfied that proper hospitality would be provided.

"Did you manage to join the work train?" Lucas asked. Too impatient to sit down like the others, he was pacing close to the corridor.

"Very easily," Little said.

"Few men wanted to," Lowell added. "They only pay two and a half dollars per day and deduct one dollar for room and board. They were not surprised when we quit."

Rachel's jaw dropped. "That's ridiculous! Those wages won't raise any zeal for shoveling snow at this altitude, for days on end."

"We'd have to double it, if we want to raise our own army," Mitchell suggested, watching Lucas.

"If we can find anyone to hire," Lucas warned. "Wyoming and Utah's mountains are not well supplied with men, especially at this season. Otherwise, we'll have to follow the usual practice and encourage volunteers from among the passengers."

"They may be very willing, if it's the only way to reach San Francisco faster."

Low rumbles of laughter answered Mitchell's sally.

Braden returned and began to set out coffee and sand-wiches. Lowell fell upon the food like a hungry locust.

Rachel eyed Little uneasily. He was quietly observing the others, looking like a parent permitting his children to argue, while knowing that the real problem would come from a different direction.

"What about the snowplow?" Lucas asked, his gaze hooded and narrow on the older man.

"The one with the work train is in good health," Little said slowly.

"But?" Lucas prodded.

"The spare—the one in Laramie—has been taken apart for *inspection,* to make sure that it stays healthy."

"What?" Mitchell sprang to his feet.

Rachel's stomach plummeted to her feet. If that was true, every turn of the *Empress*'s wheels was taking them closer to the high mountain—and the likelihood of being trapped.

Lowell took up the tale, his tone brusque and somber. "Turns out Collins and the head guy in Laramie are old friends, almost family. Collins persuaded Leventhorpe that it'd be best to look like he was really worried, just to make sure nothin' goes wrong like it did last year. So right now, that snowplow is in pieces."

Rachel tried to draw a deep breath.

Lucas looked as if he dearly wanted to tear down Leventhorpe's office on top of him. "What if we force Leventhorpe to change his mind?"

Little shook his head slowly. "It's already in so many pieces that it would take two days to put back together."

"And Collins would be long gone by then."

Someone murmured a profanity. Rachel didn't reprove him.

"Maybe a flanger will travel with us," Mitchell said, not sounding very hopeful.

Lucas impatiently shrugged the suggestion off. "All they do is scrape snow and ice from between the rails and dump it on the side. They can't cope with six inches or more of snow and any wind would just pile the snow back up again. Men would still have to hand shovel switches, sidings, and so on."

"With four hundred and fifty-nine miles between Laramie and Ogden, and talk of heavy snow at the Rockies' summit," Lowell commented.

"So we pray," Rachel said firmly.

Lucas glanced at her, startled, and began to smile, not entirely nicely. "Exactly so, my dear. Let us ask Divine Providence's assistance, that our enemies may be confounded and the Lord's blessing smooth our path."

Rachel edged along the rough trail, trying to avoid the masses of snow being hurled overhead from shovels. She had bundled herself up in men's clothing until she appeared to be a penguin, but she had no desire to be hit in the face with a mouthful of icy crystals. Given the number of men working to keep the train moving, anyone walking near the locomotives needed to be very cautious. Three dozen of them had come two days ago from nearby settlements, lured by Lucas's promise of high wages.

The rough trail had been packed down by men's feet until it was hard as marble. It would probably turn slick enough to break a man's leg after sundown. The snow beyond reached almost to her waist, deceptively fluffy and friendly, and offering no protection from the omnipresent cold. It did, however, allow her to see the one man whose movements were still as graceful and disciplined as a panther, even after two days of walking and shoveling their way across Wyoming.

Lucas was a beautiful sight, even under the heavy clothing, always shoveling at the same strong, steady beat which made other men's efforts look frenzied and wasteful.

A slow, rich warmth lit deep in her chest, sending flickers through her bones. Oh yes, she could happily watch him do even the most inane tasks for the rest of her life. Which was why she was out here, even in this dreadful weather, when every other woman had taken shelter inside by a stove. Even though a ghost walked through their marriage.

Because she'd rather look at him, under three—or four?— layers of clothing, than stay safe and warm.

She flinched once again at the realization of her vulnerability, but pulled herself back into action and worked her way forward to him. *Thank God for buffalo coats, which protected her from the consequences of her own folly.* She reluctantly lowered the woolen scarf from her face. "Care for some tea, Lucas?" she shouted.

He swung around with a rapidity which would have impressed a tiger. "Rachel? What are you doing out here? I told you to stay indoors, where it is warm."

She shrugged and began to work through her layers of men's clothing to find the flask of tea inside her coat. "Everyone else is either working, exhausted, or sick."

Lucas cast a fulminating glare at her, but bit back a scathing retort, probably because of their audience.

She did her best to look innocent and businesslike. Her excuse was entirely true: The weather had turned foul once they left Laramie, becoming an appalling mixture of high winds and cold.

It had been cold almost every day, and not the heavy, wet cold that she'd grown up with, thanks to living along the coast, which had smacked her in the face like an immense door shoving her into an ice block. No, this was a raw, bitter cold and wind that shredded her skin and clutched at her throat. When it turned that cold—as it had for a few hours last night— the train simply stopped, since no man could work in it.

The wind made it worse, driving its sharp claws down her throat to capture her breath. It had blown almost continuously, tossing the snow up until it obscured all of the men's efforts. It blasted the tiny grains of snow into blocks, as solid and icy as any glacier.

Without a snowplow, they'd been forced to clear the railroad tracks by hand. Shovel by weary shovelful, the grueling, brutal labor of cutting into, ripping a block of frozen snow—now ice—out of the drift, and hurling it away, had left men literally dropping in their tracks . . .

The train had taken two days to travel a distance that would normally require only six hours. She hated to think how long it would take to reach help.

At least they had leaders onboard, who'd kept trouble from breaking out. Lucas, first and foremost . . .

Her husband jammed his shovel down and leaned on it. "Did you bring tea for anyone else?"

"Of course." She handed him the flask.

He tipped his head back to drink, the strong muscles rippling in his throat.

Her mouth promptly dried, aching with the need to taste him. She made a small involuntary sound and turned her attention to the inanimate scenery. This was not the time or place to indulge herself in lust.

Stopped by a great snowdrift, the train fretted just before the top of the Continental Divide, in a long, gently sloping channel cut by the now frozen Green River. Still pulling only the main section, its three locomotive engines were sending impatient puffs of smoke into the gloomy late afternoon sky. Behind them—to the east—the railroad tracks swept over a bridge then disappeared behind bluffs. All around were mountain ranges, like monuments to forgotten gods: The rugged Seminole Mountains in the north; the battered Sweetwater Range in the west; the Wind River Mountains still further west; and the gentler Uintah Mountains in the far south.

Great dark clouds loomed over the mountains to the northwest, sweeping down to fill the valleys and cover the peaks. They were so thick and low that the setting sun barely tinted a few fringes—sure sign of clouds heavy-laden with snow.

Lucas handed the flask back to Rachel. "Thank you."

She tilted her head toward the coming storm. "How long until you think it will arrive?"

He glanced at it and shrugged. "Little says less than two hours, once the wind changes. After that, it will be a true blizzard with high winds and a foot or more of fresh snow."

A gale, howling outside the *Empress* and dumping snow everywhere? They could barely move forward now if there was more than a few inches of snow over the tracks. "We'll be stranded."

His vivid eyes were intent and reassuring. "We'll be safe. We have plenty of supplies and the railroad train will come for us."

She shuddered, remembering a hundred appalling stories about people lost and alone on the Great Plains during a blizzard. But she, at least, had Lucas to keep her safe. The biggest danger would probably be the delay in reaching Ogden. "I'm sure you're right. But what about Mr. Donovan? Can we still warn him?"

Lucas's mouth tightened and he began to jerk his muffler up his throat, his previous confidence changed to angry determination. "There's been no answer from San Francisco to my cables. Donovan probably hasn't landed yet."

"Oh dear." She buttoned up her coat, making sure the flask was safe inside, and turned to the next man.

The rails ran back toward the east, black against the silver snow, rippling toward the darkened sky, their purity undisturbed by any train—especially one with much poorer passengers. "How far back do you think the immigrant train is?"

His fingers drummed on the shovel's handle. "I don't know. We heard its whistle, but that could be a trick of the ear. I hope they're close."

"Why?"

"So we can share food, if they're stranded."

She spun back to stare at him.

He was watching her, his eyes hooded, veiling his thoughts. "We have plenty of provisions but they don't, since their passengers must buy cheap food at every stop while we began with enough for twelve days. Their chances of survival go up—if they find us before the storm comes in."

"They could go hungry!"

He nodded, his expression as unyielding as the mountains around them.

"And if they don't reach us?"

His voice was very harsh. "They'll be racing to find us so we'll hang lanterns on our caboose. And pray they don't ram and derail us."

She'd heard enough stories to know what that meant. "Both trains could be lost if that happens," she whispered.

He gave a single curt nod of agreement and tapped his cap farther down on his head, refusing to let his expression tell her anything else.

She bit her lip, the cold carving her bones as hard as the wind ripped her skin. They were all at risk here, one way or another—and nobody else would help them.

A cat's paw of wind from the northwest touched her face. She froze. Another sliced into her, its bitter claws raking her. She gulped, the harsh mouthful of cold freezing her throat and lungs.

Every man was standing still, staring at the onrushing storm. Lucas's expression was deadly angry, as though he wanted to do battle.

"The wind's changed," Rachel whispered.

"Yes." He almost hissed the single syllable. "Pass out the rest of your tea as quickly as you can, and go back inside. The storm may come sooner than we think."

"Certainly."

She swallowed hard and turned toward Little. *Dear Lord, please let the immigrants make it through . . .*

She'd only taken a few steps when a joyous hooting arose from downriver. Her heart leaped into her throat and she lifted her head.

In the far distance, a train was chugging slowly from behind the bluff and onto the bridge, coming through the avenue they'd carved out so painfully.

The immigrant train had finally arrived.

Lucas threw his cap into the air and shouted, "Hurrah!"

Their train blew its whistle, sending up a deep, echoing blast, and began to ring its bell in long cascades of joy, which echoed around the mountain valley. All around Rachel, other men whooped.

And the wicked winds sent a blinding sheet of snow swirling across the bluff in front of their train.

Collins leaped back up onto his railroad car and into his drawing room, his gaze automatically seeking out his son. Was his fever still much reduced? Had he left his bed?

Maitland looked up at him from the sideboard where he was pouring wine. "Is our trap well set for those pigs, Father?"

Collins briefly closed his eyes in purest relief. Maitland was not only standing; he was just as acid-tongued as ever. Thank God he was finally healing from that bitch's attack.

Outside, their train stirred and rattled harshly. A work train lacked any elegance, especially when it left train stations. But there'd been time to pick up his telegrams at this tiny watering stop high in the Utah mountains.

"Yes, all's going very well. Humphreys has cabled that he's more than willing to do anything in his power to assist me, the true legal authority for the Bluebird."

Maitland snickered happily and handed his father a glass of wine. "Oh, very well said!"

"Yes, isn't it?" Collins agreed. "We might want to award him a bonus for turning such an elegant phrase."

His son's good brow lifted, making his skin twitch and pull against his bandages. Damn the bitch, the scar underneath the dressings would always look even worse than that nearly inhuman ripple. "*Might* want, I believe, actually means *won't want* in this case."

Collins chuckled happily, committing his son's countenance to memory as something else they were owed revenge
for. "But *might want* has such a charming ring to it!"

They laughed together for a moment, ignoring the winds
shaking their Pullman and the drafts slithering over the carpet. Beyond the draperies, the world beyond was a seething
white blizzard, muffling their train's whistle as it slowly
began to head west again.

"Also, Donovan should land tomorrow in San Francisco.
Jenkins, his new telegrapher—and our good friend—reports
that he has no idea yet of Mr. Grainger's difficulties. Donovan still intends to arrive at the Bluebird on the scheduled
date."

"Oh, very well done, sir! The goat is prancing toward the
pit. Thanks to the telegraphers, we also know that Grainger
and the bitch are snowed in, unable to help Donovan and
waiting to be destroyed. Soon we shall return to Boston and
resume our accustomed leadership."

Collins bowed extravagantly to his son's applause. With
all of his enemies ready to be disposed of, life was definitely
improving.

The vestibule door creaked and groaned. It reluctantly
opened, producing a great blast of cold air followed by
Lucas. He was wrapped up in his buffalo coat, with his cap
jammed down over his ears—and so covered in ice and snow
as to be nearly solidly white.

He was alive, not frozen to death, nor lost in the blizzard.
Thank God.

For a moment, Rachel could scarcely move, her heart so
high in her throat it choked her.

Gulping back a few foolish tears of relief, she rose from
the settee, her velvet dressing gown rippling around her feet,
and went to help him. The storm hammered at the *Empress*
as if jealous of having lost its chance at him, shaking the
valiant railroad car.

While Hanscom, the Union Pacific conductor, was an excellent man, he'd already privately admitted that Lucas's money and stockpiled food were what kept the two trains alive. They were even more hard-pressed by the laborers' presence, the men who'd come to shovel snow and were now distributed among both—previously quite full—trains. After two days of being snowbound, tempers were running very short. But the half dozen Donovan & Sons' men aboard also provided a well-disciplined group, more than able to assist the Union Pacific crew in settling any disturbances to the peace.

But managing all of that could only be done by one man: Lucas. So he'd traveled through the trains and along their periphery far too often for Rachel's taste, seeing to the people's comfort and checking their condition—regardless of his own.

He tossed his cap onto the table and began to peel off his muffler, every movement accompanied by loud cracks of shattered ice. He was breathing a little hard but that already seemed to be easing. His skin was stretched taut over his face's bones, giving him the appearance of a medieval knight—refined to his purest essence by the burdens he carried.

His blue-green eyes glinted under the single lamp's light, those damnable eyes that always drew her close. Her northern devil. "You should be asleep."

Unwilling to openly admit the depths of her helpless attraction to him, she forced herself to shrug and picked up his gloves. Heavens, they were so cold as to be almost immobile. "I dismissed Braden and Lawson, so they could have a good night's sleep."

She carefully set the gloves over a basin to thaw and gathered up his muffler for the same treatment. "Did you encounter any problems among the poker players?"

"No, not this time, thank God." Lucas brushed the snow out of his hair, shaking himself vigorously. Beads of icy water flew everywhere and crystalline droplets danced onto the carpet from his buffalo coat.

Rachel eyed him anxiously. He'd returned by walking through the storm, not through the train, so he could have been frostbitten. Were there any white spots high on his cheekbones or the tip of his nose? What about his fingertips?

"Was the weather very nasty out there?" she asked softly, stepping closer to him.

Ah, no frostbite—just icy clothing and the faint scent of sandalwood coming from his damp hair.

She shivered in recognition and hunger.

He shrugged wryly and began to unbutton his coat. "What would you expect after three days of howling blizzards? A tropical beach to appear along the Green River?"

She laughed, as she was expected to, and moved closer. His fingers were stiff and clumsy from the cold. "Let me help you."

His hands lifted away slightly. "Thank you."

From this angle, he looked more careworn than battered by the storm. Her fingers still yearned to touch him.

She wasn't much more nimble than he'd been with the buttons, since she was all too conscious of his chest rising and falling stirring his woolen coat, the steady beat of his heart under her fingers, his strong legs close enough to push aside her brown velvet dressing gown and slide between her legs . . .

He was watching her, his eyes heavy-lidded and heated, watching her unbound hair curl around her neck. Maybe she should have braided it.

She gulped and finished his last button but didn't move away. "Would you like some coffee?" she offered. "Or . . ."

"Something warm and sweet?" he suggested and slipped his arm around her waist.

She automatically leaned against him, her head tilted against his shoulder. But why should she do exactly as she'd always done, especially when he looked so exhausted?

Why not try something a little different? He could only say no.

Perhaps she could entice him. Silly idea—he'd always been the one to make all the moves—but a delectable one.

Hoping to seduce him felt a little like dancing with a tiger—both exciting and dangerous.

She wrapped one arm around the back of his waist. Her other hand began to gently caress his thigh, daringly close to his hip.

Lucas froze, one eyebrow rocketing up his forehead. He stiffened, stumbling a bit when his trousers tightened suddenly over his groin, across his hip—and under her fingers. "Rachel, what are you doing?"

She smiled up at him, pleased with his reaction to her very small bit of seduction. "Perhaps something fast and smooth?" she offered, sliding her fingers closer to his fly.

He was remarkably large and hot now, almost like an iron bar from the foundry. A small wet dot touched his trousers, at his shaft's tip—echoed by a swelling pool of heat deep in her core.

She stroked the back of two fingers up and down, up and down his shaft.

He jerked and gasped something in a foreign language, not one of the classical languages. Indian perhaps, not that it mattered.

She crooned his name and encouraged him again with the same stroke, gliding her palm over him.

He was sweating fiercely, as red and flushed as though he'd been shoveling coals into a roaring furnace instead of wading through snowdrifts at the top of the Rockies. "What the devil are you thinking of, Rachel?"

"I've never watched you closely, Lucas," she mused, still fondling him, still watching her hand sweep slowly over him.

He started to say something in English. But it abruptly turned into a harsh grunt when her fingers gently cradled his balls. He cursed softly in that strange language but didn't try to move away.

"May I look at you, Lucas?" she asked sweetly. "All of you, without clothes between us?"

She petted him very, very gently, strumming the seam of his trousers—and enjoying how very weak her own legs were. Her breasts were tight and aching, her nipples pressed against her corset, hungry for attention.

His breath wheezed out and his shaft strengthened even further. "Not here, Rachel. Good God, what if someone saw us?"

Rachel shifted to face him. Now she could put two hands to enjoying him. If she unbuttoned his vest and shirt . . . Her husband was such a very handsome man.

His fingers were almost shaking when he clasped her wrist but he didn't yank her hand away.

"Hanscom is back aboard the train, amid the palace cars, correct?"

"Correct," Lucas agreed, a little hoarsely. "Rachel, I haven't agreed . . ."

"No, of course you haven't." Her voice was really very husky—not surprising, considering how fast her heart was beating. "Do you really need to?"

A low chuckle was her only answer. His hands settled on her shoulders and began to gently knead her, subtly encouraging her attentions.

"Braden and Lawson are in their quarters, so there's no one else who could watch us," Rachel observed, not quite certain anymore what she was talking about, and pulled off his shirt.

She sighed, liquid heat spilling gently from her core onto her thighs. His naked torso was truly beautiful: The sculptured form, the iron-hard muscles rising and falling, the coppery nipples nestled amidst his thick black pelt. Even the blue veins twisted under his marble white skin like a sketch showing the path to heaven on earth.

She laid her palm flat against his belly for a moment, simply enjoying the rise and fall of those rippling, hard bands of flesh. His shaft surged, as if lunging up to reach her hand.

How she wanted to knock him flat on his back and sheathe his shaft deep inside her. If he'd been naked and her heart hadn't been beating loudly enough to be heard in Salt Lake City, she'd probably have done it. As it was, she contented herself by sliding her hands around to his back and slowly down over his ass. His high, tight, ass.

"Dammit, Rachel, hurry up." He sounded as if he wanted to wring her neck. He kissed the side of her neck, stroking her back and pulling her close to him.

"Hmm." Was this what being drunk felt like—the near inability to think straight, move, or even talk? But she was panting, too, and her hips were rocking back and forth, trying to reach the fiery hot bar behind his fly. If Demon Rum had such a salutary effect on women, no one would campaign against it.

She kissed his shoulder, nuzzling and nipping at his collarbone.

He groaned and threw his head back, clearly reveling in her attentions. "Rachel," he growled, "what the hell are you waiting for?"

Startled but encouraged by his passionate response, she encouraged to work her way across and down his chest, slowly slipping out of his grasp and sinking onto her knees. His expression turned into a rictus of delayed pleasure and he clenched his fists, pounding them at an imaginary wall.

Her skin was flushed and tight, crackling with the heat coming off him.

He spread his legs like someone desperate to keep his balance—and she smiled, a slow, seductress' gleam.

She unbuttoned his trousers and slipped her fingers inside, giving his shaft long, slow pulls. He arched his back, hungrily pushing into her hand for more.

Fire pulsed deep inside her, the waves rising higher every time he pressed against her.

She slipped his trousers down his hips to display his magnificent shaft. The splendid dark crimson head was greatly engorged, reaching almost to his belly and weeping a little with eagerness. His balls were fat and heavy under their dusting of hair but starting to rise high.

She wanted to fill herself with him, starting with her mouth. Taste him, smell him, learn his textures, absorb him into her bones, starting at her head . . .

He panted, his chest rising and falling rapidly, his fists clenching and unclenching. "Rachel, for the love of God, will you stop kneeling and do something?"

She tossed her hair to one side and bent her head. A slow swirling lick over his tip brought the lovely, familiar, salty taste and his hips surged forward.

Her core clenched in agreement. She repeated the caress, lingering over him, polishing him in wider circles, swirling in more patterns. She'd always enjoyed doing this, savored the fires burning hotter and deeper inside herself.

Lucas's fingers sank into her hair and kneaded her scalp. "My dear lady, you are so very skillful."

She hummed, hunger rising hotter and faster through her blood. She stretched her jaw wider so she could take more of him into her, managed to bring his entire cockhead into her mouth, licking and sucking the greatest delight in the world. *Oh yes . . .*

His knees almost buckled and he groaned with pleasure.

She hummed her approval when her body remembered old skills and took even more of him down her throat. She stroked his ass and between his legs, finding all the wonderful sweet spots which made his breath catch and his hands snatch at her head.

Up and down, up and down, matching the rhythm to her breathing, the beat of her heart, the fire blazing in her core . . .

And then she had him entirely inside her mouth and throat. He jolted into climax, throwing back his head and howling in pleasure.

The uninhibited passion in that cry tumbled her into rapture, shaken to her foundations and tossed to the stars.

She leaned against him afterward for balance, feeling very warm and relaxed.

Even if his late mistress still held his heart, having his body could be very, very enjoyable.

Chapter Ten

The high mountain valley was a beautiful scene, which would have inspired any painter. The sky above was a clear, crystalline blue, touched by a few wisps of cloud from the distant peaks. The frozen river curved elegantly along the valley floor, framed by the high bluffs and crossed by a graceful trestle bridge. The temperature was warmer today, leading to a gentle chorus of slowly melting snow and ice.

The two trains waited patiently, light trails of black smoke drifting from their smokestacks. Dozens of men worked industriously at clearing snow from the huge icy drift in front of a great locomotive, plumes of white flying like egret feathers above their heads as they dug. A handful of other men, barely visible through field glasses, tramped farther afield with rifles on their shoulders, hunting antelope and rabbits, in the hopes of varying their fellows' diet.

Children found wondrous ways to play amid a small grove of cottonwoods nearby, under their mothers' watchful eyes.

All in all, it was a landscape remarkably full of active people—with Rachel Grainger not counted anywhere among their number. She yanked her buffalo coat higher up around her ears. At least outside, she had the illusion of sunshine and warmth.

"I could walk down to the cottonwoods and play with the children," she suggested, trying to sound reasonable. She was standing with Lucas on the *Empress*'s rear platform, which allowed them a good view and the illusion of privacy.

She glanced up at him between her eyelashes, trying to charm him. "I'm sure their mothers would be glad of the assistance, after so many days cooped up inside. I promise I wouldn't go inside the grove, so I'd still be visible from the train."

"Rachel, you know very well that everyone is out there because it's the only way to stay warm. We should have enough to eat, but we're running very low on coal. We can't let the palace cars freeze, yet the engines may not have enough to reach the next station."

"Then let me go out into the sunshine." She put her hand on his arm pleadingly. "You could use the *Empress*'s private stock of coal for something else—perhaps the stoves in the emigrant train's family car, where the children are."

Just let me stretch my arms in the open, Lucas . . . I've spent three days caged inside that wooden prison, while the howling winds reminded me of Collins's Ledge.

Lucas shook his head, as implacable as ever. "No. Remember the lady who broke her leg when she stepped through the crust of snow and caught her foot between hidden roots and boulders in there? I won't risk you having a miscarriage."

What sort of clumsy idiot did he think she was? And as for a miscarriage—it was such an utter impossibility as to be not worth even discussing.

With her nerves already on edge, her usual diplomacy slipped through her fingers. "I'm sober, Lucas, unlike her, and I swear I'd be careful."

"No." His face softened slightly. "I'll take you for a walk this evening after dinner."

When she'd be unlikely to find anything to exclaim over but would very likely be battered by another round of that omnipresent arctic wind. She tried to appear enchanted, but no doubt failed miserably.

He misread her appalled expression. "You needn't worry about the stench from the emigrant train."

"Excuse me?"

He shrugged. "Its railroad cars are manufactured with a single convenience at each end, even though there are two adults for each seat. They weren't built for longer than the minimum run."

She gaped at him, opened her mouth to demand an explanation, and shut it.

He went on briskly without providing any further details. "I asked Braden to form a work party to clean it as much as possible—starting with the family car. There's too much chance for disease with so much filth around."

She made an instant decision but, before she could voice it, Lucas spoke again, his voice harsher than usual. "You're not to go anywhere near that train, do you understand?"

She stiffened, startled at being addressed in that peremptory tone of voice. "Why not?"

His expression hardened into granite immovability. "I won't have you risking your life or the child's."

"I am not pregnant."

"You might be."

She opened her mouth to expostulate with him. She was very healthy and her pregnancy—if one existed—was less than a week old. Surely scrubbing floors couldn't possibly injure her health, assuming she was careful not to become too tired.

Mitchell appeared, loping up alongside in the cleared path, his normal urbanity gone. "A fight started among the shoveling gang farthest from the engines. Something about Mississippians not having dealt an honest game of faro last night to the Texans."

Lucas muttered something about damn fool Southerners, which Rachel pretended not to hear, and tossed the dregs from his coffee cup into the snow. He gave her a quick, hard kiss. "Stay inside and warm, wife."

A moment later, he was gone with Mitchell, somehow managing to look unrushed although moving very quickly.

Inside and warm. How many days had she been doing that? Didn't he understand how much it reminded her of Collins's prison?

If she helped at the emigrant train, she'd still be inside and warm.

Rachel gathered up both their coffee cups and went back into the *Empress*. "Braden?"

He immediately faced her and came to attention, a tray of dirty breakfast dishes in his hands. Those very, very perceptive—and extremely polite—eyes acknowledged her. He bowed slightly. "Yes, ma'am?

Even after years away from the British Army, he was still very much a soldier and formidably alert. What did she possibly have to worry about if he was her escort, as he would be at the emigrant train?

"How are the preparations for your work party coming?"

He eyed her warily. "To the emigrant train?"

"Of course. Do you have sufficient supplies? What about personnel?"

His gaze, previously quite cordial, promptly turned flat and unrevealing. "We have more than enough supplies, ma'am, but are limited in the number of staff."

What an extraordinary phrase, *limited*. "Why?"

"Volunteers were requested, ma'am, and none have stepped forward."

None? Her eyebrows flew up. Three overcrowded filthy railroad cars and *nobody* except their own exhausted passengers would help him clean? They were admittedly very dirty, but she'd seen volunteers turn out for far more distasteful duties.

"The weather is good and there is much to be done elsewhere." His tone was overly dispassionate.

She had no difficulty unraveling this description and finding a possible cause for the problem. "Do you know if any disease has been reported on the emigrant train?"

He betrayed no surprise, of course. She suspected that he'd

perfected that expression while explaining night raids along India's North-West Frontier to younger soldiers.

"Fever and the grippe, which are to be expected given the weather." He paused, somehow managing to look even more stolid—a sure sign of nerves on his part.

She came alert. "Yes?"

"There's a young boy, perhaps five years of age. He's suffering from a sore throat, runny nose, cough, fever . . ."

"And?" she demanded.

A muscle ticked in his cheek. "And a rash."

Goosebumps raced up Rachel's arms. "Measles?" she breathed.

"We don't know yet."

If he had measles, they'd have to quarantine every other child onboard—and every adult who hadn't already survived that dread pestilence. The worst impact of contracting it would fall on pregnant women and their unborn children, but only if the mothers weren't immune. Good God, how that disease could kill and kill and kill . . .

Rachel shuddered. "It could be an ordinary rash," she said firmly. "Combining that with the grippe would explain everything."

"Yes, ma'am." Braden didn't sound entirely convinced.

The child had to have a combination of simple problems, exacerbated by foul conditions. Anything else would mean an epidemic, which could kill dozens of the people trapped here.

She murmured a quick prayer to Divine Providence and started planning how to care for the little darling. After nursing Elias, the practicalities rolled off her tongue.

"Has he been moved into someplace separate? We'll need to make him comfortable, of course. Cleansing everything will be vital, with carbolic soap if at all possible."

He frowned, color slowly fading from his face. "Are you considering going there yourself?"

"Who else will, if they think he has the measles?" Rachel asked simply.

He looked even more appalled. "Mrs. Grainger, you must take excellent care of yourself."

She smiled reassuringly at him. "Braden, please relax. I'm very sure I've had the measles. In fact, I've tutored small boys just before they came down with it—yet I stayed healthy. So there's no danger to me. But if you don't want to come . . ."

His shoulders went back and he slammed into attention. "Ma'am!"

She cocked an eyebrow at him. "Do you swear, by your mother's grave, that you've had the measles?"

He clicked his heels, drawing himself up into an even more rigidly formal attitude. "I swear, by my mother's and grandmother's graves, that I have had the measles, ma'am."

"Then we are agreed," she said briskly. "We'll go over to the immigrant train and make sure that the poor little boy has the best possible care."

"Yes, ma'am."

She pretended not to hear his muttered prayer that Master Lucas wouldn't be angry, probably because she was whispering the same thing.

Rachel stepped outside and took a great, healing breath. It was so late in the day that few people were visible except the shoveling gang laboring to move the trains forward. The setting sun cast purple and gray shadows across the snow, turning the high mountain valley into a twilight world. Frigid its air might be, and cold enough to snatch at her lungs—but it was also pure, since she was upwind of the emigrant train.

She'd thought the stench on the outside had prepared her for the harsh reality of the railroad car's interior. But she'd been so, so very wrong. Filthy beyond belief in the most animalistic fashion was the only way to describe it. No wonder the poor boy had been sick. Thank God, they'd washed him up, and found him and his mother a clean place in the baggage car with a sympathetic clerk.

Now that she'd finished scouring the convenience, Rachel

simply planned to return to the *Empress* and burn every article of clothing she wore. She'd long since lost every drop of food in her stomach. She pulled her blanket cloak around her more closely against the wind and started to trudge forward. At least, she'd had enough sense not to bring her precious buffalo coat on this work.

"Rachel."

The deep, rough voice made her jump. She whipped around. "Lucas?"

He was standing just behind her, feet planted wide apart. His fists were clenching and unclenching at his sides. Two bright spots of color burned high on his cheekbones. By the look in his eyes, he could have murdered anyone who stood in his path and laughed for joy afterward.

Oh dear Lord. Rachel's skin turned absolutely frigid. For a moment, her fingers tightened on her blanket before she resolutely loosened her grip.

"What the devil have you been doing?"

She eyed him warily. But she had done nothing wrong. "Scrubbing the convenience."

His voice was very gentle—too gentle. "How dare you disobey me and risk our child."

Risk? What on earth was he talking about? She tried to reach him with logic, using the pattern of all their years of correspondence. "There's no danger. I've had the measles before."

He gripped her arm, his fingers sinking into her soft flesh like iron claws. "Are you completely certain that the boy's problem is the measles? That you've had it before? That being immune will protect my child?"

She stared at him. "Your reasoning is absurd! I have followed the counsel of Boston's finest physicians, yet you are asking questions that would shame a country quack. Are you so blinded by guilt for a dead child that all you can see is a flickering chance of illness?"

"Yet if that disease occurs, my child will die! However

small the chance may—or may not be—the potential cost is huge. Do you care so much for another woman's babe that you won't give a thought for your own, madam wife?"

She flinched, remembering the horror stories of miscarriages and distorted fetuses, after an expectant mother had been touched by measles.

But it was silly to quail at that, since the odds were so very, very slight.

She rallied, forcing her hammering pulse to slow. "The chance of that is small, compared to this boy's illness. He lacked people to help his family care for him. Would you have asked your child to go untended?"

"*My* child will *never* be untended in his lifetime." Lucas's eyes glittered like a tiger's, daring her to challenge him. His fingers tightened into her soft flesh.

Her breath slammed in her throat, as if contact with a predator had banished generations of civilization in an instant. She stiffened her spine and glared at him.

The silence stretched, neither of them yielding.

A deep whistle sounded in the valley below. Then another, and another.

Someone shouted. Their trains hooted, and blew their whistles long and loud, calling out surprise and pleasure. Echoes tumbled over each other throughout the surrounding valley.

Lucas stilled, listening.

"Where is it coming from?" Rachel asked desperately.

"East?" he muttered. "But there are no plows there and nothing else could have reached us so quickly."

He turned to stare, his expression raw with hope. She followed his look, their earlier animosity forgotten—at least for the moment.

A massive train chugged slowly into sight. A great bucker plow led the way, pushed by three closely coupled locomotives. The bucker plow itself was shaped like a great naval battering ram, with a steel-shod prow, heavy timbers, and an upper deck for its skipper to command its usage. Before it, mountains of snow frothed and fell back, like ocean waves before a ship of the line.

Following that came two sturdy freight engines, also coupled together, pulling another small train, which included enough coaches to house two hundred men, some cooking and provision cars, a coal car, a water car, and a caboose. Men hung out of the windows and marched alongside, waving their caps and shouting greetings.

It was a snowplow and its army was fully capable of opening the transcontinental railroad track.

The sight snatched Rachel's breath away. "Thank God, we're saved," she murmured.

"How the devil did T.L. do that?" Lucas demanded simultaneously.

She glanced at him. "T.L.? Your father? What does he have to do with this?"

"Look at the engine immediately behind the plow. Which railroad did it come from?" Lucas's eyes narrowed, focused solely on the enormous plow.

She squinted. "Pennsylvania?"

Impossible. Well, barely possible if someone with great power had forced that superb railroad to immediately send one of its most prized assets across half the continent. But still . . .

She looked again. "The *Pennsylvania* Railroad sent a snowplow to *Wyoming*?" Her voice ended on a high note.

"Correct." A muscle ticked in his jaw. "What the devil will I owe him for this? He can't demand anything from me any more."

"Perhaps it's a gift." She might be furious at Lucas on her own account, but she could still be rational.

Lucas shook his head, turning pale beneath his tan. "How did he manage to persuade the Union Pacific to allow it on their line? My word, the blow to their pride!"

"He'd need a very powerful hold on them, or a very large

bribe," Rachel agreed. "Something to do with those big hearings in Washington, perhaps?"

"How the Union Pacific is entangled in the Crédit Mobilier scandal?"

"But Elias said your father had kept himself away from the Union Pacific's crowd."

"No. But those hearings could bring down the railroad and much of Congress, even possibly the administration. The Union Pacific will need allies."

Their gazes met, linking them with much of their old camaraderie. "More than enough reason to join forces," Rachel said softly.

"Indeed," Lucas agreed and firmly took her filthy hand in his. "With due *caution*, of course."

She flinched slightly at the warning to her, but set her chin and met his stare, look for look. She'd do exactly the same again, given the chance. If she was the only one who could help a child, she'd do it.

Maitland threw his head back with a sigh of relief. "Thank God, we're finally out of those damn mountains."

Collins smiled at him fondly. His son's spirits were improving daily, along with his health. He'd even had the energy for an evening among the lower orders in Ogden, enjoying blood sports and a cheap whore, who Collins had paid off afterward in gold. But he'd have shelled out double the amount to see his son so cheerful, even laughing, while he practiced that bitch's future punishment.

"Just a couple of days to Nevada and more mountains," he reminded him.

Maitland shrugged. "But our mine will be there and our friends. After we take care of Donovan, we'll have its riches to turn against the bitch. And, given just a little luck . . ."

Were Maitland's wits working again, too? "Yes?"

"That husband of hers will follow us and we can kill him there, too."

Finally, you've realized that . . .

"Splendid idea, son. We'd need to lay our hands on the bitch first. Otherwise, his family would claim everything through her, saying something about how the grieving widow is expecting his child."

Maitland frowned. "Pity. I was hoping to simply kill her immediately but, very well, we'll snatch her."

"And you'll teach her true obedience," Collins purred.

His only son's smile was a true one, which lit his eyes and his mouth. Collins would not have tolerated it directed at his late wife, but it was perfect for the bitch.

"Yes, I will need to do that. Immediately and thoroughly." Maitland lifted his chilled glass of champagne in a toast. "To the Bluebird, Father!"

"The Bluebird!"

They drank deeply, in perfect harmony.

Where the devil had Rachel gotten herself to now? Had she found another charity case to risk her life for?

Lucas leaped back into the *Empress*, scanning every corner of the drawing room. All the curtains were open, yet he hadn't been able to see her from outside, where the sun had set. If she wasn't here, dammit, he'd turn the entire train upside down to find her.

It was bad enough that he'd been delayed for so long, chattering interminably with his train's conductor, the Union Pacific roadmaster, and the Pennsylvania Railroad conductor about how best to utilize the shoveling gang he'd hired. For all he cared, they could take the lot and have them dig their way to China, if it meant he'd have his hands on Rachel five minutes earlier.

When he found her, he was either going to wring her beautiful neck or ride her into the ground, so she'd know who she belonged to and whose orders she had to obey. Both options appealed to him.

Braden straightened up from trimming a gas lamp, its fellows casting a warm golden glow over the room. "Good evening, sir. Would you care for some dinner? Lawson saved some very fine antelope steak."

Lucas waved the suggestion off as unimportant, even after a long day's brutally hard work. "Has Mrs. Grainger dined?"

"Yes, sir, and has retired to the main bedroom."

"Thank you."

He brushed past without another word, not about to respond directly to Braden's superbly blank expression.

He gave a single hard knock on his bedroom door and went in.

"Braden? Did you have a question?" Rachel poked her head out of the bathroom. "Oh, *you*."

Her disgruntled tone left no doubt as to her mood. She also looked delectable. She wore a flowered silk wrapper, which clung suggestively to her damp form. Her chestnut curls were piled loosely up, with a few tendrils escaping to draw attention to her slender neck and alabaster skin. Her cheeks were flushed and she smelled delicious. His chest tightened, his lungs heating.

Lucas pounced. In a single, swift movement, he grabbed her by the wrist and pulled her into the bedroom. An instant later and he had command of her other wrist, which he manacled with the first in one of his hands. He slammed her up against the wall, braced against a solid section of walnut paneling. "Yes, it is I—your husband." He slid his leg between hers, boldly parting her silk robe.

She wore nothing underneath and she squirmed slightly, deliciously over his leather trousers. His heart slammed against his chest, sending a matching pulse through his cock. It grew, lying fat and heavy inside his trousers—close to her but not close enough.

She gaped at him. "Lucas!"

"I'm glad you remember who I am." He caressed her cheek lightly with the backs of his fingers. "Because you have to know who's giving you orders so you'll know who you have to obey."

She frowned, clearly not inclined to submit easily. "Lucas," she began.

She was hardly in a position to argue, though. "I'm sure a few moments more will remind you of some of the activities done with your husband," he said sweetly. "Such as this . . ."

He nuzzled and licked the pulse point on the inside of her wrist, the one that always weakened her knees—and made his pulses sing in anticipation.

She gasped and sagged slightly before snapping back erect. "Don't be absurd!"

"Or this . . ."

He bent her arms to one side, opening her lovely throat for his kisses and teasing nibbles.

His passionate Rachel moaned and writhed, helpless before one of her favorite forms of loveplay.

His cock surged forward, growing in heat and size inside his trousers. His balls were fat and heavy, swollen with seed, pulsing with the same mad current that ran through veins and muscles and bones, demanding he hold her forever.

"Or this." His voice was so deep and rough it seemed to belong to someone else.

He abruptly released her wrists and caught her by the hips, sliding her up the wall until his aching cock pressed against her belly.

Her golden eyes blinked open, dazed. "Lucas?"

Gritting his teeth against the urge to yank—and destroy one of her few articles of clothing—Lucas undid her robe's belt. The slippery silk fell open, baring her. She had perfect breasts— firm and large enough to fill a man's hand—but not a bounty that distracted from the elegant lines of her waist. And as for the wonders that were her nipples . . .

He raked her with his eager gaze. "Oh hell, yes, you're beautiful."

Her nipples firmed, lifting upward as if demanding more attention.

He chuckled and she blushed. "Lucas, please."

"Exactly." He took the first one into his mouth and enjoyed it, thoroughly, leisurely.

"That's not what I meant," she protested weakly, wriggling against him in a highly suggestive fashion.

He raised an eyebrow at her, in no mood for maidenly vapors. "You're my wife, Rachel. Are you saying you're not enjoying yourself?"

His thumb slowly rubbed her nipple. She panted, her eyes closing.

He raked his teeth lightly down her neck. Devil take it, if his own body would slow down and give him a little more time, he might be able to teach her a few lessons, instead of simply wanting to jump on her. "Rachel?" he reminded her, no doubt sounding damn harsh.

"Anything, Lucas." Her eyelids fluttered. "But don't we need to lie down first?"

"Hell, no!"

He fumbled at his trousers' fly. Only instinct and long experience took him past blinding need and overly tight cloth long enough to free his cock. It sprang free, fiery hot, slicked with his juices—and snug against her satiny smooth belly. The same place where their child would grow.

He lifted her by the hips. His cock slipped between her legs, gliding between her intimate folds. "Wrap your legs around my waist, Rachel."

Her eyes opened wide with shock. "Are you joking?"

He was about to be rendered insane by her hot, sweet juices . . . "Dammit, Rachel, just do it!"

She obeyed, settling herself firmly for a very long ride.

Thank the Almighty, he had her against a very smooth piece of wall there against the corridor wall and beside the door. It was also extremely well polished, of course, as befitted anything aboard the *Empress*.

He groaned something wordless, his pulse hammering in his veins. His balls were fat and tight, tucked up high and aching for release.

He surged forward, sheathing himself in her, and slammed her against the wall. She shrieked and clung to him, her channel enfolding him in the hottest of welcomes.

He rode her thoroughly, desperate to stamp himself on her, pounding over and over against the wall. Instinct dictated his timing, not sanity nor his own body's needs. Did one climax shake her or two? Or three?

But she was still hot and willing, gasping for breath and chanting his name, when he brought her up the last, long climb to rapture, her exquisite body still caught between him and the wall. He was panting, heat streaking through his veins, and his seed boiling in his balls, desperate for release.

He nipped her shoulder in her favorite spot and sent her over the precipice into ecstasy, her voice breaking on his name.

That note of pure desperation unleashed him. He roared his triumph and climaxed, flooding her with his seed—trusting her with every hope he had for a tomorrow.

She was half-asleep afterward, when he brought her carefully down, totally disinclined for conversation.

Lucas was glad of her unaccustomed silence because he had no words to offer. Instead, he was full of the unsettling suspicion that this time, they truly had created a baby and he'd tied himself to a woman who took risks he abhorred.

And that he might be falling in love again—this time with a woman whose heart belonged to another man . . .

Two days later, Lucas was only willing to bet on one thing: Riding Rachel at all hours of the day and night might be extremely pleasurable for them both, but it would not make her yield an inch on any subject she considered to be a matter of honor. In fact, her idea of diplomacy was to not mention such difficult topics, just as she was doing at the moment while they rode down the last canyons toward Ogden.

A patch of sunshine swept through the *Empress* and passed over Rachel, where she slept in one of the custom-designed recliners. It illuminated her chestnut hair until she seemed an angel too pure for mortal men and then the sunlight vanished.

The beautiful Pullman shook, rattling and vibrating, matching the wheels' clickety-clack. The train raced downward through the narrow gorge, sweeping out over every hairpin turn until it seemed ready to brush the snow-covered trees on the opposite side. It slowed occasionally, gathering itself for each longer, steadier passage along the hairpin's leg until the next tight corner. But always, always, it offered its passengers a superb view of the tumbling, icy waters below and the fantastic spires and cliffs beyond.

Lucas paced the drawing room's length, paying no heed to stupendous sights he'd seen dozens of times before. They had no part in the decision he had to make now, while they were still hours outside Ogden.

He and Rachel had never spoken directly about their fight over her behavior aboard the emigrant train. He'd certainly never apologized for dressing her down. She'd behaved abominably by endangering their unborn child when she'd exposed it to the measles. On behalf of their baby—if not now, then the one which would someday exist—he could not—and would not—allow her to risk herself.

He shuddered, remembering the last time he'd seen Martha—her features so incredibly still, her skin translucent with great purple bruises coming up underneath.

Ogden was where they'd change trains for Nevada. After that, they'd travel for two days across trackless, appalling deserts to reach the Bluebird Mine and finally confront Collins. God willing, he'd have an answer from Donovan to his telegrams by then. But if not, he'd face Collins on his own.

In either case, did he want to take Rachel with him? She believed Humphreys, the Bluebird's manager, would obey her orders and spare Donovan, if he heard them from her personally. But who truly thought Collins's henchman would behave in such a civilized fashion? Was that slight chance enough to wager Rachel's life on it?

Or worse, what if Maitland Collins brutalized and killed Rachel as Ambrosia had been destroyed? Removed all semblance of her as a woman until she was only a lump of flesh, barely visible in a pool of blood?

A cold sweat broke out over his body, tightening his gut worse than any charge into battle. He pounded his fist into his palm, not seeing the Witches' Rock when it flashed past.

No, never!

He could not do it. He would be breaking his oath to cherish and protect her, if he did so. Rachel, who had no more idea of how to protect herself than a day-old kitten did.

So he had to keep her behind, even if it meant physically forcing her—which she'd see as an unforgivable betrayal, given how she'd been imprisoned by Collins. Rachel—would refuse to discuss any disagreement on a point of honor, which she'd undoubtedly consider this.

He came to a halt, staring at rocks as granite hard and twisted as his choices—and as bleak as his future.

That brief taste he'd had of a warm, comfortable home was exactly that—brief. He needed to set it aside now before the memory set roots too deeply in him. It was a small price to pay for his wife and child's safety.

Chapter Eleven

Rachel closed her eyes and tilted her head back, unabashedly basking like a lizard. Ogden, thank God, was sunny. It was also undoubtedly very windy and cold at this time of year, but it had brilliant green trees and *distant* snow-capped mountains. All in all, it held bountiful pleasures to enjoy while recovering from Lucas's latest bout of possessive lovemaking—and preparing for the next.

She smiled at some very delectable memories, reminded herself not to lick her lips in public, and settled herself more comfortably onto her bench at the big Ogden train station.

The *Empress* had been uncoupled from the Union Pacific train and shuttled to the waiting Central Pacific train, with many short, repetitive hoots and bells, clanking and clacking of wheels and rails.

Once they'd arrived, Lucas had been quickly greeted by several big, tough Donovan & Sons' teamsters. He'd politely introduced her to them, before leading her to this seat to rest. Other Donovan & Sons' men from Utah now guarded her, while he was still absorbed in conversation.

She frowned slightly, watching her husband more closely with the railroad car's distraction out of the way.

Now that she thought about it, his expression was very harsh. Had they said something to anger him? But he'd been abrupt ever since he'd woken her up from her nap onboard the *Empress*, by making such passionate love to her.

So whatever his concerns were, they'd appeared before Ogden. Even more unsettling, his old friends—Little, Lowell, and Mitchell—had gathered around and were vehemently arguing with him about something, only to be shaken off.

Her brows knitted, while she considered possible causes.

Surely it couldn't be her fault. Oh, they'd had words back in Wyoming about how she'd scrubbed that emigrant train. But she hadn't brought up the subject again and neither had he. Diplomacy forbade discussing something one wouldn't apologize for. She could not regret acting with true Christian charity back in Wyoming.

"Rachel, please come with me." Lucas stood before her, blocking the thin sunlight.

Rachel shaded her eyes and squinted up at him. Big, strong, everything a protector should be . . .

"We're invited to lunch with my old friend Taylor at the Donovan & Sons' depot." Something about his tone sounded a little unusual.

Rachel pursed her lips, considering it, but couldn't put the difference into words.

His voice sharpened. "Rachel?"

She could describe this mood with a single word: Peremptory.

Well, why not go? Dining with company and away from the train would be very pleasant.

She held out her hand to him. He accepted it and lifted her to her feet. An instant later, he had her hand captured under his on his arm.

Her hair ruffled slightly on the nape of her neck. None of the other men were with them. In fact, Lowell and Mitchell had turned their backs and were facing the *Empress*.

"Have you known the depot manager long?" she inquired as delicately as possible. She hadn't felt this uneasy since she'd been on Collins's Ledge.

"Almost ten years. Taylor and I served together in the Army. I helped him obtain the job with Donovan & Sons."

So he was someone who owed much to Lucas, who would undoubtedly do a great deal to return the favor.

Surely the only reason she could possibly feel chilled was the brisk breeze coming off the snowcapped peaks . . .

Once they reached the street, Taylor came forward immediately. A weather-beaten, burly fellow with the look of a canny bloodhound, he appeared an honest man, but not one whose loyalty ran in the most conventional paths.

Rachel strolled down the boardwalk between the two men, her stomach icing over faster than the mountains' summits and firmly told herself there was no necessity to calculate escape routes. Lucas, after all, had sworn to protect her with his life.

The large Donovan & Sons' depot stood only a few blocks away. It could almost be called a fortress, with its stout stone walls, narrow windows, and iron-braced doors. Men, wagons, horses, and mules moved past in startling numbers, most of them laden with packages and crates and all of them in a rush.

Lucas immediately swept her close to his side and away from a particularly enormous dray, heavily laden with barrels, and pulled by eight mules. Rachel clung to him, far too grateful for this ordinary example of his protectiveness.

Taylor raised his voice to be heard from the other side of the entrance. "I'll take these cables down to the office to be sent off."

Lucas nodded his thanks, not bothering to shout over the clamor, and swept Rachel onto a long inner corridor, away from the great central courtyard. Here the central square broke into a smaller nook, with two sides composed of the corridor and the last made up of obviously private stables. A vegetable patch slept away the winter, while a handful of goats placidly chewed some hay. She could glimpse the Central Pacific's offices through the stable's windows.

A guard stood where the nook opened into the central courtyard, where he could watch both the stable and the great warehouse beyond.

This was obviously an extremely well protected, yet very quiet place.

Her heart began to thud in her chest.

Lucas opened a door at the corner and ushered her in very formally, without touching her.

Rachel took three steps and found herself in the center of a small private suite. It held a cot, chest, table, and chair, plus a hand-stitched copy of the Lord's Prayer, all lit by a hanging oil lantern. A convenience and small hip bath could be glimpsed in another, even tinier, room next door. Everything was immaculately clean.

A single window showed the goat pen.

The entire suite was less than half the size of her quarters on Collins's Ledge.

The tiny space grayed, becoming infinitely distant, and she forced it back into focus. Surely her presence here could not mean what she feared.

"What is this place, Lucas?" She was proud of how normal her voice sounded.

"Where I want you to stay while I'm gone, Rachel." Lines were graven into his face, as deep and unyielding as the mountains high above. His blue-green eyes glittered, as frosty as their ice. "My darling, will you please stay here while I go to Nevada? You mean more than my life and I am sworn to protect you."

"What if I say no?"

His jaw set hard. "You must stay here. No matter what it takes."

She searched his face, desperate for a glimpse of the man she'd come to trust. He could not betray her like this. "No! You can't mean that. You can't lock me up in here."

Brackets deepened around his mouth. "It's the safest place for you. Collins will never steal you out of here. The walls are strong and the men will guard you. Taylor's wife will stay in the depot with you."

Her throat tightened. Her skin was colder than the snows in the Wasatch. "But—what about the Bluebird? You need me to talk to Humphreys!"

"Do you truly believe that anyone who'd been plotting with Collins for a year will meekly turn over a new leaf as soon as you walk up to his door? Can you ask me to risk your life by taking you exactly where Collins will be looking for you?"

She flinched, making a helpless sound. His logic was as implacable as his eyes. Tears gathered and she blinked them back fiercely. She revolved slowly, staring at the cramped quarters, her skirts whispering over the floor like lost hope. "How can you expect me to live here, for any amount of time? I'll die, Lucas."

"You can walk outside, as long as you stay within the depot."

"At least when Collins locked me up, I could see the ocean and the far horizons!" she hurled at him.

He flinched slightly but didn't back down. "You escaped from him. Worse, a villain could have stolen you, if they'd known where you were. I will not take *any* chances with your life."

She grabbed him by his rough wool coat's lapels. "Lucas, life is composed of chances. I'm willing to gamble."

He firmly took her hands away. "I am not."

Good Lord, why wouldn't he understand? She stepped away from him, ran up against the chair, and turned back. "Will you do the same thing if there's an epidemic of cholera or measles a year from now, when this is over and there's no danger from Collins?

He hesitated, the affirmative written across his face.

She could have thrown something at him. "Lucas, if you always insist on hiding me away whenever any danger comes near, I'll never be able to breathe. I cannot live like that; no woman can."

"Can you honestly expect me not to do my best?"

She bit her lip, the small pain echoing the larger ache in her heart. He'd proven to be a northern devil, but not for the reasons she'd expected. "Lucas, if you do this now, I will never be able to trust you again."

Agony flashed through his eyes then vanished. "I know that—but your life is more important to me than how you view me."

If logic wouldn't reach him. . . She discarded pride and sank to her knees. Tears blinded her. "Lucas, please . . ."

He made a single, rough sound. "Rachel—just try to understand and forgive me." He was gone an instant later, the door slamming behind him.

She stared at it, the sound ripping through her like her own agony.

Catullus had had the right of it:

> Odi et amo, quare id faciam, fortasse requiris?
> Nescio, sed fieri sentio et excrucior.
> "I hate and I love. Why do I do this, you require
>   an answer?
> "I don't know, yet, I feel it happening to me. I feel
>   the fire and am crucified."

Rachel curled up on the floor in a ball and wailed. She never knew how long she cried, only that she did so until she was exhausted, with her eyes and throat red and raw. A glance in the bathroom's tiny mirror showed a wreck of a woman.

She gulped, appalled at how far she'd fallen since she'd left the station.

She glared at her reflection. Like hell.

She liked the sound of that forbidden word so much, she repeated it again—like *hell*.

Lucas thought she was so helpless that she needed to be locked up in a cage like a canary. She'd prove that he was wrong. She'd escape from here and she'd make it to the Blue-bird, where she could help foil those nefarious plotters.

After that, maybe one day she'd find peace again studying the classics.

The first step was eliminating the ruined woman in the mirror.

Rachel was bitterly glad that the chest contained several clean handkerchiefs, enough to blow her nose and wash her face. No one had come in, which was another blessing.

Next she took stock of her resources, as she'd learned so painfully to do on Collins's Ledge. There was food on the table—a simple meal of sandwiches and fruit, but at least something which would travel well. She also still had gold and jewels hidden around her corset, since she'd never lost the habit of secreting them. It would be a little clumsy and embarrassing to exchange a jewel for a train ticket, but it was certainly possible.

A minute later, the food was packed into the basket it had evidently arrived in. Two more minutes and she'd sliced through the stitches holding a single small ruby onto the corset and hid it in her basket.

The next step was to escape, a task easier announced than accomplished.

She grimaced and tiptoed over to the door. After long minutes of listening, she was confident enough to open it a crack and peek out.

Nobody was there.

Was everyone convinced she had so little gumption that she'd stay in her prison cell, rather than run? So spineless that they didn't need to set guards?

Rage stirred hotter, speeding her pulse and tinting the world red. She'd teach them a lesson: She'd escape this cage and prove that she was braver and stronger than they'd thought.

She slipped out, easing herself through the door like a shadow. A very wary look told her that the guard was watching a wagon with a large team of mules being turned around in the central courtyard. He probably thought she was too heartbroken by her husband's departure to cause trouble this soon. If she ran *now*, she might just make it to the stables without being seen.

She said a quick prayer under her breath, picked up her skirts and her basket, and went as quickly as possible down the corridor—without ever hesitating or looking back. Time was, after all, of the essence. In any event, what could the guard do that Lucas hadn't already done to her? Shooting would be a mercy.

She whisked into the stables, with their door to the Central Pacific offices and the railroad station, and leaned against the wall, sweating far too profusely. A couple of horses poked their heads out of their loose-boxes to study her curiously. The light was filtered and golden, warm with the familiar, homey scents of a well-run, clean stable.

She listened, straining to catch something over the pounding of her heart.

She gathered herself for the last dash to the railroad station. She'd do her part to help save William Donovan's life, of course.

After that? No matter what it took, she would not live with Lucas Grainger.

Lucas braced himself on the ornate brass overhead rack and stared out the window at the uncaring piles of rocks known as hills. Maybe, if he tried hard enough, he could convince himself he was calculating men and equipment for any necessary assault on the Bluebird, spurred on by his current stark surroundings.

God knows, the Great Salt Lake was a harsh enough sight with enough salt crusted along its shore to look like a snowdrift. Yet even the recent blizzards hadn't quieted the alkali in the air, which ripped apart men's lungs and had earned this area the sobriquet of The Great American Desert.

A small voice whispered that, if Rachel was here, he'd be playing chess with her or laughing or purring after another tumble in her bed . . .

He kicked the inoffensive chair next to him and swung away. He'd traded her safety for her love so he'd best start working on guaranteeing her safety.

The train wheezed to a stop at Promontory, permitting even more alkali to swirl over the *Empress* from the Great Salt Lake only a few hundred feet away.

Unlike every other passenger, Lucas swung down onto the platform, telling himself it was for sentimental reasons. After all, this was where the two railroads had joined, thus uniting a continent. The alkali dust immediately burned into his lungs.

Surprisingly, the train lingered at Promontory. In fact, the engineer placed the locomotive into a waiting state, until it barely seemed to hum. The conductor offered no explanation except railroad business. Apparently a guest of the company would join them, which required that the entire train be delayed for his arrival.

Lucas took great delight in cursing the ancestry of the arrogant, selfish newcomer. It was far better to think about that than a future without Rachel, or an ice-cold Rachel sitting across the table from him.

Finally, another locomotive approached from the east, chugging along at great speed. The conductor chivvied the passengers back aboard, at least the few who'd braved the frigid winds with their burden of raw dust.

Lucas lingered on the platform, confident that he could board the *Empress* within seconds once he'd satisfied his curiosity. His instincts stirred, for no reason that he could name.

His train eagerly began to make steam, ready to race on.

The new locomotive pulled in, its whistle and bell loudly announcing its arrival. Its conductor handed down a slender lady with chestnut hair and a queen's proud bearing.

Rachel? Here? Impossible. His heart stopped beating *Good God, it was her.*

His heart lunged back into action. *How the hell would he keep her safe now? And how the devil would he keep his heart safe?*

She sailed down the platform, carrying a single small basket, and halted in front of him.

Lucas instinctively drew himself up and looked down at her. "How the devil did you get here?" he inquired, as haughtily as possible.

"I told the district superintendent that my husband and I were honeymooning on his business trip. He left me in Ogden to rest but I grew lonesome after only an hour. Given my tearstains—" her tone hurled calumnies at him for having forced those marks on her—"the superintendent believed me. He was very sympathetic and loaned me his inspection train to rejoin you."

Her glare drilled him to the bone, an expression that Sherman would have been proud of. "I am going to the Bluebird Mine," she announced. "If you try to stop me, I will simply find another way. Do you understand?"

His mouth tightened. There was nowhere between here and the Bluebird to leave her. He could take her back to Ogden—but that would give Collins even more of a headstart and time to plot Donovan's death. He couldn't do that. He'd have to bring her along and plan to bundle her up safely, guarded by some of the additional Donovan & Sons' men who'd joined in Ogden.

He nodded abruptly, heartily disliking his options. "Understood. Come on." He put his hand on the stair rail.

She stayed firmly fixed on the platform.

"All aboard!" called the conductor, from closer to their locomotive. Its whistle blew, signaling its imminent departure.

Lucas lifted an eyebrow. "And?"

"We will have separate beds, even if I have to sleep in the drawing room."

He tensed, cut to the bone by this publicly announced rejection. Somehow he'd always believed they could build a future together, thanks to their mutual enthusiasm in the bedroom. "Separate beds? Why?"

Her golden eyes held all the warmth of sunlight glinting on a siege gun's muzzle. "Because you are not a gentleman and do not deserve a wife's company."

She considered him that low? For having done his best to protect her? Having his innards blown apart would have hurt less than hearing that.

The world grayed for an instant.

Her train's whistle blew sharply, signaling its departure. Bells ringing, its wheels clanked into action and it began to back up, slowly at first then faster and faster. Their conductor came hurrying toward them, prominently displaying his watch. "All aboard!"

Lucas drew himself up proudly, determined not to let her see what she'd done to him. But he never had, and never would, force himself on a woman.

"Very well."

The simple phrase tasted like ashes.

William Donovan strolled back into his San Francisco townhouse, holding hands with his wife. Abraham and Sarah Chang, their houseman and his wife, came forward immediately. William promptly dismissed them so they could go shopping in Chinatown. This would be Viola's first Chinese New Year in her own home and everyone wished to make it a splendid celebration.

The house itself was a small place that he'd owned for years and would soon be replaced by a much larger establishment suitable for children. But this home had the advantage of a central location and his office on the main floor, where Jenkins, his telegrapher, kept him in touch with all his business doings.

It was uncommonly quiet at the moment, with few loud

clickety-clacks coming from inside to bear witness to Jenkins's diligence. Still, it was currently during the man's brief afternoon break.

Not that William was paying attention to Donovan & Sons' affairs at the moment, given how his wife's enormous dark blue eyes were studying him, while her slender fingers strolled up his arm. The howling winds outside had whipped brisk color into her cheeks, emphasizing her mouth's sweet sensuality, which was perfect for urging him into ecstasy. By all the saints, every man would be married if they knew a lady like her.

"I wish we'd heard from Lucas Grainger. I'd be much happier about his safety, if he'd cabled us as he promised to."

William nodded silently, his own happiness slipping into worry. Dammit, it wasn't typical of his friend not to come through. The Army had lost a future general when he'd resigned.

"But this does provide us," Viola commented softly, "with more time to . . ."

His attention switched straight back to the center of his world. "Improve our techniques for connubial bliss?" he suggested.

She gaped then laughed and popped him lightly on the cheek. "You are entirely too much of an Irish devil to be allowed out in public. You're lucky I adore you."

She leaned up for a fond kiss. He caught her around the waist and pulled her closer, losing himself in a joy that never grew old. "We could go up upstairs," he murmured, a few minutes later.

"If we do that, you'll be late for your appointment with Huntington," she reminded him. Her voice broke when he lightly scraped his teeth over her throat. Her neck helplessly arched back to allow him more room to excite her.

He rumbled happily and enjoyed her sweet flesh a little more before reluctantly withdrawing. "You're probably right: We'd better wait until after I speak to that poor fool who only has a railroad to worry about, not a beautiful wife. I can carry you off to my bed when I can spend an entire evening enjoying you undisturbed."

Her eyes were closed, her skin flushed, and she was definitely panting. William observed these signs of carnal passion with wry satisfaction, well aware their counterparts existed in himself. He caressed her cheek lightly. "How do you wish to spend these moments, sweetheart?"

Heavy eyelids slowly lifted, revealing her deep blue eyes filled with passion—and he tumbled head over heels into love yet again. His fairy queen who'd blessed this Irish lad with her life and love, who was all of his living kin.

She blinked, untwined her arms from around his neck, and straightened his lapel. Her hands lingered overlong, stroking his chest, before falling away.

He grumbled silently, but saw the wisdom of her choice and stepped back.

"Well, we might want to consider names for our children," she commented.

William lifted a quizzical eyebrow. From the bedroom to children was all too short a step, after all—but naming the little ones before they were conceived?

"What did you have in mind?" he asked, genuinely curious, and leaned back against the wall next to the office. "I'd always thought of naming them for our family and friends."

She knitted her brows, looking enchanting. He clenched his fists lest he grab her and kiss the furrows away.

"How did you receive your name? I don't believe it's a common one for Irish Catholics."

William snorted in derision. "Hardly, since it's that of the Protestant king who defeated and banished the last Catholic king. But I was named for my grandfather's partner during the Ninety-seven Rising, who saved his life more than once. My family believed it was more important that he was an Irish patriot than that he was a Protestant."

"Would you want your son to be called William?"

He shrugged. "Not my firstborn. Joseph perhaps for my father, or Gerald for my grandfather. Or maybe Morgan for my best friend."

Her eyes widened. "You'd accept an English name?"

"If it's a name that means family and love, Viola dear," he commented, deliberately being as mild as possible in order to tease out her opinions.

How important was this to his Southern belle? Her family always chose Shakesperean names for their children, preferably ones with links to great literary themes or possibly prior generations of their lineage.

"What about something Irish?" She stamped her foot. "Something that will remind your son he's a Donovan whose family came from County Cork, not just another boy born in North America?"

Was she thinking of a more common name, such as another Patrick or Michael? "What do you have in mind?"

"Brian would be a good start. For Brian Boru, the high king who defeated the Vikings. Then there's Brendan, for Saint Brendan the Navigator. It'd be only fitting if your son had wanderlust," she added tartly.

He roared with laughter before adding between gasps, "Or Donal for the two great medieval regents."

"Or Roark, or . . ."

"You've a great many good names spilling off your tongue! Let's not lose them all to the moment's competition."

He pushed the office door open and a quick glance satisfied him that Jenkins was still absent. The room was compact, barely large enough to hold a big desk, a large swivel chair and a small straight chair, plus a small table. Like the rest of the furniture, they were high quality, comfortable for large men, and extremely durable. A narrow cot, typical of a telegrapher's office but atypical of any other type of office, was pushed against the wall behind the door.

It also sported several windows, on each side of the house's southwest corner, which were currently allowing some pleasant breezes to sweep through. The garden beyond was tiny, but provided an excellent view of the neighbors' overgrown foliage.

He sat down at the big desk with its infinity of cubbyholes and litter of papers. Where was a blank pad of flimsies? Almost gone? Dammit, what was the fellow up to, allowing basic supplies to run so low? He'd already spoken to him about his drinking.

He handed Viola the pad and a pencil. "Well, write them down."

"All of them?"

"Of course. We must protect our unborn children's interests," he intoned piously.

She sniffed. "Only if you do so, as well."

"Certainly." He cast a dubious look over the desk. There was no other pad in sight. Well, the backs of old cables would have to do. "Henry, for your brother. Or Richard, for your father."

"Very sentimental choices," she approved. "But you haven't mentioned any daughters."

"Neither have you."

"Brigid, perhaps. Does Jenkins always eat at his desk? And do so like a pig?"

She held up a yellow flimsy, its penciled message almost obscured by grease.

William frowned, wiping his own fingers on his handkerchief after encountering similar examples. He pulled a handful of telegrams from the cubbyhole labeled MISC for miscellaneous, gambling they could be most readily ignored.

"Telegraphers are usually dedicated to their jobs, which means they stay at their post day and night," he commented, handing her his handkerchief. "But every cable he's handed me was immaculate."

Viola harrumphed. "You might want to speak to him. Uncleanliness like this will quickly invite the lowest forms of vermin."

William nodded absently, a chill sliding down his spine. In his hand lay a single telegram, which had been sent from Omaha less than a week ago—by Grainger.

Viola immediately caught his shift in mood. "What is it, William?" She leaned over his arm to read the few words, her hat's proud feathers tickling his cheek.

Collins and Humphreys were plotting treachery at the Bluebird.

Why hadn't he known? Jenkins had to be in on it. Or at least damn well bribed.

Rage stirred, crystalline bright.

"Why, that low-down, stinking scum." Viola spat.

Soft footsteps sounded just beyond the closest window. The breeze shifted abruptly, teasing papers out of the wastepaper basket, as if someone had blocked the breeze from the tiny garden outside.

William touched Viola's arm. She nodded, the barest movement of her head. Thank God, she was closest to the door and could escape. If anything happened to her . . .

At least he had his dirk. Here in San Francisco, it was uncommon for gentlemen to wear any weapons at all and almost no one knew he had it.

A great rock smashed through the south window. An instant later, another shattered the west window.

Time stretched like taffy, until every movement, every detail became crystal clear.

William immediately dove under the desk, pulling Viola with him and covering her with his body.

A pair of shots plowed into the wall, where his head would have been if he'd still been sitting in the chair.

Silence fell, broken only by the telegraph's erratic ticking.

His knife was ready for immediate use—should the coward show his face.

"You'll never get away with this, Jenkins," William called, calculating the distance to the door. If he could only distract the bastard long enough to get Viola clear . . .

A rough laugh was his only answer.

Jenkins was on the west side of the house. Perhaps if he watched that window . . .

He glanced at Viola, asking permission. Her mouth held very tight, she nodded slightly.

He touched his fingers to his lips, then to hers. She gave him a brief, genuine smile and crossed herself. He drew his crucifix out from inside his shirt, kissed it, and rolled quietly, cautiously out from under the desk, free to hunt a killer.

"Why are you doing this?" he called.

Jenkins laughed bitterly. "You never recognized me, did you, Donovan?" He'd shifted to the south window now? The echoes were very indistinct on that side of the sunken garden. "You bought my father's business and left him a worthless drunk, who drowned walking home from the saloon. Now I'm here to see you ruined as well."

"Johnson of Hangtown Freighters? Did you change your name?" William frowned, thinking back through the years.

"That's it. You destroyed his pride and he became a worthless wreck. My mother changed it when she remarried. I kept my foul stepfather's name so you wouldn't recognize me."

William nodded silently, remembering the fast-talking fellow with the whining wife. "Johnson agreed to an honest deal. Otherwise, how would he have had the money to lay about in saloons for five years without doing a day's work?"

"Are you calling my father worthless?"

A fusillade of shots shattered the plaster over the desk. William cursed his errant tongue for risking Viola's life by telling the truth too quickly.

Outside, the neighbors had finally started to raise a fuss. But it would take time to form a search party and the slender, nimble Jenkins could easily slip all but the tightest cordon.

"As one man to another, let my wife go. She has no place in this." William took up his position between the two windows, his long, deadly blade in hand.

For the first time, Jenkins hesitated before answering. "Very well."

William glanced back at his darling and jerked his head toward the door. Tears trickling silently down her face, she slipped out of the room without another word, crouching low the entire time.

More determined than ever to kill the bastard who'd put that expression on her face, William waited. Jenkins would have to come in close to kill him.

Gravel crunched on the path outside.

William continued to wait, his breathing steady and his pulse regular—as they always were during a fight.

Jenkins's head popped up at the west window, silhouetted against the setting sun. He pointed a heavy Army Colt at William. "Damn you, Donovan, your sharp business practices will cost you your life—before you sire another generation of . . ."

William threw his beloved dirk. It sank into Jenkins's throat, slicing through flesh and nerves and bones.

The traitor collapsed instantly, dead before his head could strike the garden paving.

Running feet sounded outside, coming down the path. William spun immediately toward the sound, reaching for one of the weapons he'd have carried in a less civilized place.

The feet slowed and approached cautiously, their existence almost hidden by the neighbors' loud excitement over talking to the police.

William shook his head. Ah, the innocence of law abiding citizens . . . He turned his attention back to his beloved, law-abiding but wise wife. "Viola? You can join me now."

He snatched a blanket off the cot, put his hand on the sill, and leaped down onto the garden path. Explaining this to the neighbors would probably be best done with Viola's assistance. She had a knack for charming cantankerous males.

Viola stepped around the corner, carrying her beloved shotgun. She came to a halt and frowningly assessed the crumpled corpse. "You already killed him," she accused her husband. "I was planning to hand him over to the law and cheer at the hanging."

"Yes, dear. As I'm sure you recall, he *had* fired a gun at you." He smiled wryly and discreetly covered up the late, unlamented Jenkins. His darling was entirely capable of any amount of bloodthirstiness, whenever it was needed to protect her loved ones.

She sniffed haughtily, but allowed him to wrap an arm around her waist. She leaned against him confidingly an instant later. She was shaking, damn the traitorous wretch for having frightened her!

"I thought I'd died a thousand deaths when I saw you under the desk, with the glass all around, knowing he was out there," she admitted.

He tightened his grip on her. "So did I, sweetheart."

The neighbors started to crash through the foliage toward them.

"We have to leave for the Bluebird tonight," Viola remarked, her voice slightly muffled by his coat.

William's heart skipped a beat and he stiffened. Risk her life so soon after almost losing her? "*We?*"

"Of course. You and me, plus as many of your best men as possible." She read his appalled silence quite accurately. "Don't give me any nonsense about leaving me in San Francisco. I'll simply follow you by the next train."

"I'll lock you up."

"You can try."

He'd have to try to change her mind along the way, although his chances were slim. Viola could make a Missouri mule look reasonable.

"At least as far as Reno, of course," she added briskly. "I'm not optimistic enough to think you'd take me into battle at your side."

He snorted softly at his own overprotective folly. He'd misread her need—and his!—to always be together, as a desire to accompany him into the coming battle. Viola had fought Indians and worse; she knew far better than to go where she'd only be a hindrance. He acquiesced as graciously as possible. "It will be a pleasure having your company in Nevada, Viola."

She pressed herself closer to him with a small, relieved sigh, just as the neighbors reached them.

Chapter Twelve

Rachel strolled down the boardwalk and tried to pretend an interest in Reno's frozen sights. Just behind her paced her two guards, Peter and Paul Hawkins. They were Donovan & Sons' men from Ogden, taciturn brothers who monitored her every move whenever she left the *Empress*.

The Sierra Nevada Mountains rose shockingly fast to the west, their summits dazzling the eyes. Below them, their steep flanks, the low ridges at their feet, and even the tiny humps of sagebrush—all had vanished under a heavy mass of snow and ice.

According to the talkative Central Pacific stationmaster, storms had come in from the north more frequently than usual this year, never quite allowing the previous storm's deposits to fully melt. Instead of the typical icy mud, now Reno's inhabitants slogged through a half-dozen feet of solid snow and ice. In Virginia City, at over six thousand feet, miners were supposedly using snow tunnels to cross between buildings because of the much worse conditions there.

Rachel shrugged slightly and moved on, turning away from the sun glinting off the frozen Truckee River. However narrow and cold those structures were, they couldn't be any worse than the atmosphere inside the *Empress* had become since she'd reluctantly returned to Lucas. For the first day, she'd at least had the consolation that he'd need her help to protect William Donovan. But yesterday, they'd received Donovan's cable, announcing his telegrapher's treachery. Donovan was now racing to Reno to meet Lucas, so they could jointly confront Humphreys and Collins.

And after that? Well . . . She'd withdrawn behind an impenetrable shell of rigid politeness, harder and deeper than the one she'd worn after Elias's death. Her eyes and ears, even her skin seemed divorced from her brain. She ate because food was put in front of her. She'd ignored the excited planning for Humphreys's demise because it meant nothing to her.

Even when Lucas had asked her what she wished done with Collins, she'd simply shrugged and told him to do what he thought best. He would do exactly that anyway, no matter what she suggested.

Hurt had flashed through his eyes at that and she'd been briefly glad. He deserved to feel pain for having treated her—utterly betrayed her!—in the one way she couldn't tolerate. His countenance had turned as expressionless as hers and he'd bowed, before turning away.

He'd slept, these past two nights, in the bunk in the office. Everyone else tried to pretend they hadn't noticed.

A distant corner of her mind told her that her current mood was only grief and shock. But it was a tiny voice, unconnected to the vast, ravaging terror that awoke her every night screaming from nightmares when that tiny room in Ogden blurred into the cellar on Collins's Ledge . . .

She paused to draw her buffalo coat more closely around her. The winds were very bitter this morning, screaming out of the mountains as though they came directly from the North Pole. The old-timers were muttering darkly about another storm coming in before sunset. At least she was dressed for this weather, with her sturdy walking dress and flannel petticoats.

Bells were ringing, somewhere near the station, but not at the station. She dismissed them.

"Ma'am?"

She turned back to face her two escorts, surprised at their interruption, since they'd always been very patient. They'd never complained about her penchant for wandering as far as possible from station houses during stops, only occasionally getting others to help watch her, albeit at a distance.

Paul Hawkins looked around, his eyes searching the shadows. They stood on a narrow boardwalk on a side street beside a general store. It was darkly shadowed, almost an alley, yet perfectly respectable. Nobody else was in sight, probably because they had enough common sense to stay out of the weather.

Both men were wiry, weather-beaten, dark-eyed and dark-haired westerners, who clearly had guns very close to hand. His brother Peter was the taller one and slightly more talkative. "Mrs. Grainger, can we head back to the *Empress* now?"

She frowned. She'd only been away from it for fifteen minutes. "Very well."

She smiled a little wryly at him. "Sorry I lost track of time."

"That's quite all right, ma'am." Peter's lips curved in a smile meant to be reassuring, but it didn't quite reach his eyes.

An enormous knife whipped into Paul's neck from behind. He gurgled once and dropped in his tracks.

A blur of silver flashed past her head and into Peter's throat. A knife hung there, vibrating rapidly.

His eyes widened but instead of trying to pull it out and save himself—oh, dear Lord, instead of trying to save himself—he went for his gun.

Rachel was suddenly so cold she couldn't move.

Peter's breathing was liquid and bloody, but he somehow brought his Colt up, still in its holster.

A woman was screaming somewhere, long and high.

He fired his gun and black smoke blew back across his shaking hand. His eyes were barely focused and the front of his coat had turned crimson. He fired his Colt again and sank onto his knees.

Maitland Collins stepped out behind him. "You bastard, you cost us one—no, two—of our men."

People were shouting but not close enough. Someone tried to grab Rachel, but she elbowed him somehow and started to run for help.

Maitland shot Peter in the head. He crumpled over his brother, as alike in death as they'd been in life.

Rachel gasped, tears lancing through her, and slowed.

A rough-handed fellow seized her and pulled her back against him. He pressed a thick wad of cotton over her mouth, heavy with sweet-smelling chloroform, and hoisted her over his shoulder.

She tried to fight him, but her heavy skirts hampered her. Before she took her third breath, she was asleep.

The *Empress*'s dining room was ablaze with light from her chandelier and sconces, reflected from mirror to mirror until the entire room seemed on fire. Armed men stood around the walls and filled every seat at the table except one, where an elegant lady sat. Braden watched from the doorway, still every inch the old sergeant and ready to help in any way possible, with Lawson behind him. No one spoke, for words were not needed.

A whistle blew in the distance, long and lonesome, and a conductor announced his train's departure for California. Wheels clanked into motion, shaking the *Empress*. Wind rattled her windows, as though impatient to set her on her way. They had already started to howl louder and louder, strengthened by the northern storm sweeping in from Alaska. The last few days of relative warmth were over.

Lucas said a small, quiet prayer that Rachel wasn't out

there somewhere in the elements. Surely Collins had to know he needed to kill Lucas and make her a widow before he could solidify his hold on the Davis fortune.

He cleared his throat and finished his account with the worst news. It was, after all, his duty.

"Peter and Paul Hawkins are dead, although they took two of the attackers with them."

"May God rest their souls," Mrs. Donovan murmured and crossed herself. Donovan's hand tightened over hers before he echoed the silent prayer.

"Amen," went around the room.

"Donovan & Sons will, of course, look after their families," added Donovan.

Lucas nodded, recognizing the public confirmation of the popular but hard-earned corporate pension. "But with a fire in the roundhouse," he went on, "there were no locomotives available to follow the kidnappers."

"Why, those—" Viola Donovan exploded onto her feet, a deceptively fragile, blond volcano.

Her husband patted her arm. "Mrs. Donovan, we're here to decide how best to destroy them. We don't need any additional names for them."

His words were tinted with his native Ireland, an unusual sign of strong emotion. Lucas smiled faintly, almost tempted to pity Rachel's kidnappers.

She sniffed and reluctantly sat down, flipping her train out of the way with a very aggravated snap.

"A posse left immediately but they haven't reported finding anything," Mitchell added.

"Telegraphers passed the word up and down the line. No account of them there, either," Lowell finished the report from the back, where he stood against the wall into the corridor.

"Your opinion of that, Lowell? You're the only one here who's seen Mrs. Grainger, the Geiger Grade—the toll road—

and the railroad's right-of-way. You might be able to guess where they could hide her."

Lowell straightened, looking almost hesitant, and the man next to him shoved him forward. A San Francisco fellow stood up and the youngest man present sat down at the table for the first time.

"Mrs. Grainger is a slender lady and very strong," he said, obviously choosing his words carefully. "I can think of a dozen places to leave that private train and hide her, within the first ten miles. There are even more hideouts closer to the Bluebird. She's a little tall but, unfortunately, this is the perfect countryside to disappear in, especially with this wind to wipe their tracks."

There was a collective growl.

Lucas went on stonily, finishing the description of her condition. "The sheriff found the cotton they'd used to drug her. It smelled as if an entire bottle of chloroform had been poured over it."

Mrs. Donovan's eyes widened. "Oh, the poor lady!"

Men growled and guns shifted in holsters.

The cold fingers around Lucas's heart, that had been there since he'd first heard the shots fired, deepened. His darling Rachel, staggering or collapsed and in agonizing pain from that drug? People had also died from it, since it could unexpectedly stop one's heart.

Donovan's gaze flickered over him before he rose. "We'd best decide how to rescue her, lads. We know where and when one of the ruffians will appear. I'll wager we can persuade him to talk. What say you?"

A roar went up.

"I'd be glad to help." Little's calm words slipped into the quiet immediately afterward.

Lucas stared at him, shocked out of his heartache. He'd guessed his old friend had the skills to persuade even the most reluctant to speak—but to volunteer for that unpleasant task? Lowell and Mitchell wore the same expressions of shocked disbelief as he did, even though they'd only known the big Ute Indian for a few months.

Donovan's lips curved mirthlessly. "Thank you, friend. We all serve as we must."

He rose and flipped a big map open across the large dining room table for everyone to see. His wife promptly began to weigh down its corners with salt cellars and other tableware, while Lucas automatically helped her. The others crowded forward and even those seated leaned forward to see.

"This is a map showing the route from Reno to Virginia City by train. It also displays the locations of the biggest mining claims and hints at the higher mountains."

Lucas looked over it, hunting the Bluebird. Ah, there it was—south of Virginia City and Gold Hill.

Donovan's finger traced a thick black line. "The railroad's route is essentially that of a fishhook, with Reno at the top or eye, Carson City at the bottom, and Virginia City at the sharp tip. While always handsome, the engineering required for the miles from the Carson River into Virginia City is particularly breathtaking."

"Literally," Lowell muttered, which evoked some laughter.

"Humphreys, the Bluebird's manager, is expecting me shortly before lunch today, when he'll undoubtedly try something uncivilized. I don't believe he knows I'm aware of all of his plans, although he's certain I suspect he's stealing from me," Donovan went on.

"And from Mrs. Grainger," Lucas put in. "It's why we were here. She has the good fortune to be Donovan's partner."

Mitchell walked his fingers across the map, measuring distances. "Do you think she'll be at the Bluebird?"

"Humphreys is an extraordinarily clever man. It's amazing I caught his thievery," Donovan said, rather bitterly. "He's not stupid enough to be involved in kidnapping a white woman. No, that's his partner's doing—Collins."

"Who tried to kidnap her back in Omaha, remember, Mitchell?"

Lowell's face came alert. "He's the one who sabotaged the snowplow back in Laramie."

"Exactly."

Lowell slapped his leg. "He deserves killing for that alone. Two trainloads of people nearly died for it."

A horrified gasp stirred the air.

"So we need to capture them both, plus Collins's son, Maitland, who's brutalized women for years," Lucas finished.

Viola Donovan shot Lucas a sideways glance at the last statement. He met it stonily. If he ever had the chance to disembowel Maitland Collins, he'd do so gladly, just for the bastard's attack on Rachel.

"But how can we invite everyone to the party?" Donovan mused blandly.

Some dry chuckles went up at that description.

Lucas came alert, like the others. He'd never been to Virginia City before so he, too, was relying on Donovan's ability to plan.

"Reno and Carson City fall in a north-south line but the railroad track isn't straight, because of the mountains. Instead it bends sharply east at Steamboat, where you can catch the Geiger Grade over the mountains into Virginia City."

Over the mountains—on these roads with a storm coming in? The hair on Lucas's neck stood up. "One group takes the railroad and the other the toll road?" he questioned.

Donovan's face was almost expressionless. "Correct."

Lowell studied his boss, his usual blatant hero worship completely absent. "The Geiger Grade is an extremely steep road, sir, known for its high winds and snow. It's likely to be even worse than usual today."

Lucas's mouth tightened. "Which is why Humphreys won't be expecting any guests from that direction."

Donovan gave him an edged smile. "Exactly. But not many men, just enough to get onto Mount Davidson above the Bluebird. The mine's very high up, which is how she got her name."

"Sharpshooters," noted Mitchell. "I'm in."

"Yes, you'd be able to see any men leaving the Bluebird for hiding places around her. However, you could break your neck before you've gone a mile on the Geiger Grade," Donovan warned.

"I'll go," said Lucas.

"And I," added Little, almost simultaneously. They smiled at each other, old Army memories rising to the fore.

"And I," said Lowell. "You'll need a guide who's ridden the Geiger Grade before."

Other men's voices rose, but Donovan's strong tenor cut through them effortlessly. "Enough! Four men only as sharpshooters. The rest will come with me to the Bluebird's headquarters at its stamp mill, where Humphreys will have most of his crew. We won't show our hand too quickly there, either, so you too can have some fun."

Somebody chuckled, all too happily.

A smile teased the corners of Mrs. Donovan's mouth, although her hand continued to clasp her husband's.

"Any other questions?"

"How will you reach it, if she's that high on the mountain?" Lucas asked, comparing terrain, distances, and the weather.

"There's a private rail line, which runs from the main line to the stamp mill. It serves both the Bluebird and her abandoned southern neighbor, the Gold Drop—here." Donovan tapped the map.

Lucas's eyes met his old friend's in a flash of complete communion. An abandoned mine could be a very useful hiding place for blackguards.

"I'll give you a copy of this map."

"Thank you."

Donovan looked around. "Get something to eat and try to take a nap. Sharpshooters will depart within the quarter-hour."

Lucas rose, glad to finally be taking action so he could forget the terror freezing his veins whenever he thought of Rachel. Dear God in heaven, the agony of seeing the kidnappers' train disappear into the distance, while the roundhouse burned behind him, taking all hope with it . . . "We have to leave now, if we're to meet you there. The yardmaster's promised us a locomotive from Carson City, but we'll have to find horses."

"I brought some with me from California."

Lucas's hopes went up. "Some of the ones you bred?"

Viola Donovan laughed, the musical sound rippling through the air. She had her hands affectionately wrapped around her husband's arm, as though reluctant to be parted from him for even a minute. "Are there truly any others for him?"

"Not for this," Donovan admitted. "We've a depot in Virginia City and you can exchange them there, if you have the need and the time."

"Thank you." They clasped hands, silently but with real emotion. This plan had a chance of working—not much, but a little.

Rachel hid her face in her hands, praying that the headache would continue to leave her. Collins hadn't bothered to tie her, rightly figuring that the chloroform's aftermath would incapacitate her for a very long time to come.

At least it was dark in here. If she'd had to look at bright lights, such as a chandelier, the agony in her head might have exploded into full-fledged life and left her moaning on the floor, unable to do anything. As it was, she could at least sit up and notice her surroundings—and remember.

She forced back the nausea that threatened to rule her. If she could think, she could fight. Peter had fought. She owed it to him and his brother to do her best. Oh, dear God, she owed it to Lucas.

She was in a tiny, dusty room that was very cold, although not frozen. Heat was coming through the floor and there was a faint draft. Men were talking somewhere about getting up steam. Perhaps they were a locomotive's crew, even the one that had brought her here.

Villains.

Another bout of dizziness rose up but this one was smaller. She fought it down and continued trying to notice and remember everything. When she escaped, dearest Lucas would want to know where she'd been held so he could bring these brutes to justice.

He'd been right, after all, and she'd been so terribly, terribly wrong. Men had died for her arrogance. She'd thought rational discourse would rule everywhere and violence meant nothing.

Folly. Utter, complete, nonsensical folly.

He'd tried to guard her from the worst side of men and she'd given lip service to his precautions. The one time she'd treated his precautions casually because she'd been furious, villains had caught her—and killed innocent men.

She cringed, drawing into herself until her arms were clasped around her knees, and rocked herself, moaning. Dear Lord, it would be justice if she saw the two Hawkins brothers, lying on the boardwalk in their blood, every night in her dreams for the rest of her life.

Next to that, jealousy of Lucas's dead mistress and worries over his future fidelity mattered nothing.

She wanted Lucas back. She wanted him to hold her and cuddle her and tell her that the nightmares didn't matter, before kissing away the pain.

She loved him. Arrogant and high-handed though he was, he was the only man who made her heart sing. If he wasn't in her life, she'd go maimed and empty for the rest of her life—no matter how many men she could buy with Old Man Davis's money.

But how could she live with a man whose idea of showing

his love was to continually cage her, to wrap her up in cotton wool whenever a single cloud showed on the horizon? Could he give her enough room to thrive, if he was sure that she'd remain with him, unlike Ambrosia or his reckless sister?

Could she stay, whether or not he opened the doors to the cage?

Sweet Jesus, it was cold and blowing harder than Satan could have whistled up a hurricane. Lucas hunched his shoulders, grateful for the buffalo who'd given him this coat. He had the best gear in the world—buffalo coat, fur cap, felt boots, heavy mittens—and he was still freezing, while climbing to the top of Geiger Grade. The gale seemed to have a wicked eye for finding every crack and crevice, before slipping inside. If he hadn't been wearing layers as Little had taught him years ago, he'd have fallen off his horse from pure misery.

Thank God for Donovan's skills as a horse breeder, too. Mostly Morgan, part California Barb, and just enough Thoroughbred to handle Lucas's weight, the black gelding treated this unforgiving road like an interesting ride through a park. He was completely sure-footed and hadn't even shied when a tree branch broke overhead. Lucas would have given a thousand dollars for a horse like him in the cavalry.

Their little party had been the only ones on the road for the past two miles, proving the good sense of the rest of society.

Lowell's hand went up and Lucas slowed, stopping alongside him. "What is it?"

Lowell pulled down his muffler. "We can check our gear here before we begin the descent."

His usually daredevil countenance was entirely serious.

Lucas nodded. "Good idea. Rest your horses for a few minutes, too." Once they reached Virginia City at the mountain's foot, speed would be the best guarantee of surprise.

He swung down and thoroughly checked his gelding, paying particular attention to every strap and buckle. Even though every bit of tack had come out of Donovan's personal stable, this had already proven itself to be a ride for not taking chances. He gave his horse a little water, safely stored in an insulated canteen.

And he worked very hard not to think about how empty the *Empress* had seemed without Rachel in it. Facing the private Pullman where he and Rachel had been so happy, whose every inch offered up happy memories, had been agony. Such as when she'd neatly trounced him at chess and blushed so deliciously when he'd flirted with her, or moan passionately when he savored her sweet breasts. Or the delightful shock on her face the first time he'd brought her to rapture five times in one night.

But the same small box of wood, padded with velvets and silks, ornamented with carved woods and the finest crystals, also hurled bitter memories of her coldness over the past two days. Of how she'd look at him every time he opened his mouth as though she was waiting to hear how he'd lock her up again. Or how she'd draw back so not an inch of her skin or her skirts touched him. Or how her conversation was a model for deportment at a royal banquet, but nothing like the camaraderie they'd shared for so many years.

How could he return to it?

He had betrayed her trust.

If he'd done his duty, instead of flinching from how much she hated him, he'd have guarded her better today—and she wouldn't have been kidnapped.

He'd failed her, as he'd failed Ambrosia. If she died, as Ambrosia had died . . .

It was all he could do not to shout at the uncaring wind.

He glanced up gratefully when Little joined him.

"When I was a young man," Little said quietly, "I loved my wife very, very much."

Little was looking straight ahead, the lines in his face as

deep as the ones carved in the Sierras. "We were very, very passionate and we fought sometimes."

Lucas held his breath, instinctively knowing that Little had never told this story before.

"After one such fight, I went hunting in the mountains. While I was gone, another tribe attacked and kidnapped my wife, as well as others. I followed as soon as I returned, but I was too late. She had been injured in the attack and slipped off a cliff during the trip back to their camp. She was killed instantly, but I still blame myself."

He turned his head to look at Lucas, tears glinting on his cheeks. "I never returned to my people or the life my wife and I had shared. Instead I joined my mother's people and became one of their warriors, occasionally taking refuge from those memories in firewater. Now I ask you not to make the same mistake I did. Even the oak bends a little before the wind."

He inclined his head and strode off, his back straight as an arrow.

Lucas exhaled slowly, rocking back and forth on his heels, accepting the lesson.

He was in love with Rachel. He'd sworn never to fall in love again, but clear-eyed, golden Rachel had stolen his heart before he'd noticed. Quite possibly before he'd arrived in Omaha.

He knew he'd endure anything to have her come back to him. He didn't give a damn if she'd been outraged—although his revenge on the bastards who'd done it to her would be vicious. He simply wanted her alive and in his life.

Given that, what more could he offer? His pride that wouldn't let him admit mistakes—or discuss a crisis with her in advance? After all, she might have stayed in Ogden, if he'd asked her in advance. Maybe.

Most of all, he'd have to give her the freedom to live her life the way she wanted to, to go where she wanted and take the risks she wanted to. Even with the children.

He'd have to risk their lives in order to have a marriage with Rachel. Or he could do as other men did and trust them to Divine Providence, while he devoted himself to cherishing their mother in every possible way.

But he loved her and that was the only possible way to prove it to her.

He blew out a breath. The wind immediately whipped it away, tossing a few, fat snowflakes in its place.

Snow already? While the toll road had been cleared, it was still icy in places. If it snowed, they wouldn't be able to see the treacherous ground underfoot.

Little rode up, his dappled gray Appaloosa almost disappearing against the ice-shrouded rocks. "Ready?"

Lucas nodded and swung himself into the saddle. He gathered up the reins and rode forward, the others falling in behind.

They reached the lip of the road and a chance gust of wind threw itself against them. They paused instinctively and the clouds briefly opened, allowing Lucas a glimpse of the Geiger Grade. Brutally steep even with enough switchbacks to make a wagon master curse continuously, the mountain bordered it on one side but the other was a sheer plunge, which ended on rocks hundreds of feet below.

Hell and damnation, it was worse than any tale he'd ever heard, especially in this weather. If he lived through this, he'd damn well spend every day of his life doing his utmost to convince Rachel of how much he adored her, no matter how difficult.

Because this ride would be the best possible preparation.

A dry chuckle bubbled up at his own stupidity. He'd allowed his own fears to box him into a corner and lose the woman he loved.

Life was short and worth any risk, as his first sergeant had told him time and again. Sometimes the only way forward was straight ahead, if standing still would buy him nothing.

Lucas kneed his big black forward, trusting to his mountain-loving Morgan blood, with the old joy of combat singing through his veins.

The gelding's ears went back and he tucked his tail in tight, making very clear his low opinion of his rider's taste in routes.

Lucas simply slouched down in the saddle, as he'd done so many times on so many long cavalry patrols, pulled down his cap, and prayed.

The black shook his head, sending his tack ringing. He stepped out onto the Geiger Grade and began to warily pick his way down through the compacted, rutted ice.

Chapter Thirteen

The great headlight flashed across the Bluebird's stamp mill, eerily bright through the lightly falling snow, and disappeared, cut off by a fold of the mountain. They were on the mill's fourth floor, high enough that the brutal noise of crushing rock didn't ruin all conversation. It was a superbly built wooden structure, strong enough to withstand years of shaking from the dozen great stamps crushing rock below.

Looking at the office's lavish furnishings and Humphreys's diamond jewelry, Collins strongly suspected that the Bluebird's books had been cooked even more than he'd suspected. A Brussels carpet he could excuse, but just how much had it cost to buy and deliver that massive, seven-foot-tall, pier glass window? But that discussion could wait for another day, after they'd dealt with Donovan and Grainger.

Collins leaned forward to catch the last possible glimpse of the train. "Donovan is exactly on time."

"He probably had somebody watching the clock for him, to make certain." Maitland snickered.

"He is one of the most cunning businessmen of his generation. Don't make the mistake of underestimating him." Humphreys, surprisingly dapper for such a burly man, spun away from his window and faced the others. "He'll have at least one trick up his sleeve."

"But we have the greatest card of all—Rachel Davis," Collins pointed out.

"True. We just have to kill Grainger quickly so his family won't kick up a fuss. After we're done here, we'll leave from the Gold Drop mine before Donovan's friends seek vengeance."

"When I will have the opportunity to teach that bitch some manners?" Maitland purred.

Collins lifted an eyebrow at his son, wary of his blatant anticipation. "Remember—we need every man for the coming fight with Donovan. There'll be time enough for her later."

Maitland smiled charmingly and spread his hands, his wound's red seam splitting his face into an appalling demon's mask. "Of course, Father. Revenge is a dish best served cold. Very, very cold."

Rachel cautiously lifted her head. Good—both eyes were open and her spine was vertical, yet the dizziness was receding. Even better, the terrifying migraine that had made her heart stutter was now merely pain, an intense agony that lived behind her eyes. She could tolerate that for a very long time, since her blood beat strongly and steadily through her veins.

Her face was numb with cold, echoing the room's temperature, and she slowly rocked, tucking her mittened hands into her armpits for warmth. She'd long since pulled her scarf up over her mouth. Neither Collins had visited her since she'd arrived, so they'd never tied her up—not even in the beginning. They had to be wagering on that heavy dose of chloroform they'd given her.

Thankfully, he'd let her keep her buffalo coat and everything else she was wearing. Dear Braden had made her carry her mittens in an interior pocket. She'd almost certainly need them outside.

Satisfied the movement wouldn't cause any additional discomfort, she braced herself against the wall and slowly shoved herself onto her feet.

Another wave of dizziness touched her when her knees locked under her. She tensed, terrified—then forced herself to relax and breathe slowly, steadily, as Elias had taught her. He'd survived far longer than anyone had thought possible, thanks to controlling his pain far better than any of his doctors with their drugs. The multiple doors refocused into a single one and her pulse settled into its old, sober beat.

Rachel swallowed hard, setting aside that hurdle, and looked around for an escape route.

Nobody had checked on her since her arrival, at least not that she'd noticed. The locomotive crew was now loudly speculating about overtime pay, given the winter's heavy workload.

Even so, she didn't intend to walk out the single door, if she had any other choice.

The room itself held no furniture, only a few crates and some heavy tools, one of which looked like a complicated wrench. She needed two hands to hoist it experimentally; good heavens, it must have been designed to open recalcitrant valves on mining equipment.

She swung it—and had to brace herself to control it. But she could do it, enough to break a window and climb onto the roof. After, of course, cutting an "X" in the glass with her diamond-studded mourning brooch to reduce the noise.

Two very dusty, dormer windows showed a developing storm, with strong winds tossing pine needles and pine cones past. Occasionally, a gust would veil the windows in white but, so far, it hadn't started snowing. At least, not here. She had no guarantees on what the weather was like higher in the mountains.

From that side, she could faintly hear the thundering beat of great machines constantly pounding. A stamp mill, perhaps?

She leaned closer to a window and looked for her own opportunities. Here she was three stories up, with no roof until the first floor. However, the snow had drifted close to the big, wooden structure. The snow drift's edge had been sharply cut, almost turned into a wall, next to a door in the mill. Just beyond that gaped the dark mouth of a snow tunnel, its destination invisible against the white landscape.

If she stepped into it, she didn't know if she'd find herself with friends or enemies. But wasn't that the truth no matter where she went? At least she'd be somewhat safe from the elements.

Or she could try to escape through the door and find another way out. Smash through it with the wrench? She put her hand on the wood, testing its strength. It was far too heavy.

Perhaps she could unscrew the hinges, as Anglesey Hall's carpenter always did when he wanted to repair doors. But with what?

Nothing offered itself.

No, her only hope was the window. She'd have to jump out, slide down that roof, make it through that tunnel—and pray.

It was a moment's work to unpin her brooch and mark the glass, echoing one of Elias's childhood escapades. She hefted the great wrench again and smashed it against the glass, heaving it more than swinging it. The glass immediately broke into a great star and silently fell into the gale, spinning like lost spirits. She rolled the wrench over the wood, grinding it down until the edges were as smooth as possible.

The winds clawed at her face, spitting snow at her, reminding her of what was to come. Childishly, she stuck her tongue out before she dragged over a crate. She'd do whatever was necessary to escape and rejoin Lucas. One day, she'd see her mother and Mercy again, too.

Shifting the crate revealed an elegant firearms case of a distinctive size and shape, with a crate of ammunition hidden behind them. Long guns—rifles or maybe shotguns.

Maitland must have left her in the storeroom without bothering to see what else was here.

Shocked, she sank back onto her heels and began to think, harder and faster than ever before in her life.

She'd learned how to handle a shotgun years before, mainly to keep varmints away from the chickens when Old Man Davis visited his country home. He traveled light at those times and every servant had to do double—or triple—duty. It had amused Elias to make sure she retained her grasp of the basics, although she was hardly excellent.

Could she use one of these against a man?

Maitland had murdered Peter and Paul Hawkins in cold blood. This was a frontier country and she'd need something to defend herself with.

She bent her head and prayed for wisdom in using an instrument of death. Then she wrenched the lids off the two boxes, ignoring her overworked muscles' heated protests.

The long guns had been stored ready for a moment's use, not in the layers of grease needed for long storage. Even better, they included a Greener shotgun, the best of the best and the type she was familiar with.

Shotgun slung over her back, she gathered her skirts and clambered onto the crate, grateful she'd worn such a sturdy, simple promenade dress. Ruffles would not be the best companions on this journey.

Her skin was cold underneath the buffalo robe, yet her pulse was running as steady as her determination. She didn't give herself time to reconsider before she pulled herself through the window and stood up, bracing herself in the window frame. The winds battered her, cutting at her face.

An instant later, she released her grip and jumped. She thudded onto the roof, snow and woolen skirts lifting up around her, and slid down again faster. She dropped again, face first, into the drift and scrambled out as quickly as possible, gasping for breath and her heart pounding.

She crashed through the snow into the tunnel and pressed herself against the side, trying to calm down enough to listen.

Nobody sounded the alarm from within the mine building

she'd just left. A locomotive somewhere close by was peace-fully turning over, as if ready to leave on a moment's notice. Probably for Maitland and Collins.

Beyond the tunnel and the area immediately around the mine, the snow lay six feet deep, far too deep for her to walk through without snowshoes.

The only way to go was straight ahead, through the snow tunnel. A faint light glimmered deep within, probably thanks to the shreds of daylight being filtered through the snow. It was enough to see by, but not enough to remove its resemblance to the cellar on Collins's Ledge.

Rachel gulped and brought her Greener to the ready. Gritting her teeth, she turned away from the mine and started walking.

Lucas shifted forward another inch. Little moved with him, matching every flex of hips and thighs. Not an ounce of snow tumbled down the mountainside.

While exhilarating in a fashion that he'd no desire to experience again, the damn ride down Geiger Grade had taken longer than he would have liked. They'd left the horses a few miles north of here with a friend of Lowell's, who'd grinned happily upon seeing him. He'd also provided four fine pairs of snowshoes, which had brought them quickly and silently over the last leg.

They'd arrived here above the Bluebird thirty minutes later than planned. Donovan was due any minute. If Humphreys had sharpshooters, they were already present—and ready to kill Donovan.

Their position was high on Mount Davidson, naked on a particularly barren slope, and one false move could betray them or start an avalanche. Ten feet away, Lowell was tucked behind a boulder, sighting in landmarks. Twenty feet back, Mitchell had silently killed Humphreys's only sentry and was now tucking him into someplace invisible until the weather settled down.

If it ever did, given that the wind was now blowing fast enough to wipe out a man's tracks within five minutes. Snow trickled insidiously down Lucas's neck and sought new places to nestle inside his wrists. But he was warm enough to fight—warmer than he'd been in the Army—with his woolen balaclava to protect his face and his double layer of gloves and mittens. He was also grateful he'd been out hunting several times with Little back in Colorado so this wasn't his first trip of the season on snowshoes. Otherwise, every leg muscle would be aching from lifting the damn things and his hips from keeping them wide apart. But they were absolutely silent, a deadly advantage when hunting men.

Little mimed a bird's wings and pointed at a burst of light below, which matched thundering noise.

Lucas nodded. The Bluebird Mine with Donovan's train sweeping its headlight across the landscape. It turned suddenly to Lucas's left—on the north—darkening the great beam, before it reappeared again, pointing at the Bluebird. The private track coming up from the main line to the Bluebird and the Gold Drop was a Y-shape, with a deep gorge at the base of the "Y," just before it reached the main line. Even for a mountain railway, it was an extraordinarily twisting piece of track. An engineer would have to stay very alert to keep his train on that line.

Lucas frowned, tracing the railroad track to the south. Had he seen embers floating into the sky there, near the Gold Drop? Perhaps light coming from a window?

Yes! A train was waiting there, hidden on the Gold Drop's southern side and out of sight from the Bluebird. Only Lucas's position high on the mountain had let him spot it. That must be how Collins and Humphreys planned to escape after killing Donovan, since he had numerous friends in this town.

A frigid gust blasted him, swirling snow over him and Little. He wiped it away and caught a flicker of movement, of red and black checks against dark boulders. The man shifted again, revealing a rifle trained on the railroad tracks leading up the Bluebird.

Lucas's eyes met Little's. Humphreys had at least one sharpshooter.

Another man stretched briefly, pushing his arm out to one side. Humphreys's second sharpshooter.

Were there any others? They'd need to take them out within another minute or so, even if that brought down a hornet's nest on their heads.

Lucas glanced around. Lowell was in place, prepared to shoot down anyone who came out of the Bluebird after them. Mitchell had disappeared into his spot, higher on the mountain and ready to cover them all.

He looked back down at the Bluebird, ready to start the attack.

But a tall, slender man slipped out of a door on the south side, where Lucas could clearly see him. He was superbly dressed, in a fur coat that a Russian nobleman would have been proud of.

Maitland Collins? What the hell was that devil up to now?

He glanced around secretively, as if making sure no one was watching, and vanished into a snow tunnel. He must have locked up Rachel at the Gold Drop, the next mine south, damn him.

Lucas's hands tightened, desperate to rend the smiling bastard into a thousand pieces. He ground his teeth and fought himself. He could not run after Maitland now. If he did so, Humphreys's sharpshooters would be alerted and dive for cover, no doubt emerging in time to kill Donovan. He had to stay here long enough to do his duty and fulfill his mission, no matter what his heart screamed at him.

The train's headlight flashed again.

The first sharpshooter was in position, ready to fire at the small depot in front of the Bluebird. The second one had an even better line on Donovan's arrival.

Lucas took aim. Little did the same at his side.

The train's whistle blew, the sound echoing around the mountain.

The wind dropped away in the same instant, as though blessing Lucas's choice.

Lucas immediately fired and Little did the same, the shots blending into the whistle's notes.

The would-be assassins slumped forward onto their rocks, crimson trickling onto the snow.

Donovan's train chugged into sight, bell clanging and wheels screeching.

Lucas waited tensely, desperate to see how soon he could go after Maitland.

William stepped down from his private car, the whistle's last echoes dying around the high valley. He kept his head high, waiting for any more shots than the two he'd counted, his pulse steady.

Time stretched and snapped back to normal when the Bluebird office door opened.

Grainger had taken out two sharpshooters. Would there be treachery inside? His lip curled. Very likely.

Best to get this affair over with quickly. He'd promised to return to Viola this evening. This was the first time—and the last, if he'd anything to say about it—that he'd ever leave her for a fight.

He strolled forward, smiling, as dapper as could be in his finest London tailoring, fresh bought on his honeymoon less than a year ago.

Humphreys offered him a hand, beaming across his face. Sweet singing Jesus, where had the man gotten the money for a sable coat? The Bluebird on her best days had never paid that much, especially not to her manager.

William shook the traitor's hand. "A pleasure to see you again, Humphreys."

He deliberately didn't introduce the two men with him, treating them as secretaries not worthy of names. And he certainly wouldn't mention the others hidden aboard his private car and its baggage car.

"It's been far too long," Humphreys agreed. "Donovan, this is Albert Collins, principal trustee for the Davis Trust."

William kept his gaze polite and his greeting cordial. If he had to choose whether to turn his back on Collins or Humphreys, he'd probably pick Humphreys—a choice he wouldn't have made five minutes ago. But Collins was deadly, both in intelligence and physical presence. Even more troubling, something angry and dark paced behind his eyes which seemed to have nothing to do with William. He was quiet after the initial exchange, allowing Humphreys to take the conversational lead—and William would have wagered a month's income that Collins deferred to no man. His eyes strayed south occasionally, ignoring Humphreys's smooth offerings of liquid refreshments once inside his office.

The hairs on the nape of William's neck stirred. Grainger was free to leave his post on the mountainside, once all of Humphreys's sharpshooters had been dispatched.

But what the devil else was going on out there?

If she ever built her own house, every room would be as large as possible. At least every room that she entered.

Rachel took another step and another, careful to do so as quietly as possible. The air here was cool with a crisp bite to it whenever she came close to a tunnel wall. She guessed that there were several feet of snow above, all shimmering and reflecting light into the tunnel.

The inside was uncommonly still, as though time itself had stopped. Every sound was magnified, until even her skirts brushing against the wall had sounded like an army. She'd finally chosen to walk down the center, where she could move almost silently. She suspected that men's boots would sound uncommonly loud. Heaven knows they'd left tracks.

The floor was covered by a soft layer of snow, which

showed every step that anyone had ever taken. Humphreys's men had apparently been carrying heavy goods out of the Gold Drop for months. Was that mine still capable of producing? At this moment, did she care? Not in the least, especially when she was still close to the Gold Drop.

Footsteps echoed through the snow tunnel, moving hard and fast from the Bluebird. Their owner was whistling. Maitland.

Rachel stiffened, goosebumps running up and down her skin.

Two more sets were walking toward her—from the other end.

Oh dear Lord, she was trapped.

Maitland came around a curve in the snow tunnel and stopped. He smiled silkily and the raw red line clawed his cheek. His eyes glittered in the eerie blue light above the Colt in his hand, pointed so steadily at her. "Good evening, Mrs. Davis."

Rachel straightened her spine. "Mrs. Grainger," she corrected him, looking down her nose.

He sneered, which did the most appalling things to his face. "Mrs. Collins-to-be."

No matter what he looked like, it was only justice for how he'd behaved to her, to her sister, and to all the maids. To say nothing of murdering the Hawkins brothers . . .

He strolled toward her, still holding the gun. The other men were running now.

She brought the shotgun up to her shoulder. "It's loaded and cocked."

He laughed, its evil confidence echoing through the tunnel. "You'll never be able to look a man in the eyes and kill him."

Her hand trembled. Oh dear heavens, was he right?

"I saw you murder Peter Hawkins and leave him to drown in his own blood." She'd have nightmares about that for years.

He waved off her accusation with his free hand. "You

owed me that for this face. Do you know how many women this scar will cost me?"

Was that all murder meant to him? The saving grace of anger steadied her. Time slowed until she could hear each individual beat of her heart, feel every compression of her lungs.

"Murderer," she whispered.

He rolled his eyes. "What do I care? But if you grovel well, I may allow you to live six months after the child is born."

Quick as thought, she raised her shotgun and blasted both barrels into the tunnel's roof over Maitland's head. It shattered into a thousand pieces, raining ice shards over him in a crystalline dance. The deep boom echoed up and down the long, dark stretch. It rang through her head and shook her bones, staggering her.

Light flooded in for an instant. In the center, Maitland stared at her, his mouth open and his eyes wide with shock and horror.

She backed away instinctively.

Before he could move, an ocean of snow flooded over him, burying him to his knees, then his shoulders and his head. His shot went wild, into the sky, its report outweighed by the thunderous avalanche of snow. Drowning him, as he'd drowned Peter and Paul Hawkins.

Now he could answer to Divine Providence for his crimes. The footsteps slammed to a halt behind her.

She spun around, frantically fumbling in her pocket for shells. Heaven help her, she needed to reload . . .

Two men glared at her, both of them aiming Colts at her. One of them spat a stream of tobacco juice at the pristine wall. "Should we kill her now or take her to the boss?"

"Now. She's obviously a threat."

The color drained from her face, but she kept her head up.

A rifle spat twice in quick succession from somewhere over her head. The two guards fell forward, neat holes drilled in their foreheads.

Rachel choked and spun around, finally getting the shells into her shotgun. Surely if she stayed calm, her stomach would relax. This was the West, not Boston. She had to be strong, if she was to live here with Lucas. Somehow.

As if her thoughts had created him, his beloved voice spoke. "Rachel! My God, I died a thousand deaths when the ground collapsed before me and I saw you."

He dropped into the tunnel and wrapped his arms around her, holding her as tightly as in an iron vise.

She clung to him, allowing herself to shake for the first time. Even the damp buffalo fur of his coat was precious. "I thought I'd never see you again."

He kissed the top of her head. "I have to take you to safety."

"Yes, of course." She gripped her shotgun, ready to go with him.

He raised an eyebrow. "No arguments?"

Tears touched her eyes. "None. You were right to have always been so protective."

His mouth twisted. "You're generous—but we can speak more later. Come along; I'm putting you on the train."

William strode out into the stamp mill. If he had to choose one place to cause trouble anywhere in a silver mine, it would be here. The immense building was a single large room, with a forty-foot ceiling and floored as superbly as any ballroom. A half-dozen square openings in the floor allowed great columns of steam to rise to the ceiling, like Aladdin's genie.

The great crushers stood on the highest platform. Taller than a man, they were able to reduce the hardest rock into fist-sized chunks. The next platform contained a row of half-ton stamps, which smashed the chunks into a fine paste using water. Finally the vanners, amalgamating pans with their deadly liquid mercury and other chemicals, settling tanks, and boilers each had their separate platforms and played their own roles in chemically separating the ore from worthless rock.

The Bluebird's second greatest resource, after her silver ore, was the spring which allowed her to perform all these steps on her own premises—unlike the other mines which had to haul their ore down to the Carson River.

None of the platforms, nor the steps between them, had railings, of course. Like the tunnels and shafts inside the mountain, a stamp mill was a place where the devil took the hindmost.

The day shift had ended just after William's arrival and no later shift had started, making the big room an eerily quiet place for someone used to the typical earsplitting din. Only a few men were present, who looked chosen as much for fighting ability as for mining.

William, Humphreys, and Collins had first inspected one of the hoisting shafts. They were still standing near the steam vent which marked it, just as a vent marked every shaft. Collins was with Humphreys and William but he was lagging well behind, away from the steam vent. He looked around and turned back, quickly disappearing outside. A sturdy man who'd had an earlobe torn off in a fight followed him a few minutes later.

Blessed Mary preserve him, may Grainger have eyes in the back of his head for that devil's doings.

"Here's a sample of that new ore I was talking about," Humphreys remarked. He handed William a chunk of rock, which one of his men brought down from the stampers. "What do you think of that rich strip of blue muck running through it?"

William lifted a quizzical eyebrow and looked at the rock more closely. Unlike gold which was much easier for amateurs to test, neither the color nor the thickness of the muck told everything about the amount of raw silver in a chunk of ore.

Silver ore varied a great deal in color and its color usually matched its origin. Comstock silver ore was usually blue and softer than most region's ore.

But this chunk wasn't. It had more gold running through it and the silver streaks were narrower and harder. It looked like a rich grade of Arizona silver ore, not Nevada.

"Hmm, very interesting," he said noncommittally.

His two men came alert. One of them edged toward the door. The other moved upstairs.

Humphreys tilted his head, never having heard him use that expression before. "Do you like it?"

"I haven't seen anything exactly like it here before," William said truthfully. The Donovan & Sons' man closest to the door mimed needing to relieve himself and slipped outside. The other one had his back against the wall, in an excellent location to cover the room. "What did you want to do with it?"

"Send it to hell."

He grabbed William by the waist and shoved, striving to throw him through the five-foot opening and down the two thousand-foot drop. Quick as lightning, William hooked his foot around the other's ankle and heaved, catching him off balance and throwing him. They both rolled away from the vent and the fight was on, going at each other like the skilled wrestlers they both were.

From the corner of his eye, William could see several of Humphreys's men, who'd been peacefully handling equipment and mildly displaying pieces of rock, charge the Donovan & Sons' man by the wall. Another fight started, while others of Humphreys's men laid bets on the outcome.

Then the door opened and a wedge of Donovan & Sons' men charged in, shouting, "Donovan! Donovan!"

The melee was on, fought amid the great vats, between the platforms, and up and down the stairs with men taking advantage of every bit of cover, every difference in elevation to use blades or fists or feet against another. Few bullets were fired, not with so many allies nearby and so many vats full of mercury.

William had little time to watch, for he was in one of the best fights of his life, with every dirty trick completely acceptable. He was panting and bloody by the end, circling the steam vent with his father's dirk in one hand.

Humphreys feinted but William countered, not allowing himself to be tricked into taking that great plunge.

The bastard was tiring now, his reflexes slower. William parried and twisted the other man's wrist, then released and stepped back away from the opening.

His enemy staggered backward. One foot found nothing and his hands went up, searching for something to hang onto.

William watched, unmoved. It would take time and a considerable sum to restore safety to the Bluebird's operating conditions, given what he'd seen in the hoisting shaft and elsewhere.

A dread realization flashed into Humphreys's eyes. He fell screaming, seared even as he plummeted.

William crossed himself. He'd light a candle and have a Mass said for the man's soul at the first chance. It was a great pity to see greed destroy such a fine engineer.

The melee was growing quiet, with Humphreys's men either surrendering or dead. The ones beyond caring were laid out in a corner.

Little, Grainger's friend, dragged another corpse in and stretched him out with the rest. It was the fellow with the torn earlobe who'd followed Collins out of the room.

Mitchell carefully washed himself up at the spring. If William knew anything about that Virginian, he'd done twice as much fighting as most and showed it half as much.

Lowell climbed down from the ceiling, where he'd obviously defeated somebody on the four-foot-wide beam which spanned its length.

William shook his head and laughed ruefully. Jesus, Mary, and Joseph, would the lad ever grow up? Did he really want to see the day when that happened?

A man screamed outside, like a soul in direst agony.

Grainger? Collins? William couldn't put a name to its author. Ice ripped into his veins.

Chapter Fourteen

Lucas treated the unsettling echoes like ill-advised dinner table conversation—something to be ignored.

"Gentlemen, please allow me to explain a few matters." Lucas smiled at the locomotive crew, his rifle held prominently in front of him.

They stared at him from the engine cab, clearly considering him a dangerous nuisance. "Which are?" the engineer growled.

"Being men of sense, you heard the gunshots and have decided to make your departure."

Two short nods answered him.

"But I suspect you earlier brought my wife here against her will." Lucas's voice was silky soft.

"We would not!" "Never!" the men shouted back.

Rachel stepped out from behind the shed and carefully walked to Lucas's side, trying not to slip and lose her balance on the ice. The wind was blowing almost hard enough to push her over, certainly enough to numb her face if she was outdoors for any amount of time. The storm had finally decided to deliver snow, instead of merely tossing it over the landscape.

"You?" "Your wife?" Their voices mimicked surprise.

"You read the cables," Lucas reminded them, his voice laced with steel. "You know a woman was kidnapped."

There was a very unhappy silence.

"What do you want?" the engineer demanded.

"If you take my wife and me back to Virginia City, your participation will be forgotten."

"We were hired . . ."

"*Now* or there's no deal."

They grumbled but acquiesced. "Very well. Use the private car at the rear," the engineer added.

Lucas inclined his head. "Thank you," he said ironically.

He handed Rachel up the stairs and into the small palace car. It was elegantly equipped in a very masculine style with an abundance of brass, including brass spittoons at every aisle seat. But she was given no time to compare it to the *Empress*.

The train jerked into motion an instant later, sending Rachel into an undignified heap in a chair. Still, she automatically tucked her mittens safely into her coat. The train's whistle blew loudly, peremptorily warning all comers of its approach, underlined by the loud clanging of its bell.

Lucas caught himself on the chair's back before swinging himself into a chair across the aisle from her.

Rachel glanced at her husband. She'd left her shotgun on the settee closest to them, as had he, although he still had his Colt. "Virginia City?"

He shrugged, packing his cap and mittens into his coat. Like her, he hadn't taken off his coat in the chilly palace car. "It's only a few miles away and you can stay with the Donovan & Sons' staff there. I can return in a few minutes to help Donovan."

She nodded, determined not to ask any more questions. God forbid he tell her that she'd have to stay in another cell.

The train's wheels whirred, not the usual comforting rumble. It leaned into a corner—and moved faster, instead of slowing down. Someone ran along the roof overhead.

"Brakeman?" Rachel queried.

Lucas nodded, although his face turned still and harsh.

The train stretched for another corner and slowed slightly this time. But the wheels still weren't turning properly, only sliding like a sleigh. The brakes were working somewhat but not the wheels—on an icy, twisty, downhill track during a winter storm.

A great whistle blew in the distance, long and deep, followed by a bell.

But if their train could stop before they reached the junction, they'd be safe.

Rachel reached out her hand to take Lucas's.

The rear door was wrenched open, revealing a wild-eyed Collins. He pointed a Colt at them, as though he'd rather use it than take his next breath.

"You!" He spat on the floor toward Rachel. "You killed my boy."

Lucas made a convulsive movement for his gun before his hand dropped away.

Rachel's throat closed, understanding what he couldn't say and would probably never explain. He would never take the slightest chance that she might be harmed. No matter what, she'd have to make the first move. *Oh, dear.*

Collins stepped inside, balancing himself easily against the jolting, swaying car. He was, after all, a sailor and accustomed to similar terrifying conditions.

Ahead, brakes screamed but the train still slid through the next corner and gathered speed. Surely their brakes would work soon and keep them from being crushed by the larger train. Or worse, derailing . . .

"You will both die," Collins announced conversationally.

"What about the Davis fortune?" Rachel suggested desperately. She'd marry any demon to save Lucas.

Collins shook his head, tears slowing tracking down his cheeks. "Nothing matters now except seeing you two in hell, for destroying my boy. It'll be a slow death so you'll both know what's happening and why."

Not now, not when she had a chance of telling Lucas how much she loved him . . .

Collins tossed several lengths of rope at Rachel. "Tie him to the arms and legs of his chair with these."

Rachel gathered them up and squatted down before Lucas, her back to Collins. Their eyes met and his were oh, so very frustrated and angry.

She smiled at him reassuringly and glanced significantly down at the carpet beside him.

He frowned briefly before his eyes widened, an expression of purest agony appearing in them.

She'd just told him she planned to attack Collins—and he'd have to sit still.

She waited. If he moved first, her plan wouldn't work. If he did so, they had little chance that she could see.

He nodded curtly, a display of trust so pure and hard-won that her heart fell completely into his hands, without reserve.

"What the hell are you waiting for?" thundered Collins and came closer

What the hell, indeed?

Rachel leaned into the aisle, her skirts hiding her deeds from Collins. She picked up the brass spittoon by one handle—a full one, thank heavens for lazy housekeepers—and spun around, hurling it into Collins's face.

He staggered back, hands flying to his eyes, and cursed.

Rachel quickly fell prone, out of Lucas's way.

He leaped out of his chair and attacked their enemy—ignoring his Colt, probably to protect her from a wild shot on this madly rocking train. They managed to draw their knives, but lost them all too soon. Bare hands were more useful, given the need to fight for balance at the same time.

So they fought together like lions, clawing and gouging at each other. They rolled around on the floor and were thrown back and forth against the tufted, carved furniture while the train moved faster and faster. All of the spittoons rolled around the floor in an unholy mess.

Rachel fumbled onto her knees and crawled away from the fight, determined not to handicap Lucas. She found herself near the rear door and the guns, but couldn't get off a shot at Collins without hitting Lucas.

The great train's headlight was growing larger and larger, its light brighter and brighter as it flashed more and more frequently into the car. Its long, deep whistle sounded again and again.

Their train's whistle answered, bleating terrified echoes into the night. Their car's rear door was banging an agitated accompaniment. The brakes screeched repeatedly before giving up with one, last agonized scream. The brakeman shouted a warning and jumped, his voice trailing off. The train was moving so rapidly everything outside was a single, continuous blur. The crew shouted something as well before they, too, leaped.

They couldn't stop the train. It would either derail on this icy, curving track or be run over by the larger train, which was coming downhill and couldn't easily stop.

The great train's headlight shone into the private car, setting the crimson upholstery ablaze with light.

Lucas hurled a punch into Collins, making the older man stagger back for an instant. "Jump, Rachel. Jump now!"

She gulped and obeyed him. All he'd ever asked of her was unquestioning obedience. Difficult as it was in this minute, she gave him that gift.

Rachel had done exactly what he said! For an instant, Lucas was uplifted by shock and insane joy. Would he have the pleasure again? Only if he dealt with Collins.

Stronger than he'd been before, he hit the bastard in the gut.

Collins staggered and fell onto the settee yet again, as he'd done so many times before.

But this time, instead of trying to stay aboard and continue the fight, Lucas dove forward down the aisle, heading toward the back door and ignoring the spittoons. He caught the frame and pulled himself up to his feet, inches away from the open air and Rachel.

The train careened around another corner, moving faster and faster. The bigger train's headlight was as bright as high noon in the Arizona desert.

Lucas looked back at Collins down the length of the palace car.

The older man stared at him, his face battered and bleeding, death walking in his eyes. He started to stagger forward, every finger curled into a claw.

Lucas turned his back on that frozen, angry stubbornness, stepped onto the platform, and leaped into he knew not what—except that it was his only chance of life.

He tumbled end over end into the snow, immediately blinded by the fine, white crystals. They pounded him and softened him, all at the same time, until he came to rest in what seemed an enormous, frozen sand dune. He cupped his hands in front of his mouth and shoved the snow away, using the same motion he'd use for swimming.

To his utter relief, the darkness fell away and the frozen gale greeted him, blasting the rest of the snow from his body. He fought his way out, ignoring any soreness.

He'd managed to land on the last stretch of somewhat level ground before the deep, narrow canyon.

The great train's whistle blew again, almost deafening him, and its wheels screeched, shooting sparks over the white slopes.

The smaller train ignored it, cinders flying out of its smokestack as if it were racing to hell. In the palace car, Collins was standing erect, his head held high.

Despite everything he knew, Lucas took a step forward to warn the man.

The track dropped and curved, marking the start of the slope down to the main line and the gorge's lip. The engine jumped forward, as if eager for the challenge—and derailed.

It crashed into the canyon, dragging its tender and the palace car with it. Metal tore and screamed as if human. It bounced from boulder to boulder, before smashing into the base with a boom that almost sent Lucas to his knees. Black smoke burst out the canyon, licked by crimson flames.

Lucas edged forward and looked down. The gorge had become a fire pit, full of twisted, burning metal. No one could have lived through it.

"Lucas!" Rachel ran at him, half-stumbling through the drifts.

He spun and caught her to him, pulling her away from the canyon's edge. Praise the Lord she was safe.

He managed not to read her a lecture about running in avalanche-prone snow near canyons. All of that was unimportant when she was in his arms with her hair teasing his throat.

The freight train's crew finally arrived, exclaiming over the madman who'd ridden the runaway train into the gorge, and the time for private conversation was over.

Lucas slid farther down into the *Empress*'s enormous bathtub, grateful for the miracle of modern plumbing which had erased the spittoons' reek. Even Rachel had barely tolerated being near him after the reunion's first joyous rush had worn off. He could have ignored the myriad aches and pains from that ride or the dive onto the mountainside. But he had to admit that soaking them out was a pleasure.

He'd returned from the Bluebird less than an hour ago, together with Rachel and Donovan. The tall Irishman had barely waited for their train to slow down before he'd been running toward his wife, while she'd hurled herself at him heedless of bitter weather or onlookers. Rachel had nestled closer to Lucas as they watched, and he'd wondered how much she'd fancy such an uninhibited greeting. After that, they'd retired to the *Empress* where she'd chosen the smaller bathroom near the other staterooms, insisting that he'd need the largest one possible.

It was nearly midnight now and the Reno rail yard was remarkably quiet. Even the whistles and bells of passing trains sounded friendly, like neighbors calling to say hello. In the distance, a heavy train rumbled past, passing a pleasant vibration onto the *Empress*.

Like the rest of the master suite, the bathroom was an exotic fantasy—this one inspired by a Russian bathhouse. Brilliantly colored tiles in a wild variety of small, intricate birds, animals, and flowers covered the floor and every wall up to shoulder height. Above that, red damask swept over the walls and ceiling. Soft, hand-knotted rugs were scattered across the floor, while the temperature was cozily warm, thanks to the red and black stove in the corner.

He crossed his arms behind his head, plotting the best way to convince Rachel to stay with him. Surely she'd enjoy a trip to Yosemite, that legendary valley. Once there, he could talk to her—or seduce her . . .

The doorknob clicked.

Lucas cocked an eyebrow. Had she sent Braden in with some clothing?

The door swung open and Rachel peeked in. She wore a black silk robe belted around her waist, which emphasized her skin's purity and the narrowness of her waist. Her chestnut hair was pinned loosely atop her head, allowing a few curls to caress her neck. He'd swear that she wore nothing else—certainly not a corset.

His breath hitched, almost audibly. His cock promptly, predictably, swelled with approval.

Her amber eyes were a little nervous. "May I join you?"

"Certainly." He started to sit up, wondered if he should be respectable and not display his reaction to her, and decided he didn't give a damn.

He reclined against the bathtub's rim and smiled encouragingly. This would be easier if he could start by seducing her.

She drew up a stool beside him and sat down. "More champagne to celebrate with? Or would you prefer something else?"

He'd barely had two sips from his first glass, but now that she was here, he'd certainly change his attitude. "Champagne, of course."

They toasted each other and drank the bubbling gold wine, her eyes heavy-lidded and sensual.

But she caught his wrist when he started to bring the fragile crystal back toward the tray. He cocked his head inquiringly.

Her slender fingers were trembling as they touched the long bruise on his arm where he'd bounced down the hillside. "You were right to have made me stay in Ogden."

"But I should have tried to discuss it with you more."

She shrugged that off. "I'm as stubborn as you are; I wouldn't have listened to you, no matter how long you talked."

He nearly laughed, recognizing the truth in that.

"But, mostly, I should have trusted your wisdom from the start. If I had, the Hawkins brothers would still be alive." Her golden eyes were damp.

"Dammit, Rachel, you can't blame yourself for everything."

His throat tightened. He set his glass down on the tile floor and swept her into his arms, silk robe and all.

She gasped but held on, barely managing to kick off her slippers before they, too, were wet. "Lucas," she protested unconvincingly.

He ran his thumb over her cheek. "Collins and Maitland were devious, ruthless men, darling, who were determined to steal you. They burned the Reno roundhouse, simply to stop any pursuers. Until Donovan arrived, it was very hard to outmatch them."

"Do you really think so?" Hope started to flower in her expression.

He nodded firmly, unwilling to admit to himself just how much truth there unfortunately was. "Yes, I'm sure. The Hawkins brothers' deaths are not entirely your fault."

She sniffed and laid her head against his damp shoulder, her curls tickling his chin, ignoring her damp silks—and the swell of his cock against her. "Thank you. If nothing else, I avenged them."

"And very neatly indeed." He crooned to her softly, trying to ignore his racing pulse.

"So much lost," she muttered. "To think all of this started when Elias died."

"I know you married Davis for love . . ."

She sat bolt upright and gaped at him. "Love? Good God, no!"

"But he always behaved as though it was a love match," Lucas protested. "Why else would he have married you?"

She shrugged, visibly selecting her words before she began to speak. "I'd nursed Elias ever since he returned from the War and his wounds didn't disturb me. An attachment developed on his side during that time, and it grew."

"But not on yours," he probed. She'd never *loved* Davis? There might be hope for him.

She shook her head. "No. I liked him very well as a friend, but I never desired more. Then he proposed." She hesitated before continuing. "Our fathers persuaded me that I was the only woman he'd ever marry. Everyone knew that his remaining time would be very short. Elias's father was concerned about protecting the Davis assets, such as the bank accounts, horses, and great books. But my father . . . He convinced me that the Davis family servants I'd grown up with, my friends and family, could best be protected if I became Elias's wife and heir."

Lucas dared to rub her arms lightly, reassuring her—and gentling her again to his touch. "You believed him."

She nodded firmly, her face graven. "Father was entirely

correct. Otherwise, the trustees would have turned them off within a week of Elias's funeral. And Elias did better with me than with anyone else. If I'd walked away—and his health had worsened—I would never have forgiven myself. It was more than enough to trade a few years of my life for—and I found a few joys with Elias, as well."

His shoulders suddenly seemed to stand a foot taller, even though he was in the tub. He shook his head, throwing off the last of an old burden. "I love you, Rachel."

Her great eyes widened, turning as golden as a cat's. The wet silk highlighted her lovely figure and he forced himself to look up at her face.

"You don't have to say that." But she caressed his cheek, even as she spoke.

"It's God's own truth, darling. I don't know how not to hold you fast and tight—and God knows I'll probably watch over our children as though they were the only ones ever born on this earth. But I swear I'll work to let you do what you want, to go where you choose, and take chances as you please, if you'll only stay with me. And I promise to discuss matters with you, as my most trusted partner."

Joy glinted in her eyes. "I vow to always adore you and cherish you. I, too, promise to talk to you, especially when I believe the subject is difficult."

He caught her face between his hands. "My beloved wife."

Tears glimmered on the tips of her lashes. "I will do my best to be a good wife to you and to be strong enough for this frontier country. I want our children to grow up here, not in Boston where a man's future depends on his father's."

He could have jumped out of the tub and capered around the bathroom like a fool. "Thank God. I'd have lived there for you, but I'd rather build our lives here."

She laughed, the sound soft and musical like bells showing the way home through an early winter snowstorm. "My dear northern devil, would I ask you to be anywhere except the

West? Just promise me that you'll come home every night to me and our children."

"Every night, always." He kept their kiss gentle, gliding his tongue over her mouth in a symbol of sealing their new vow.

She gave a soft moan and leaned forward, caressing his shoulders. His tongue teased the seam of her lips and she sighed again, kissing and playing with him in a sweet dance.

"Can we try to make a child tonight, Lucas?"

He frowned. "Weren't we before?"

"But this time—because we love each other, not to silence some lawyers?"

She ran her tongue over her lip, looking more adorable than any dozen women had any right to. If he could have reached up into the heavens and brought down the moon for her personal enjoyment, he'd have done so.

"Of course we can, my darling." He'd simply have to learn how to be a good parent according to her terms.

He kissed her again, more intensely, pushing aside the future trial for the current pleasure. He lingered over it, enjoying the luxury of time with her, the hedonism of hot water, soft gaslight to watch her by . . .

Best of all was the knowledge that they could do this tomorrow and tomorrow and tomorrow . . .

She purred his name and stretched against him, rubbing herself over him like a cat, stroking him with her breasts and nipples until he groaned, heat spinning through him. Her silk robe might not have been there for all the distance it put between their skins.

One day, he'd feel his child's heartbeat there, just as clearly.

Water danced, exploring the tub's limits.

His nerves sang with exactly how taut her breasts were, how curved her stomach, how strong her thighs. He untied her robe and pulled it down her arms, the better to stroke her shoulders and kiss them.

She tossed her head back and laughed, sending ripples of joy through the room like the sun glinting on spring snow, while it melted

Lucas chuckled with her, more than willing to share anything that gave her pleasure—and deliberately pulled her robe completely off her.

She stretched her arms around his neck, nuzzled his throat, and stroked herself even more lasciviously over him.

Water splashed over the side.

He groaned and ran his hands down her back, his fingertips gliding over her spine and shaping her fine rump. Ravishing, oh so very ravishing.

Her sweet folds rippled around his cock, pinned between her thighs.

She moaned happily.

He almost came, fire lancing from his groin through his chest.

He gasped, reaching for some shred of logic. He could enjoy playing with a woman as much as any man. But this would never do, not for making babies.

He abruptly grasped her by her hips, making her kneel in the tub. He sat upright with his legs crossed, sending water hurtling out of the tub.

She choked.

An instant later, he lifted her up high, slipped his hands under her thighs, and brought her down across him—and astride his cock. He simultaneously wrapped her legs around his hips and bathwater exploded toward the ceiling.

She moaned and her eyes slid half-shut, arching in anticipation. "Oh yes please, Lucas."

He bared his teeth in pure masculine triumph

Slowly, oh so very slowly, savoring every fine, delicious sensation of fiery hot cock sliding into tight wet channel, he slid into her.

She moaned again and again, helping him, her inner flesh kissing him. He lifted her up and down, down and up, water wildly sloshing across the floor with every beat and her sweet voice chanting his name.

Where ice had once lived in him with the stern determination never to think about who he was with, now his cock tightened every time a chestnut curl touched the water—because she'd tossed her head in passion—or her golden eyes glazed in anticipation.

He burned for her, through her, with her.

His balls were fat and heavy, orgasm a hairsbreadth away. Yet still he delayed beyond the bounds of reason, because she hadn't reached hers.

He toyed with her pearl, coaxing it in just the manner she preferred.

She arched again, her fingers digging into his shoulders, and climaxed on a long ecstatic sob.

Instantly, he matched her, going blind as he filled her womb with his seed, the world as golden as her eyes. Rapture—and definitely the taste of heaven . . .

San Francisco, Christmas Eve 1873

Outside, the heavy winds and rain pounded at the windows of the fashionable new mansion. But inside, the big kitchen was filled with a dozen people and the enticing scents of melting butter, molasses, and pure sugar. The enormous central table was covered with square pans, each one thoroughly buttered. Some of them were full of delectable taffy, looking like spun gold under the shimmering gaslight.

Both Lawson and Braden were enveloped in once-white aprons, now much touched by flour, butter, and molasses. Lawson stood at the stove, giving careful attention to the boiling pot of taffy he was stirring. Braden bustled around, providing the eternal flow of small supplies to the partygoers.

T.L. Grainger—Lucas's father—and Portia Townsend—

Viola Donovan's niece—were assembling a gingerbread house at a small table near the butler's pantry. He'd arrived that afternoon, laden with gaudily wrapped packages, and looking surprisingly anxious under his urbane mask.

But the longer he sat with Portia, the more he relaxed and the more genuine his laughter became. And the more he and his son Lucas glanced at each other in true understanding and affection, sharing their relief that a beautiful young girl was looking less heartbroken.

Portia was genuinely smiling as she mastered the clearly unfamiliar task. She'd only slowly started to chatter since her abrupt, unexplained arrival from New York two months ago, for an indefinite stay with Viola and William Donovan. She was as blond and blue-eyed as Viola, with a cameo-pure beauty that would one day make men beg for a single smile. At the moment, however, her face was highlighted by streaks of red, green, and blue icing.

In the center of the room were the star attractions: Rachel's mother and sister.

Mother was pulling taffy with her Los Angeles rancher, while her San Francisco lawyer was tying strands of taffy into Mother's initials. Rachel had no idea which gentleman held the advantage in the competition for her mother's favors.

Mercy currently had the rapt attention of three Donovan & Sons' men. One was pulling taffy with her, one had rushed off to obtain butter for a small blister on her hand, while another was pulling taffy using a large hook embedded in the wall—and making a great display of strength as he did so, straining against the sugar in order to flex his arms and shoulder muscles. Mercy was paying only polite attention to him.

The doorbell rang and Braden marched off to answer it.

Rachel leaned against Lucas and tried not to chuckle. They were standing in the dining room doorway, which gave them some leeway for commentary. "Does Miller always show off quite so openly?"

"Not according to Evans." Lucas carefully shifted their newborn son to his other arm and pulled Rachel close, his blue-green eyes gleaming with contentment. He'd been so deliciously protective of her during her pregnancy, but not too much so. He'd even found her a classics society, where she could continue her studies.

She wrapped her arm around his waist and snuggled happily. "Maybe he'll stop doing so."

William Donovan laughed, his six-week-old son sound asleep on his shoulder. "I'm afraid not. In fact, your sister seems to have captured the hearts of more than one Donovan & Sons' employee."

"Exactly as her older sister did," Lucas said smugly. He dropped a quick kiss on the top of the top of her head, one of the little demonstrations of affection that were becoming easier and easier for him to give.

She snuggled closer and glanced at the clock, calculating how much time had to elapse until they could go upstairs together.

The front door thudded open in the wind and Braden's deep voice warmly greeted the newcomers. Rachel turned to welcome them, anticipating two of her favorite men.

Little and Lowell appeared in the door. Little was, as ever, big and quiet—but with a smile lurking behind his eyes at the sight of his godson, Lucas's firstborn.

Lowell's hair was still slightly damp and his face roughened by the harsh weather. A lock of black hair had escaped a comb's instructions to fall over his forehead, highlighting his clear blue-gray eyes. He'd come straight from hauling freight into the northern gold mines, clearly delaying only to wash. His clothes reflected it—clean but not elegant on his rawboned frame, as befitted a young man of the outdoors, not the city. He was incredibly striking but not handsome, at least not yet.

A small sound escaped someone and Rachel glanced around.

Portia was staring at Lowell like a woman, not a child, desperate to memorize every inch of him.

A shiver ran up Rachel's back.

Lucas's arm tightened around her. He stepped forward, with their son, and she gladly went with him. It was Christmas and she was united with her beloved northern devil, the greatest gift of all.

Author's Note

My infinite thanks go to the superb staff of Golden Spike National Historic Site in Brigham City, Utah, Central Pacific Railroad Photographic History Museum at CPRR.org, and to Karen Woods for the perfect quote from Catullus.

During January and February 1873, House and Senate committees investigated corruption involving the Grant administration, the ruling Republican party, and the two railroads linked by the Golden Spike—the Union Pacific and the Central Pacific. After hearing detailed accounts by the broker himself of bribery (including dates and amounts of payments to the vice-president, vice-president-elect, and congressional members), the House committee reported that only the broker and the sole Democrat named were guilty. A series of votes to censure the recipients was later narrowly defeated in public session, after blatant lobbying on the floor of the House.

All characters are fictional, including all railroad staff. All errors are entirely my own.

Please turn the page for an exciting preview
of Shannon McKenna's new book,
EDGE OF MIDNIGHT.
Available now from Brava.

"You're going down the drain, and we're sick of sitting around with our thumbs up our asses, watching it happen," Davy went on.

Going down the drain. Goosebumps prickled up Sean's back.

"Funny you should say that," he said. "It gives me the shivers. Kev said the exact same words to me last night."

Connor sucked in a sharp breath. "I *hate* it when you do that."

His tone jolted Sean out of his reverie. "Huh? What have I done?"

"Talked about Kev as if he were alive," Davy said heavily. "Please, please don't do that. It makes us really nervous."

There was a long, unhappy silence. Sean took a deep breath.

"Listen, guys. I know Kev is dead." He kept his voice steely calm. "I'm not hearing little voices. I don't think anybody's out to get me. I have no intentions of driving off a cliff. Everybody relax. OK?"

"So you had one of those dreams last night?" Connor demanded.

Sean winced. He'd confessed the Kev dreams to Connor some years back, and he'd regretted it bitterly. Connor had gotten freaked out, had dragged Davy into it, yada yada. Very bad scene.

But the dreams had been driving him bugfuck. Always Kev, insisting he wasn't crazy, that he hadn't really killed himself. That Liv was still in danger. And that Sean was a no balls, dick brained chump if he fell for this lame ass cover-up. *Study my sketchbook,* he exhorted. *The proof is right there. Open your eyes. Dumb ass.*

But they had studied that sketchbook, goddamnit. They'd picked it apart, analyzed it from every direction. They'd come up with fuck-all.

Because there was nothing to come up with. Kev had been sick, like Dad. The bad guys, the cover-up, the danger for Liv—all paranoid delusions. That was the painful conclusion that Con and Davy had finally come to. The note in Kev's sketchbook looked way too much like Dad's mad ravings during his last years. Sean didn't remember Dad's paranoia as clearly as his older brothers did, but he did remember it.

Still, it had taken him longer to accept their verdict. Maybe he never really had accepted it. His brothers worried that he was as nutso paranoid as his twin. Maybe he was. Who knew? Didn't matter.

He couldn't make the dreams stop. He couldn't make himself believe something by sheer brute force. It was impossible to swallow, that his twin had offed himself, never asking for help. At least not til he sent Liv running with the sketchbook. And by then, it had been too late.

"I have dreams about Kev, now and then," he said quietly. "It's no big deal anymore. I'm used to them. Don't worry about it."

The five of them maintained a heavy silence for the time it took to get to Sean's condo. Images rolled around behind his closed eyes; writhing bodies, flashing lights, naked girls passed out in bed. Con's predator, lurking like a troll under a bridge, eating geeks for breakfast.

And then the real kicker. The one he never got away from. Liv staring at him, gray eyes huge with shock and hurt.

Fifteen years ago today. The day that all the truly bad shit came down.

She'd come to the lock-up, rattled from her encounter with Kev. Tearful, because her folks were trying to bully her onto a plane for Boston. He'd been chilling in the drunk tank while Bart and Amelia Endicott tried to figure out how to keep him away from their daughter.

They needn't have bothered. Fate had done their work for them.

The policeman hadn't let her take Kev's sketchbook in, but she'd torn Kev's note out and stuck it in her bra. It was written in one of Dad's codes. He could read those codes as easily as he read English.

> *Midnight Project is trying to kill me. They saw Liv.*
> *Will kill her if they find her. Make her leave town*
> *today or she's meat. Do the hard thing.*
> *Proof on the tapes in EFPV.*
> *HC behind count birds B63.*

He'd believed every goddamn word, at least the ones he'd understood. Why shouldn't he have? Christ, he'd grown up in Eamon McCloud's household. The man had believed enemies were stalking him every minute of his life. Up to the bitter end. Sean had never known a time that they weren't on alert for Dad's baddies. And besides, Kev had never led him wrong. Kev had never lied in his life. Kev was brilliant, brave, steady as a rock. Sean's anchor.

Do the hard thing. It was a catchphrase of their father's. A man did what had to be done, even if it hurt. Liv was in danger. She had to leave. If he told her this, she would resist, argue, and if she got killed, it would be his fault. For being soft. For not doing the hard thing.

So he'd done it. It was as simple as pulling the trigger of a gun.

He stuck the note in his pocket. Made his eyes go flat and cold.

"Baby? You know what? It's not going to work out between us," he said. "Just leave, OK? Go to Boston. I don't want to see you anymore."

She'd been bewildered. He'd repeated himself, stone cold. Yep, she heard him right. Nope, he didn't want her anymore. Bye.

She floundered, confused. "But—I thought you wanted—"

"To nail you? Yeah. I had three hundred bucks riding on it. I like to keep things casual, though. You're way too intense. You'll have to get some college boy to pop your cherry, 'cause it ain't me, babe."

She stared at him, slack-jawed. "Three hundred . . . ?"

"The construction crew. We had a pool going. I've been giving them a blow by blow. So to speak." He laughed, a short, ugly sound. "But things are going too fucking slow. I'm bored with it."

"B-b-bored?" she whispered.

He leaned forward, eyes boring into hers. "I. Do. Not. Love. You. Get it? I do not want a spoiled princess, cramping my style. Daddy and Mommy want to send you back East? Good. Get lost. Go."

He waited. She was frozen solid. He took a deep breath, gathered his energy, flung the words at her like a grenade. "*Fuck*, Liv. *Go!*"

It had worked. She'd gone. She'd left for Boston, that very night.

He'd paid the price ever since.

Don't miss Donna Kauffman's
THE BLACK SHEEP AND THE PRINCESS
available now from Brava . . .

"Bagel?" she called out, summoning the one male in her life she could always count on. "Where are you, buddy? Mommy's home and she could use a slobbery hug." She was surprised he hadn't been waiting for her at the door, tail thumping, whining with excitement at the sight of her. You couldn't beat a dog for giving a great welcome home. "Did you get into something? Listen, whatever you chewed up, threw up, or peed on, today you get a pass. Come on out."

She let everything slide from her hands onto the small wooden bench that was currently doubling as a side table by the front door. She'd worry about all that later. Right now, the only decision she had to make was red wine or the chilled white. She'd found a stash of both along with a few bottles of champagne in the wine cellar of the main lodge while doing her initial walk-through assessment, and she brought a couple of each to her cabin. She'd put the champagne in the fridge before leaving, thinking she'd celebrate closing the deal with a little private toast. Now the white would have to do. "Might just drink the whole damn bottle, too. So there."

"I have some spare beer, if you're interested."

She let out a little scream of shock and spun around, heart lodged in her throat as she searched the far shadows at the opposite end of the wraparound porch. The light had dimmed quickly in the falling twilight. "Who's there?" she demanded, wishing like hell she had her truck keys in her hand. Not much of a weapon, but they'd have been better than nothing. They were still in the ignition, where she always left them. Though she'd been debating changing that policy with the recent vandalism. But they'd never locked things up around camp, and old habits died hard.

She tried not to think about that dying part.

She was debating just making a run for the truck, and driving straight down to Gilby's office, when the disembodied voice stepped from the shadows . . . and she froze on the spot, unable to move or breathe. Her mind spun wildly, trying to make some sense of it all. It couldn't be—

"Hello, Kate."

But it was. Eighteen years melted away in a blink of an eye. Though he'd been only seventeen the last time she'd laid eyes on him, she'd know those eyes anywhere. That chin.

And that voice. That slow, lazy, sexy-as-hell voice.

"Donovan?"

There was a pause; then he said, "It's been a long time. My condolences on your mother's passing."

She accepted the platitude with a jerky nod of her head, but her mind went immediately to the graffiti that had started popping up shortly after her arrival. But that made no sense. As far as she knew, Donovan had left the day he'd turned eighteen and hadn't even returned for his father's funeral. Did he think with Louisa gone he had some right to the place? She knew there had been some talk in the papers about her wild deal with Shelby, but certainly he didn't think— "Is—is that why you're here? Because she died this past December. The funeral was a long—"

He shook his head. "I didn't come to pay my respects, though you have them."

"Then . . . why?"

He took a scant step forward, and she was suddenly painfully aware of her appearance, which was ridiculous, but true nevertheless. He'd always had that effect on her. And it had always been ridiculous. Growing up, he'd been Donovan MacLeod, son of drunken Donny Mac, the camp handyman. Hardly a member of her peer group. Most times when their paths had crossed, he'd been in little more than ragged cut-offs, with callused hands and hair in desperate need of a cut. While she'd been clad to the nines in the latest styles, her hair and makeup nothing less than perfect, as she'd intended when she'd made certain he'd see her.

Her cheeks heated now as they always had when he looked at her with those silver gray eyes of his, somehow always managing to make her feel like the discombobulated one. This time he probably could make a case for it. She resisted the urge to push her hair behind her ears, smooth the rumpled suit jacket she'd forgotten to take off when she'd stormed out of Shelby's attorney's office.

"I read about you—your camp, I mean—in the paper."

It was the slight hesitation in his voice that snagged her attention, dragging it from past to present. He'd always been laconic, with a bit of a cocky edge. Or maybe the challenging edge to his tone had been exclusively for her. Regardless, she didn't think she'd ever heard him sound anything less than certain. Of course, though it shamed her to say that she could probably still recall every single second of every encounter they'd ever had, they hadn't exactly shared long conversations together. Most of what she knew about him had come from obsessive observation and listening to the other girls' comments.

He'd been the living embodiment of every one of her fevered, youthful dreams. The proverbial black sheep, the bad boy every good girl would die to have look at her, hold her, touch her . . . take her.

Kate had fantasized about all that and more. In fact, it was the only reason she'd bothered to come anywhere near the lake property every summer. Shelby had always been around, and he'd been just enough of a creep even then that she'd done almost anything to steer clear of him. But the lure of seeing Donovan, dark shaggy hair, rippling belly muscles, piercing gray eyes, working around camp, even if just for a weekend, had been too strong to ignore.

Now, at thirty-four, and thinking herself quite past the age of feverish sexual fantasies, it was a shock to discover just how wrong she actually was.

Here's a sneak peek at Karen Kelley's
DOUBLE DATING WITH THE DEAD
coming next month from Brava.

"Boo," a woman said in a very dry, sultry voice from behind him.

He whirled around. For a split second he thought the place might actually be haunted. But if he was looking at a ghost, he hoped she didn't vanish anytime soon because she looked pretty damned sweet as she stood in the open doorway.

No, not sweet. Nothing about her looked sweet. She was earth, wind and fire all rolled up into one magnificent woman. The combination was sexy as hell.

Slowly his gaze traveled over her. Past long black hair that draped over one shoulder to kiss a breast. She was like nothing he'd ever seen with her loose white shirt, bangles at her wrists and a multi-colored full skirt.

Selena James looked even better in color than she had in black and white.

He wondered if she knew that with the sunlight streaming in behind her, the skirt she wore was practically transparent. He didn't think he wanted to tell her. He rather enjoyed the view.

"Did I scare you?" she asked in a mocking voice, one eyebrow lifting sardonically. She swept into the room and shadows blocked the view of her legs.

A shame because he could've looked at Selena James's legs a lot longer.

"I don't scare so easily." He casually leaned against the balustrade and crossed his arms in front of him.

"But then, you've never stayed in a haunted hotel," she said.

"I can't stay in a place that's haunted since there are no such things as ghosts."

As she stepped closer, he could see her eyes weren't different colors after all. No, it was worse than that. They were a deep, haunting violet.

Her features were pure, patrician, and she was tall. Maybe five-eight. For some reason he'd pictured her much shorter.

When she breezed past him, he caught the scent of her perfume. It wrapped around him, begging him to follow her wherever she might lead. She was definitely a temptation, but one he'd resist.

She faced him and his heart skipped a beat. She was alluring and sexy. Probably the reason she had so many followers who faithfully read her column. She was like a spider, weaving her web for the unsuspecting fly. But he knew her game and wouldn't be drawn in. No, Miss James had finally met her match.

Definitely tempting, though.

Man, he'd been spending way too many hours closeted away in front of his computer while he finished his last deadline, then been consumed with promotion for his current release. Dating hadn't been a top priority.

Maybe two weeks alone with Selena was just the time off he needed.

Selena watched Trent and the changing emotions on his face that finally settled into speculation.

Would she or wouldn't she?

She'd seen that interested look before in men's eyes. Trent wasn't bad himself—even better in person than he was on television. His shoulders were wider up close and his eyes more green, the color of finely cut emeralds.

The kind of eyes, and the kind of smile, that could talk her right out of her clothes and have her naked on a bed before she realized how she'd gotten there.

Oh, yes, he was a clean-shaven devil in an expensive suit and if she wasn't mistaken, wearing designer cologne.

But she wasn't stupid, and she wouldn't fall for his charm. He'd figure that out soon enough.

Trent was a skeptic. Her enemy. He'd made jokes about her column. She could very well lose her job if she didn't change his opinion about the supernatural by the end of their stay.

Lust could not enter the equation.

She faced him once again, tilting her chin and looking up at him. He was very tall, too. "You said some pretty ugly things about me on television. Do you always take potshots at people you've never met?"

"Nothing personal."

Was he serious? The bangles on her wrists jangled when she planted her hands on her hips. "Nothing personal? You're joking, right?"

She gritted her teeth. She would *not* stoop to losing her temper. But she'd love to wipe that sardonic smirk right off his face!

His smile turned downward and it was like a thundercloud hovered over him. Well, she was the lightning bolt that would strike him down.

"I go after all cheats, not just you," he said.

"Now I'm a cheat?" *I won't lose my temper*, she told herself.

"You're bilking the public when you feed them a line of crap about ghosts being everywhere and that you can talk to them."

"And how do you know they aren't?"

He swung his arm wide. "Do you see any?" He looked toward the second floor. "If there are any ghosts here, show yourselves," he yelled.

Silence.

He looked at her. "See, no ghosts."

If there were any in the old hotel, he'd probably pissed them off. One thing she hated more than a skeptic was a pissed off ghost. They could get really nasty when they were riled.

"I wouldn't do that if I were you," she warned.